CAST A LONG SHADOW

F.R. WILSON

Edited by
PAMELA HILLIARD OWENS

Cast A Long Shadow

F.R. Wilson

DETROIT INK
PUBLISHING

Published by

Detroit Ink Publishing

Detroit Michigan USA

Cover Design by

Sydgrafix

Detroit Michigan USA

Publisher's Note:

This is a work of fiction. All events and characters in this story are solely the product of the author's imagination. Any similarities between any characters and situations presented in this book to any individuals, living or dead, or actual situation are purely coincidental.

ISBN: 978-0-9995739-4-5

Printed in the United States of America

1

Roger read the text while waiting for the light to change. "Attention - Reminder, Appointment-tomorrow, Wednesday; July 9th, 10am. Martha Scott, Patient Services: Wellington LTCF." His foot tapped the floorboard.

The passenger door jerked open. A storm of wind and black hair rushed into the car. The sudden noise and chaos stunned him. Shock replaced the normal nerdy shyness in his tremulous brown eyes. Roger jammed the cell phone between his legs like a young boy caught sneaking a peek at a Playboy centerfold.

"Drive," she screamed.

The dimple fell from his cheek. "What? Who are you?"

"Go, please," she desperately panted. Kneeling in the seat, she frantically searched out the back window. She weaved and ducked, peeking over the seat. Her breast rising and falling under her rumpled yellow sweatshirt like kernels of corn being popped, the young woman shook her head and blinked her eyes as if she was fighting off sleep.

"Look miss, I don't know what you think you're doing, but you've made a mistake. Now, kindly get out of my car." His upturned chin rose even higher.

"Honk, honk." The car behind him sounded drawing his attention to the green light. "Alright, alright," he grumbled, waving away the annoyance. Roger pulled the car over to the curb out of the traffic. "Out!" he shouted, pointing to the sidewalk.

"Please, it's ...it's my boyfriend," she said, finally looking his way. "Yeah, my boyfriend." Repeating her words as if she wasn't quite sure of what she was saying. Roger noticed the red quarter size mark that started under her left eye and trailed down the side of her cheek. It looked like she had been tattooed with a cherry lollipop.

"Look, I'm sorry for your troubles, Miss, but I'm not interested in getting involved in anybody's domestic problems." She ignored him and continued scanning the back window. Roger grabbed the door handle.

She tensed as if a blast of cold wind had run down her spine. Crawling backward, she sank on to the floor and mouthed the words, "Drive please," her eyes going from the size of silver dollars to slits and back again. When they sprang open, fear screamed from her steel gray pupils. "I'll get out. Just drive. Drive now. Please." she begged.

Roger turned and looked out the back window. A hulk of a man was charging their way racing down the street like an out of control Sherman tank. Every movement of his massive frame threatened to rip apart the fabric straining to hold him in. His hand disappeared into his jacket and came out brandishing a gun. The polished silver body gleamed in the sun like a missile. His massive arms moved from left to right and back again like a compass locating north. The gun was a divining rod leading the way to them. He zeroed in on the car and picked up speed. His extended arm was a missile turret, ready to fire.

The shining steel of the gun had Roger spellbound. He watched the charging man as if he was playing one of the video games he loved. His mind slipped into battle mode. The game was on. Roger was mesmerized, calculating the right time to counter attack and bring down his adversary before moving on to the next level. His hands hovered anxiously above the steering wheel, careful not to put pressure on it and fire prematurely. As the human artillery got closer, Roger could see the rage burning in his eyes and almost hear his growls of rage. A barrage of curse words formed in his mind. *Oh, hell,* he thought snapping out of his trance. Without thinking or taking his eyes off the charging destruction, Roger's foot slammed onto the accelerator.

Horns honked, tires screeched, curses were shouted, fingers and fists were raised and shaken as he dove into traffic. Cutting across lanes, he put a stop to all other movement but his car and the charging human tank.

Swerving to the left, he skirted around a minivan making a left turn. A hard bank back to the right kept him from going across the medium and running head first into oncoming traffic. Roger righted the car, choosing one lane instead of the whole road. The vehicle sprang forward like a panicked gazelle escaping a pride of hungry lions.

Roger's attention jumped back and forth from the road ahead of him to watching the approaching danger in the rearview mirror. The human tank raced down the street at full speed. His legs pumping like steel pistons. He stopped, steadied one hand over the other and fired. "Bang, bang, bang," the bullets made contact with the trunk of the car. Roger felt the car jerk like a child trying to escape a spanking. The tires screeched as the car lunged forward as if the bullets had been the stings from a swarm of pursuing wasps.

Burying the accelerator pedal into the floor, Roger puffed and wheezed like he was pushing the car instead of driving it. His heart raced as he willed the car to grow wings. The engine roared its obedience. Last night's tacos rose up and reintroduced themselves to his dry mouth. The air grew hot and thin from his rapid breathing. Beads of sweat rolled down his back making him wiggle in his seat as the waistband of his underwear became irritated with the deposit of moisture. His left foot was tapping out an SOS.

The car took corners on two wheels, racing through lights, regardless of their color. Honking the horn and screaming, he warned everyone that he was coming and stopping was not an option. "Out of my way. Move that

damn thing. Stop, you idiot. Don't you see me coming? This is a damn emergency!" The pitch of his voice rose with the speed of the car. Horns continued to honk like a gaggle of angry geese. People flashed their lights, though the effort was lost in the bright afternoon sun. The tires screamed their protest as he forced the car to go faster.

Zigzagging his way through the streets of Detroit, Roger ended up on the freeway service drive for Interstate 94. He descended the entrance ramp, gathering speed with the incline. Not caring about driving etiquette, he bogarted his way into the far-left lane. Racing forward, he set a new speed limit. Immune to protesting drivers, he ignored their complaints and surged forward. Speeding with no concept of what a brake was he darted pass and around vehicles like an ambulance rushing to save a life, his life. Disregarding sweaty palms, he gripped the wheel tighter. Hugging the steering wheel like a kid learning to ride their first bicycle; he held on for dear life. The Ford Fusion got lost in the beginning of rush hour traffic.

Roger sneaked a peek into the rearview mirror; afraid the Sherman tank would be right behind him ready to release an endless barrage of canon fire. He pictured the man firing round after round into the car until there was nothing left, but him riding down the road on a single tire like a unicycle. The low fuel indicator pinged and brought him back to the real world. For the first time since the shooting began Roger looked over and remembered the girl. In his desperation to get away from the human firing squad, he had thrown her from his mind.

His only thought had been run and run faster. She lay crumpled on the floor; her head and arm were splayed across the seat like a dead body floating in water. She wasn't moving. She wasn't breathing. His panic grew, threatening to burst out the top of his head. *Oh, my God, she's dead. What am I going to do?* he thought. "Hey, hey, please don't be dead," he shouted. She didn't respond. "Oh, God. How the hell am I going to explain this? They'll think I kidnapped and killed her."

Roger clutched at his shirt. His heart was beating against his ribs like a prisoner banging on his prisons bars. "I'm going to jail. They'll execute me." He pounded on the steering wheel. "No, no, no. This can't be happening." The low fuel gauge pinged again. "Oh, shut the hell up." He yelled at the dashboard. "Can't you see what's happening here? A black guy and a dead white girl. They'll lynch me." Pictures of burning crosses and a mob in white sheets flooded his mind. He shook off the images. *No! This may not be the South, but I'm still just as good as dead.* He looked up to the sky. *God, why do you hate me?*

Roger maneuvered the car into the right lane and exited at the posted rest stop. He pulled into the parking lot, at the far side under the cover of low hanging trees. "Okay Roger, think," his head in his hands and his runaway foot patting at the floorboard. "You've got a dead white girl in your car. A mad man with a gun shooting at you and ."

"I'm not dead," a voice said. Roger shifted to the right. "I just zoned out for a minute."

He watched the young woman as she slowly climbed up and sat in the seat. "You're not dead?" His voice was full of surprise and relief. He almost grabbed and hugged her.

"That's what I said." She pointed to his vibrating leg. "Could you stop doing that, please?" Before cupping her head in her hands and leaning forward.

Roger slammed his hand onto his leg. A moment of embarrassment crossed his face, quickly replaced by a frown. "Hey, you almost got me killed back there. That psychotic boyfriend of yours was shooting at us."

"My boyfriend?" She twisted to look at him, "Oh yeah, my boyfriend, right."

"Yeah, the big guy. Mr. 'Sherman Tank' back there. We were lucky to get away with just a few shots. A few shots!" He jumped from the car and ran to the trunk to survey the damage. "Damn it," he stomped the ground. "My new car! Bullet holes," rubbing his fingers across the two indentions marring the shiny speckled black lacquer.

"There're only two," she said, joining him. "No one will notice them."

Roger turned and stared at her. He pressed his eyes into tiny slits. "I will." He squeezed out through clenched teeth. She shrugged and took a step back. Popping open the trunk, a mess of open suitcases full of clothes and random items spilled out. It looked like a donation bin at the Salvation Army.

"Wow, what are you doing, running away from home?" she asked.

He shot her a hard look and shoved the mess back into the trunk before slamming it closed. "It's been nice knowing you, Miss whoever you are," he said marching back to the driver's seat.

"What? You're not going to just leave me here, are you?"

"Why not? It's a hell-of-a lot better than I found you." His voice was rough as tires on gravel.

"How will I get back to the city?"

"Plenty of cars stop here and we both know you don't have a problem with hopping into stranger's cars." Sarcasm dripped from the words. Roger slammed his door. The car made a clicking sound when he pressed the button, locking all the doors. Backing the car up, he turned around and moved toward the highway entrance, not looking back. "Ping, ping" The low fuel gauge demanded. Roger looked at the gas pump icon. "Are you turning on me, too?" he asked. "I didn't shoot you. It wasn't my fault." Pulling to the right, he eased into the gas station next to the rest stop.

Standing at the gas pump while the tank filled up, Roger fumbled with a pack of unopened cigarettes. He flipped the small box between his fingers turning it over and over, examining them as if he wasn't sure what they were.

"Those things will kill you," he looked up to see her leaning against the gas pump. Her voice was as gentle as the expression in her soulful gray eyes.

"So will bullets. I've got a couple of those in my trunk, remember? Besides, since you're going to die, it might as well be from something you enjoy."

"Look, I'm sorry about the unorthodox way we met. I know it was wrong of me to get you involved. I wasn't thinking. I was scared and desperate. I just reacted. I needed help. I reached out." The words seemed to be hard to say. "When I did, you were there. Thank you. I owe you."

A door closed in her eyes as if she realized something had escaped and she was trying to keep the rest from getting out.

"Yeah, that's me, 'handy dandy Roger.' If you need something, he won't mind. He's got nothing better to do. He's got no life, no dreams," he said to the pack of cigarettes never looking her way.

A puzzled look crossed her face. "What is that supposed to mean?" He didn't respond. She leaned down to meet his eyes. "Look, let's start over. Okay? Roger, I'm Na'Taya, Na'Taya Latten. Thank you for being such an all right guy. Someday I hope to be able to return the favor." She turned and walked toward the rest stop.

Roger returned the nozzle to the pump and drove the car toward the highway entrance ramp. He opened the pack of cigarettes, lit one and blew out a long stream of stress filled smoke. The image of Na'Taya filled his side view mirror. He watched her slender frame moving the short distance across the parking lot. Her jeans hugging her like a second skin. The arms of her over-sized sweatshirt flapped like wings. She looked like a graceful bird coming in for a landing at the picnic table. She landed, tossed back her shoulder length hair and laid her head over crossed arms. She looked so vulnerable, like a kid waiting for her forgetful parents to pick her up. He tried not to care.

It's not my concern, not my problem. I've got enough of my own, he thought. Roger blew a cloud of smoke at the mirror to block out her image. For a few moments, the mirror fogged up. When it cleared, she was still there. He smoked and watched. Swallowing a deep sigh, he shifted the car in gear and rolled across the lot to the rest stop and parked near her.

Sitting with the car locked up, Roger watched her for several more minutes before he lowered the window. He was forcing out a breath as if he had to push the resistance out of the way before it would allow him to speak. "Come on. I'll give you a ride back to the city." She raised her head. Her eyes were cloudy like the sky before a rainstorm. There were no tears. But, painted on her face like strokes on a canvas, was fear.

They stared at each other for a long moment before she rose and walked to the car. "Thanks," she whispered taking a seat and offering half a smile.

"It would be wrong of me to leave you stranded out here on the highway. My mama raised me better than that. I guess I can't blame you for somebody else's crazy." He pulled onto the highway and headed east, back toward Detroit. Na'Taya stared out the window. Roger stared at the road.

"By the way," she said never taking her eyes from the window. "I'm not a white girl. My father was Egyptian and my mother was Haitian Creole."

His eyes went wide. "Oh, you heard that."

2

Roger clicked on the radio. A song by the rapper Current blurted out. "My time is short. My focus is clear." Na'Taya reached over and flipped it off. "Hey," he said, "I was listening to that. What do you have against music?"

"Nothing," she said in a voice that matched the harshness in her eyes. "Just not them, that's all."

"Them? Who's them?" She didn't answer.

"Current may be a local boy, but that dude is headed for the big times. He's getting a sickening amount of play and his concerts are sellouts. You may not like him, but you're going to be hearing a lot of him."

"Sell out," she laughed continuing to look out the window. "Grr."

"Was that your stomach?" She ignored the question. Roger pulled off at the next exit and headed for a group of buildings.

"Where are you going? I thought you were going to take me back to the city?"

"You're obviously hungry and I would like to get the taste of last night's tacos out of my mouth."

"I don't have..."

"Don't worry. My treat." They took a booth in the back of the restaurant. "Order whatever you like." He said from behind his menu.

"Okay, I'll have the Maine lobster, caviar brix, and I'll wash it down with a magnum of *Dom Perignon*." Roger dropped his menu and stared at her.

"Just kidding. Since you're being so magnanimous, I thought I'd test the limits." She wiggled her head and giggled. Her eyes sparkled like summer stars.

He liked her laugh. It reminded him of the joy you see on a baby's face; unconditional happiness. Roger returned the smile. Na'Taya ordered chicken fingers, fries, and a coke. He ordered a burger, fries and coffee. "What do you have against Current?" He asked between slurps.

"Nothing against him, personally. It's the people he works with. They aren't exactly as advertised."

"You know him?" He scooted forward in his seat.

"A little. I was working on his latest video. That is before," She quickly grabbed her drink and hid behind the glass.

"That's cool. What was it like?"

"Don't be so impressed. All I did was walk around in a bathing suit all day long popping my fingers and smiling like an idiot. There were dozens of us. I was nobody special. Just a face in the crowd." A sharp edge had crept into her voice. "I don't want to talk about them."

"Is that why your boyfriend...?" He pointed to the mark on her face.

Na'Taya reached up and touched her cheek, grimacing from the tenderness. "He's not my boyfriend. I don't have a boyfriend."

"But, you said the guy chasing and shooting at us was your boyfriend?"

"It was the first thing that popped into my head, all right? I was just trying to get away from there."

"Who is he then? Should I be worried? Should I be looking over my shoulders?"

She bit at her lips. Her eyes darted about searching for the right answer. "He works for Calvin Michaels at Majestic Music. His name is Spade." Her words were snappy and sharp. "He's one of..." she stretched out the words adding a head shake to punctuate them. "...the posse.

One of his bodyguards they send out with the performers. They aren't interested in you. They don't even know you."

"Okay, but that doesn't explain why he shooting at you? At us? What have you done that's worth a bullet?"

Na'Taya squirmed in her seat. She shook her arms and ran her hands up and down them as if she was cold. "I can't talk about this. Trust me when I say you don't want to get involved." She leapt up and rushed to the ladies' room.

What the hell is going on? What the hell are you doing? Roger thought. *You're a few days away from being free. Don't let yourself get sucked into somebody's else's drama.* He patted the air in front of him like he was pressing it down. *Stay on the edge.*

When she returned, Na'Taya buried her face in the plate of greasy food and didn't make eye contact.

"I'm sorry," Roger said. "I had no right to dig around in your personal business. Whatever is going on is your affair. Not mine. Keep your secrets."

Her mouth twitched. "I'm sorry, too. I don't mean to be so you know. But, you don't want to get involved in this. I don't want to be involved in it." She seemed surprised by her own words. "Let's just keep things light, all right?"

He leaned back, popped a French fry in his mouth, and called for more coffee. "That's fine by me."

Na'Taya concentrated on her meal and tried to mask the discomfort that radiated from her like heat from a flame. She finally spoke looking up with jerky sneak peeks. "Why is your trunk full of suitcases and stuff? Are you living out of your car? I mean it's all right. I've been there. I understand how things can go south sometimes and you've got to do what you've got to do."

"I thought we were going to keep things light? That's rather personal, don't you think?"

She shrugged her shoulders. "Hey, don't answer if you don't want to. I was just making conversation."

Roger caught his reflection in the window, translucent and stoic; showing everything, but telling nothing. Unknowable. Untouchable. *What the hell,* he thought. *I'll never see her again. Who cares what she knows or thinks about me?* Leaning into the table and smiling he said, "I guess you could say in a way, I'm homeless. I gave up my apartment and my job last week. I've been staying in a motel and living out of my trunk ever since. I'm planning on leaving for California in a few days; after I settle a few things." A tone of pride shored up his words. "Sunshine and orange trees," he boasted.

"Why don't you just stay with family or friends until you leave?" She asked pointing at him with a French fry.

Typical mid-class thinking, he thought sizing her up. *Thinks everybody else has a sweet suburban family to fall back on.* Roger tapped his spoon on his coffee cup. "My life is not that ordered. I don't have any family to speak of. Only a brother and I can't stay with him. As for friends, I'm only good with people from a distance."

"Don't you get along with your brother?"

"It's not that. Henry is different. He has medical problems and lives in a facility for special-needs and..."

She interrupted his sentence, her eyes lighting up as if someone flicked on a switch. "You're leaving him behind in some God-awful institution and moving thousands of miles away?"

"It's not like I'm abandoning him." His defenses flared. "I'll be able to fly back if they need me to."

"Yeah, if the institution needs you, but what about if your brother needs you? What about when he needs someone around who cares about him, not just someone who's paid to care about him? What about when he wants to see a friendly face or needs some comforting?" She huffed a breath, flaring her nostrils. "When he needs someone who genuinely cares?" Her eyes narrowed. "That is if you do care?"

Roger gagged on the accusation, nearly spraying out a mouth full of coffee.

"You don't understand," he said, shaking his head "I've always been there for Henry. “It's just since our mother died last year, everything has fallen apart. He's falling apart. Henry needs more than I can give him. I can't take care of him anymore. I just can't be everything he needs. Besides, half the time he doesn't even knows who I am. It won't matter to him if I'm here or in Timbuktu."

His words became more a plea than an explanation.

"I'm trying to do what's best for him .and what's best for me." He added, gripping the edge of the table like a defendant on the stand defending his life. "What about me? This may be my only chance to have a life of my own." He read her judgment. Her eyes seem to look straight through him as if there was nothing of substance, nothing of merit to him. The disapproval hit him like a slap to the face. Her unblinking stare was a condemnation and a rebuke. The irritation rose in his voice.

"Don't judge me. What do you know about it? You're just a kid. You can't understand what I've had to deal with or what I've been through. The decisions I've had to make or the things I've had to face. You probably have a nice suburban home you can run back to and let mommy and daddy make all the complications of the real world go away. I don't have the luxury of playing at life. I have to live it, complete with all its warts and wrinkles."

Na'Taya sat up in the booth. She seemed to grow six inches. Tilting her head, she looked at him in the most condescending way. Her cheeks were puffed out like an engine building up steam before it mowed down whatever was in front of it. Instead of exploding, she leaned back and dropped her fork clinking onto the plate. Laying one arm on her leg and the other on the table she continued to grow in stature. Her fingers drummed a slow beat on the Formica top. A sardonic smile eased across her lips. She spoke slowly at first, punching each word as if she wanted the words to feel the pain she was experiencing by saying them.

"When I was ten years old, my father's family summoned him home to Egypt. His village was a little hot dry wasteland in the south of the country. A dry hole in the desert. We should have known something was wrong because my father was pensive and aloof the entire trip there. Totally different from the happy giving man we knew.

From the moment those bastards looked at my mother and me, you could see the disapproval on their faces.

For the next three years, his relatives, who were everyone in the village, called my mother *tilk alkalbat alnuwbia* that's Arabic for 'that Nubian bitch.'" A hardness solidified in her eyes like cement setting. Her mouth twisted as if she had sucked on a lemon. The pace of her drumming increased with each word she spoke.

"We were treated like servants, slaves even. Despite my father's protests, they isolated us and took every opportunity to belittle and disrespect us. My father was conscripted and forced to do work he didn't like or want to do. We rarely ever saw him. When we did, he was moody and depressed. They worked my mother and me to exhaustion. When she got sick, they worked her harder until it killed her." She paused, drew in a deep breath and snickered.

"I was locked away and told only after she was dead. It was the judgment of Allah, they said. When I cried and begged to see her, they beat me and told me, it was wicked to question the workings of Allah." They then tried to marry me off to this lecherous old bastard. He was 55 years old. I was 13, 13years old." She punched the table with her fingertips.

"They beat me when I wouldn't do it. My father protested, he was threatened with death. They told him, "I was a woman and it was my responsibility to produce the next generation." Na'Taya made a sound somewhere between a laugh and a sob.

"Two months later my father and I managed to escape. I don't know what he did to secure our way, but it troubled him the rest of his life. He would never talk about it."

She leaned forward and used her finger to make swirls in the ketchup as if she was plotting a way out of the maze of emotions she was caught up in. "We made our way to Europe and eventually back to America. I was born here. I'm an American citizen; it wasn't that hard for me to get back in. My father had to seek status as a political refugee. If he were to return to Egypt, he would be killed.

We were separated for three years before he was allowed legal status and released from detention. The time there broke him. In the meantime, I drifted from one hell hole of a foster home to another."

"My father was an engineer, but for the next few years I watched this gentle educated man..." She swallowed a sob and raised her chin as if she had propped it up with a stick. "I watched him be reduced to cleaning toilets and washing dishes until he just gave out. His pride destroyed, his heart broken, and guilt eating at his soul, he withered away. Before he died, he said, "Lualiwa, I wanted to give you and your mother the world. I am sorry I wasn't strong enough." That was three years ago. I've been on my own ever since. So, don't try to whitewash me with your hard life bullshit. We all carry burdens we wish we didn't have to bear. You never know what hides in the dark spaces in someone's life. We all cast long shadows." She went quiet, letting silence and unshed tears speak for her. The intensity of her emotions crackled around her like fireflies.

It was a few moments before Roger could speak. "I'm sorry. I didn't. It's just that you're so beautiful,"

"Oh, so what, you're trying to bed me now?"

"No, it's not that."

"What's wrong, Roger?' She teased. "You don't like girls?"

"Yeah, I like girls!"

"Then I guess I'm just not good enough for you."

"No. I mean yes...I mean no, not that," Roger pounded his fist on the table causing the dinnerware to rattle. He looked around at the eyes attracted by his actions. His neck drew down like a turtle retreating into its shell.

"Stop yanking my chain." He protested in a whisper. "I was empathizing, that's all." Roger took a few moments to catch his breath. "I know what it's like to see someone you care about fade away."

Na'Taya popped a French fry into her mouth and chewed slowly. The glint in her eyes and an up turned corner of her mouth told him she knew she had won the point.

3

"Shut the door, Spade," Calvin combed his goatee with his fingers. His practiced demeanor and well-groomed facade hid his wealth of past indiscretions, fiery temper, and an over-developed ego. A master of reinvention, he had gone from shop lifting juvenile, to teenage drug dealer, to adult con man and now an entrepreneur; sitting at the head of a burgeoning music empire. Michaels had the intimidating ability of making his every idea seem possible and his every word sound like a threat or an order.

Majestic Music was his dream. Since his days of growing up listening to the music of the Motown stars, the Miracles, the Temptations, the Supremes, Stevie Wonder, the Four Tops, the Vandellas, and his favorite, Marvin Gaye, he had dreamed of eclipsing Barry Gordy's success and creating a music empire that would make Motown Records look like a hobby project. Calvin Michaels started by acquiring what he considered a proper building. "Not that lousy clap board house that Motown started in," he'd say. "But, something worthy of being called a headquarters." That was why Majestic Music sat on the main thoroughfare, Woodward Avenue, right in the middle of the growing Midtown area of Detroit., an up-and-coming section of the city that housed most of the city's cultural attraction; an area caught up in the gentrifying craze. The three-story brick building had tall ceilings, wide grandiose windows, and the look of established respectability. Being within walking distance of the Detroit Institute of Art, The Wright African American Museum, The Detroit Science Center, The Main Library, Wayne State University and numerous galleries, restaurants and entertainment venues gave his address heft.

"Where's the girl?" he asked, scowling with disapproval.

"She took off, Mr. Michaels." He lowered his head. "Hopped in a car with some guy."

"Some guy? What guy?" His face crunched up like a deflated balloon. He began opening and closing his hands like hungry jaws. "Do you know who this guy is?"

The big man shook his head. "Never seen him before, Mr. Michaels. She must have called him. It looked like he was waiting for her."

"Did you try to stop her? Did you get a good look at the guy? How about the car? Give me something here." He demanded.

"Yes sir, the car was a black Fusion. A new one. I didn't get a good look at the guy, but I tried to stop her. She took off running. I chased her and yelled for her to stop, but I even fired a couple of shots at the car to try and stop them."

"You did what?" His eyes narrowed.

"I uh, shot at the car a couple of times. I wasn't trying to hit no one. I just wanted them to stop the car." He swallowed. "You know, I thought I could scare them." He hunched his shoulders and cracked a nervous one-sided grin.

Calvin Michaels lowered his head and massaged the bridge of his nose. He looked up shaking his head. "Spade, I know you guys did what you wanted to in the military. But, this is not some Iraqi village where you are the law and the power. You can't just do whatever you want here. If you go around shooting guns in the street, you have to expect to draw attention; unwanted attention. We are a legitimate business, not some hood gang fighting for turf. You are supposed to be the head of security. I expected more discretion from you."

"You said you wanted the girl. When you yelled for me to get her. You made it sound important. I was just trying to follow your orders."

"By bringing the law down on us? Think, man. I don't need that kind of notoriety. We've got some delicate matters going on around here. I don't want the wrong kind of people looking to closely at us. Their attention is supposed to be on the music. I want them looking at the acts," he added with influence. "...not my security personnel. You've got to do better or I'll have to find someone who can."

Without knocking, Michelle flung open the door and sashayed into the room. A breeze of lavender and patchouli swept through the room.

"I told you there was something wrong about that girl when she showed up with her nose stuck in the air. When I first saw her, alarm bells went off." Her voice was as sharp as her perfume was pungent.

"When are you going to learn to pay attention to my instincts?" She continued smacking her lips and shaking her head. "You never could resist a tight ass." She added plopping down in a chair in front of the desk. Michelle had a face of calm assurance, hiding the temperament of a pissed off mongoose. Even when she complimented you she left paper cuts.

Calvin shot her a sharp look. "Wait outside for a moment Spade. Ms. Hightower and I have something to discuss."

Spade smiled at her. "Hello, Ms. Hightower." She gave an insincere smile and then forgot he existed. Spade saw the exasperation on Calvin's face and hurried from the room.

"Listening at keyhole?" He asked.

"I couldn't help but hear you. You were literally shouting. The walls around here are so thin. Besides, I'm not the problem. This new eye candy of yours is."

Calvin sighed. "She's not my eye candy. She's just one of a dozen girls hired to be on the set. We'll find her.

I'll send Spade and Disco to bring her back." He shifted in his chair. "Who brought her here in the first place?"

"The crew says she came in with Samel's nephew, Rala. They also say she's sharing an apartment with that girl with the blue hair,

Yvonne." Michelle spun the large diamond ring on her finger. "What do you think she heard?"

"I don't know how long she was there. She could have heard everything Samel and I said. Or she could have heard nothing. Even if she did hear something, what is she going to do with it? Who is she going to tell? Who knows, she could turn out to be someone we could use."

"Please, don't be so damn naïve. That one knows what she was doing. Her overhearing you was no accident. The only asset she will be is to herself and whoever sent her. If your focus wasn't always on how to get them out of their panties, you'd know that."

He leaned back in his chair and gave her a hard stare. *One day I'm going to kill this bitch,* he thought. Calvin smiled and cleared his throat. "You think she could be working for someone? May be the Feds?"

"Don't know. Could be any number of things."

"She's been here a couple of weeks. She could have learned a lot in that time. Maybe even pieced together some incriminating facts." Calvin said, thinking aloud. "Then again, if she had learned anything concrete, the law, if that's who sent her, would have already been all over our asses."

"If she is an infiltrator that means somebody is building toward something," Michelle said. "They may be trying to find a weakness by acquiring some inside information. Who knows what the game is. Maybe, it's not the law. Could be some of your old gang rivals. Or maybe, we're being double-crossed on the other end. Samel or one of his people could be playing both sides. He may be checking up on us and doesn't want us to know it. After all, Rala did introduce her. Besides, isn't she one of them?"

He shrugged. "I don't know about all that. But, it's not likely Samel or his people have anything to do with this." He waved off the possibility. "They're true believers. Those guys go down with the ship."

"All rats abandon a sinking ship, Calvin. And they generally are the first to know if the ship is sinking," She leaned toward the desk. Her red lips pressed together making her mouth look like a razor cut in the middle of her face. "Samel thinks that he's so clever. Maybe, it's him who's being played and he doesn't know it. If so, perhaps we can turn the tables and kick him to the curb, undermine him while he's being played. We could move in and take over ourselves. Even though I did broker this alliance, I've never been very happy playing second string so to speak."

"There may be something to that." Calvin said. "When you first approached me and I met him, he was as solid as sure money. I was certain we could do business. Lately he's been vague and cagey as if he's playing at something he doesn't want me to know about." Calvin raised his brows. "Are you sure about your information on him?"

She gave him a serious smirk and said. "I'm telling you. We can cut him loose and deal directly. We just have to find out who his sources are."

"I hate to admit it," Michaels said. "But something about this whole operation always troubled me. Bankrolling this enterprise hasn't been cheap. Samel has been too easy about the money. There's got to be something else at play. There are simpler ways to handle this business. We've got to figure out what his long game is."

Michelle leaned back and crossed her long shapely legs. Calvin tilted his head to get a better look. She smiled at the gesture and hiked her dress an inch. "Why does it really matter, as long as we get what we want? All we have to do is put a plan in place in case things start to double back on us. I don't want to be left flapping in the wind." She paused raising one brow. "First things first though, the girl, then the plan."

"We may be fretting about nothing. She might be just somebody who was in the wrong place at the wrong time."

"I don't care what her part is, I don't trust her, Calvin. I'm not willing to take the chance. She's got to go. If we're going to move forward, there can be no ambiguities to deal with."

"Michelle, when have you ever trusted anyone?"

"I did once." She snickered leaning toward him like he had just told a bad joke. "We know how that turned out, now don't we?"

"We aren't going down that old road again, are we? Remember, you weren't the only one who lost out in that deal. Things didn't turn out the way anyone planned, but we survived. That's the..."

"The most important part?" She drummed her lacquered nails on the arm of the chair and ran her tongue across her teeth. "Remember, we didn't all survive." She instinctively touched her stomach and gnashed her teeth. "There are still things that aren't settled between us. You do realize this, don't you?" She pointed a blood red fingernail at him like a dagger.

Calvin closed his eyes and nodded. *Yep, gonna do it.*

Michelle lit a cigarette, exhaling a stream of smoke through her nose that made her look like an angry teapot. Her words were harsh and full of venom. "I'm not going down just because you can't figure out which head you should use to run your life. Just deal with the girl. I'll deal with Samel."

He exhaled a heavy breath. "Nobody's going down if we keep our hea...our cool. We'll find her and put a cap on this." He bobbed his head putting a period on the conversation.

"Now, to deal with some real business, what's the latest on the concert? Any problems? There's less than a week till show time."

Michelle brushed off his concerns. "You read my report, didn't you?" She stared till he nodded then she continued. "Then you should know your concerns are un-necessary. Everything is going well and set to go off as planned. After this show, Majestic Music will be a major player in the market. Majestic Music will be on everybody's lips. Detroit will once again be the music capital of the US, maybe even the world."

Calvin gave a cautious smile. "I must admit. This has been the best idea you've ever had. I was skeptical at first. I never thought you could get through the red tape and make it happen. I don't know what you said to convince them to allow this concert before they tear down the bridge, but you've proven yourself again." He said a reluctant, "good job."

"As usual, you underestimated me. I told you I could make this a reality. Now that the new bridge is handling the bulk of the commercial traffic I knew they would jump at an opportunity to do something historic with the old one before they put it to bed. This way it's a win/win for both of us. They get their grand send off and we get a great venue. Believe me when I say this is only the beginning. I have ideas that will blow your mind. Once this goes off the world will be ours for the taking. We can dump this risky back alley stuff and go totally legit." Michelle rippled her fingers like a centipede walking down her hand.

"Don't worry about the concert. I have all that under control. It will be an event the world will never forget. Just keep your best suit pressed. The media will be on your door steps begging to talk to you." She swept her hand through the air as if she were writing in the sky. "The Majestic Man, Calvin Michaels." She added with a frown, "just deal with the girl."

Calvin gave a hesitant smile, matching her suspicious smirk. He rose and went to the door, "Spade, in here."

Six feet four inches of dark chocolate muscle lumbered back into the room and stood before the desk. "Yes sir, Mr. Michaels." He sounded like a foghorn.

Michelle sitting behind him, slipped her foot out of her spiked heels and ran her stocking foot up the back of his leg, tickling his butt with her toes. His eyes widened in surprise. He tensed, but didn't move. Calvin peered around him and scowled at her.

"Michelle," he said. "Why don't you go see if you can make contact with our friend. Make some subtle inquires. Even though we know subtlety is not your strong suit." He managed a half frown, half smile. "Give it a try. See if you can find out something we can work with, that is without giving too much away." He waved her away. "I need to speak to Spade, alone."

"Party pooper," she faked disappointment., rising and patting Spade on his bottom. Michelle winked at him. An echo of laughter followed her out the door.

"Mr. Michaels," Spade said. "I...I"

"Don't try to explain. You're a blade of grass up against a tornado. I understand. You either go with the flow or get mowed down." Spade nodded his agreement. Calvin smiled. *Yeah, I'm going to kill that bitch and love doing it.*

Recovering from his fantasy he said. "Go to the diner next door and get Disco. You two go to Yvonne's place and find that girl. What's her name?"

"Na'Taya."

"Yeah, pretty girl, light skinned, grey eyes, black hair," He cupped his hands as if he was holding a melon. "...tight ass? That's her, right?" Spade agreed with a smile. "Find her and bring her back here, discreetly. I need to have a talk with her." He pounded his finger into the desk. "Do whatever it takes, but bring her ass back here, ASAP. Don't disappoint me, again."

"Yes, sir. I got you, Mr. Michaels."

"Your gun," Spade produced his 9mm Kahn. "Get rid of it and get another. You know the rules. Once a gun has been fired, it's destroyed and replaced." Spade turned toward the door looking at the gun as if he was going to have to put down his favorite hunting dog. "Don't draw attention to yourselves." Calvin added. He motioned with his head. "Go."

4

Michelle stepped off the elevator, nodded to the guard, and strolled into the apartment. She stood before the floor length windows admiring the view of the Detroit River and the skyline of Windsor, Canada that lay before her. Rotating from left to right she gave a devilish smirk to the Ambassador International Bridge just a mile down the river.

A thin wisp of clouds passed under her making the scene look like a faded old photograph. The clouds reminded her of the dreams she had growing up in the cramped quarter of the Jeffries Housing Projects. In those days, the idea of living in a castle in the clouds was her favorite fantasy; living far above the desolation that was her childhood.

A gentle kiss landed on the back of her neck. "To what do I owe the pleasure of your company?" Samel's hands traced the curves of her body, riding the slope of her back, curving around her slender hips and resting in a firm embrace around her waist. He nipped at her ear, humming softly.

"Do I need a reason?" she purred.

"For you my iron rose, there is always a reason. Ever since the day we met. I have been impressed with your..." He ran his eyes down her frame. "...your determination." Another kiss on the neck. "M-m-m," he smacked his lips as if he had taken a bite out of her. Nimble fingers brought down the long zipper in the back of her dress. "This is not a bad thing, only a fact."

Michelle let the dress fall to the floor. She guided the bra and panties that followed to join it. Stepping out of the circle of silk and lace, she turned and faced him, a stony expression of fake submission on her face. Her brown eyes cold and calculating.

Samel grabbed her hair, snapping back her head until she was staring up into his haunting pale brown eyes. "Do you love me?"

Michelle combed her fingers through his curly cold black hair. She stroked his square chin and ran the back of her hand across his neatly trimmed beard. "As much as I can." She shrugged matter-of-factly. The hollow emptiness of her eyes offered nothing. The corners of her mouth angled up into a facsimile of a smile. He accepted her answer with a kiss. Her hands slide inside his robe and wrapped around his neck. Rising on her toes she returned the affection, slowly sucking on his thin lips and probing his mouth with her tongue. Spreading her arms, she pushed the robe off his shoulders. They stood skin to skin locked in each other's embrace. "A bit of pleasure before business?" she suggested, pressing her body tighter into his. He lifted her into his arms, nuzzled her neck and walked to the bedroom. The afternoon was spent in smoldering laughter.

Stretching from under his arms, Michelle asked. "Have you seen the revised numbers for the concert? I authorized a distribution of three thousand free passes." she shrugged. "A charitable gesture. It will look good in the press releases. As well as garner us some goodwill in the public eye. I'll show you the break down later."

"Brilliant as usual. You, my dear, are truly inspired."

"It will make things a bit more crowded, a bit more hectic, but..." She rippled her fingers. "I assume that means you approve."

"Approve? Of course, I do. What's the saying, the more the merrier?" He ran a hand down her body, starting at the crest of her neck, traveling down between her august breasts and ending at her navel.

"Anything that will get more bodies on the bridge I can't help but approve of. Diversifying the crowd will increase the impact." He kissed her breast. "But then, anything that you do gets my seal of approval."

"That seems a rather pedestrian response. It's rather general and unappreciative. It doesn't speak very highly of my skills, now does it?" She fluffed her hair, faking irritation.

"My love, your skills cannot be determined by singular actions. You have talents that are immeasurable."

"Oh really. Do tell. What would those be?" She raked her nails down his thigh.

"Come now. For one, you mold people the way a potter molds clay. The night we met, you had your Ambassador standing against the wall like a trained puppy. He stood obediently, never making a sound, while we danced the night away. And the way you lead Michael is nothing short of Pavlovian. It's as if people are marionettes and you, my muse, are the puppet master extraordinaire."

She turned over on her stomach and looked away. "I was merely an arm decoration at that party. It was agreed that I would accompany him only with the understanding that my actions and intentions were to be my own." She bent her head and tossed back her hair.

"As for Calvin, he is easy. Show a dog a bone and he will follow you into hell. Offering him the chance to be the next Barry Gordy," she smirked. " .and for Majestic Music to be the next Motown make anything we offer irresistible. Old dreams have a strong pull. Calvin has always dreamed of being something bigger than what he alone is capable of."

Michelle smiled. "I'm supposed to be here pumping you for information. We are making plans to push you out of the way and take over." His eyes widened. She laughed. "I suggested to Calvin that maybe we should take over the operation, and that you are superfluous, an unneeded appendage." A spark ignited in her eyes. "We need to keep him hungry. To wag some red meat in front of his hungry eyes; to feed the dream. It makes it easier to lead that dog if he feels there's a treat at the end of his trick. Besides, this rouse won't be needed for long. D-day is right around the corner." She sat up in the bed.

"Oh yes," her voice dropped. "Speaking of stupid hungry dogs; you must have a talk with that nephew of yours."

"With Rala? What does Rala have to do with...?"

"Who do you think is responsible for introducing that girl, Na'Taya into our notice?" She said the name as if it tasted unpleasant.

"Are you certain of this?" A tilt of her head answered his question. A roughness entered his voice. "He is careless to the point of distraction. His embracing of American culture has made him weak minded and addle headed. Unsupervised freedom and abundance are like a narcotic to some. I blame myself. I have been too liberal with him."

"We need to know about her. To know for certain if there are any reasons to be concerned about her presence. She's an unknown. I do not like unknowns."

"I will deal with him. It is time that he started to behave like a man and stop acting like a spoiled greedy child." Samel furrowed his brow. "It seems you were right about my coming to the studio. Despite Calvin's need for reassurance, it was a mistake to go. How was I to know that the environment had been compromised?"

She nodded her agreement. "She may have heard enough to bring curious minds into our sphere. Hopefully not enough is known to put the pieces together. If she does, we could be headed for difficulties."

"I will not accept that. We have planned for too long to be stopped inches from the finish line." He sat up and waved his hands above his head, dismissing the entire notion. "This could be nothing. If it is anything, it is a warning to be more diligent. With only days to go, we must move with deliberate caution."

"Don't downplay this. We have to make certain there is no threat to our plans. I accept some of the blame for this. I suggested Calvin. I knew he would be a good front man. But, I should have watched him more attentively. An ambitious Black man trying to make magic happen in a struggling city is a good cover. People have a tendency to give dreamers more leeway. There are so many new enterprises happening in Detroit these days that it can be easy to get lost in the boom. We just have to keep an eye on Calvin's exuberance. He does not pay attention to details. He likes to think of himself as the big picture type, things with him have a tendency to slip through the cracks. He's ruled by a dreamer's sensibility, a distracted libido," she paused, adding, " .and good taste." We can't let his recklessness and paranoia give away the game."

He cupped her chin and turned her face to his. "Do I hear some of the history you two share bubbling to the surface?"

"Please," she scowled, rising and wrapping herself in a robe. "I know him. We grew up in the same jungle. I understand him. It would be better if you stayed away and let me deal with him. You just handle the main event." Her expression became pointed and severe.

"Calvin is a means to an end. When he has served his purpose, he will be discarded like used tissue, with just as much afterthought. He's needed only because there must be someone left for the authorities to focus on. I couldn't think of a more deserving," she added through clenched teeth, "...dear."

Samel gave her an over the shoulder glance. "I certainly hope I never do anything that will turn that creative wrath of yours on me."

Michelle leaned over, kissed him and traced her fingers along the neat edge of his closely trimmed beard. With her other hand, she made him tense by firmly grasping his member and squeezing.

"Don't worry my love, I won't let you." She disappeared into the bathroom.

Appropriately preened and coifed, Michelle entered the main room. It was a large, sparsely-furnished room with a plush mocha colored velvet micro-fiber sectional, a couple of red and brown striped wing-backed chairs, a large chrome and glass coffee table, and a sizeable cherry mahogany desk placed before the floor to ceiling windows and a leather upholstered desk chair. "Now that the pleasantries are over, shall we handle some real business before I return to other matters?" She handed Samel a stack of papers.

"All twenty thousand tickets have been sold and accounted for, which was actually no feat. They were practically sold out the day we announced the concert months ago. Here's the breakdown of the three thousand free passes." She pointed to another paper.

"One thousand to radio giveaways, a thousand to public schools, and the last thousand to hospitals and health care facilities. Counting the army of people, we will need to pull this off: technicians, stagehands, extra musicians, security and such, there should be an estimated audience of over twenty-five thousand. The eyes of the world will be our witness."

"Good," he nodded. "I will need those numbers to show our employer. At five thousand dollars a head they will want an accurate count."

Michelle acknowledged him and continued. "The television rights will garner an estimated viewing audience of thirty to forty million in the US alone. Worldwide, we will reach an audience of a billion plus. This will be the most watched, the most spectacular event in decades. Working out the logistics, we decided to place the main stage in the center of the bridge. It will straddle the international border. Half of the stage will be in America and the other half will be in Canada. It's an impressive 150-foot long section. The expanse stretching into Canada is painted red and the American portion is painted blue with a white 30-foot stripe between the two. That's for the headliners.

So, while the artists are performing they will be performing in two nations at once. There will be two minor stages, a 100-feet long, each about a quarter of the way on to the bridge from the entry points of each country. All the secondary acts will be performing there; novelty bands, dancers, acrobats, magicians, you name it."

She moved to the window and fully opened the drapes, turning to face downriver toward the bridge. With a flurry of arm movements, she continued.

"Musical acts covering every genre and singing in dozens of languages will perform. All the performers at Majestic Music will be there: Current, Top Hat, and the rest; they will headline. I have also received commitments from some of the cream of musical royalty agreeing to make guest appearances. Veda, the Mansions, the Rusty Nails, Katherine Hubbard, Quinton Hill, and on and on." She strutted back and forth in front of the window like a spokesmodel. "Did I mention that Darwin Cann will be the MC? Performers from Majestic cohosting, of course." Michelle rested her hands on her hips as if she had just shown the grand prize.

"The Detroit Symphony Orchestra will provide some musical accompaniment. We will be video and audio taping the event for future sales. As the concert rolls to its climatic end and the sun begins to ascend, an impressive display of pyrotechnics will light the night sky, refusing to let the day end." Her arm swept a wide arch.

"An armada of ships, bearing the flags of every country on the planet, will be anchored around the bridge, floating back and forth up and down the river like a royal flotilla. My dear, the world is coming to Detroit! We have to make sure that we do not disappoint." She giggled showing her own satisfaction. Samel beamed and applauded like an exuberant contestant.

"I am still turning down investors. Everybody wants in." she added. Her foot kicked an imaginary ball. "Corporate sponsorship has never been even easier to obtain. They are outbidding each other like kids vying for the last cookie in the jar. They can smell a winner and this one reeks of it. I have turned down all politicians. A general statement was issued stating that this event is open to one and all, so we are shunning any and all political or religious affiliations." She stopped and smiled. "We aren't discriminating against them they just aren't allowed to sponsor us. At least not directly."

"The International Concert of Love must be open to one and all. Shouldn't..." Samel interjected.

"Just wait," she signaled. "I am sure you will love this. Since there are so many interested in being a part of this, I have made further modifications."

"Such as what?"

"To foster goodwill and not offend. I am throwing the politicians and the religious groups a bone. A couple of weeks ago, I convinced them to turn the entire riverfront into a giant party. They jumped at the idea and immediately began to make it happen. There will be booths and kiosks set up the entire length of the riverfront; shooting out from downriver west to the Ambassador bridge and east to Belle Isle Park, on both sides of the river, the American side and the Canadian side. Dozens and dozens of companies and organizations will be on display. Belle Isle has been appropriated to become a super tailgating party. The good thing about it is, I didn't have to do a thing, but suggest it. Religious groups, and politicians have joined with all kinds of companies to throw their money and influence around to make it happen." Michelle posed triumphantly. "Can I throw a party or can I throw a party?"

Samel swept her into his arms. "You are a genius. This would be the concert to end all concerts, too bad we'll have to cut it short before the end." He faked a frown. Samel began waltzing her around the room. "Ambassador Bridge is falling down. Falling down. Falling down. My fair lady!" he sang. They glided about the room in a gale of laughter.

5

Samel kissed Michelle on the nose. She straightened his tie and laid her hand over his heart. He nodded and smiled before stepping out and letting the elevator doors close. "Find Rala," he said to the guard at the door. His voice was dripping with sarcasm. "Check every strip club in the area. No doubt he's in one of them with a fist full of dollar bills and a belly full of cheap whiskey," he added through clenched teeth. "Drag him here if you must."

An hour later, Samel sat behind the large mahogany desk that dominated his office. Rala, red-eyed, and reeking of liquor stumbled into the room. "Hey uncle, you wanted to see me? What's up?"

Samel rose from his desk and walked over to the dark-haired young man dressed in a jogging suit and dark glasses. With an open palm, he back handed him across the face. Rala sank to his knees. Samel adjusted his tie, smoothed his cuffs and returned to his desk.

Rala looked up in shock, a fire of hate erupting in his rusty brown eyes. An expensive pair of shades laid broken at his feet. Wiping the back of his hand across his bloody lip he asked. "What was that for? I was just out having a little innocent fun."

Samel sat rigid and serious as a military statue with a look of disgust plastered on his face; his voice as cold as the ice in his eyes. Twisting his neck, it popped like a finger snapping.

"I have had enough of your mindless, school boy antics. It is time you accept your responsibilities and started acting like a man. You are not some American street thug. Your wanton womanizing and careless disregard for propriety may have put everything in jeopardy. All our planning and preparation could come crashing down around us because of your thoughtless actions." He reached into the humidor on his desk and retrieved a cigar. His eyes alternated between the Havana and the double-bladed guillotine. He rolled the cigar between his fingers. With a butcher's precision, he sniped off the tip. The sound of the blade cut through the air.

"Get off your knees. Stand up like a man." Samel said, sounding like a parent who just viewed a failing report card. Rala eased his slim frame into a chair, still nursing his bleeding lip. "Tell me all you know about this girl, this Na'Taya," he demanded. "When and where did you meet her? How long have you known her? What do you know about her?"

"Na'Taya. Who's Na'Taya?"

Samel's eyes narrowed to slits. His lips pressed so tight together, his mouth seemed to disappear. The cigar snapped in two. Tossing it into the trash, he retrieved another. Taking a deep breath, he continued. "The young woman you introduced to the crew at Majestic Music."

"Na'Taya." He repeated dabbing at his lip, looking up as he picked her face out of the mosaics on the ceiling. "I've introduced several cuties to that place. They always need new girls for the videos. Oh, Taya. That Egyptian chick. Yeah, I remember her. The one with the gray eyes and great ass." He casually waved his hand. "She's nobody. Just a little tease I met. She's good looking and I thought I could score some points by getting her in. I knew they would like her, that's all."

Samel leaned forward. "She's Egyptian?"

"Yeah, at least her father was, I think that's what she told me. He and her mother are both dead, I think."

"Go on."

"There's nothing else to tell you."

"Where did you meet her? At one of your strip clubs?"

"Naw, she's way too tight-ass for that. I met her at .I met her at the new club downtown, I think. Yeah, she was with some friends and she sort of latched on to me. We started talking. I turned on the charm. We had a couple of drinks. I made my move." He snickered. "But, she was like I said, a tight ass. Just a tease. I introduced her to the crew in the hope that I'd get on her good side and maybe make a love connection." He snickered again.

Samel's cold stare ended his laugh. "Is she a Muslim?" Rala shrugged his shoulders. "Was she wearing a hijab?"

He shook out a no. "What's so important about another freak? They're thousands just like her out there."

"This one may be different. Did it ever occur to you that your meeting was a bit too convenient? That it might have been a set up? That you are not as charming as you think you are?"

Rala lowered his head and waved it like a shirt flapping on a clothing line.

"There is the possibility that she was planted to make contact with you and get an introduction into our affairs."

His mouth gaped open as the possibilities flooded into his mind, "That bitch. You mean that sneaky bitch used me. She never had any intention of...She batted her big sad eyes and smiled at me like a cobra." He looked up at his uncle. "I'm sorry, Uncle. I never thought."

"That's the problem. You don't think." Samel lit his cigar and puffed up a cloud of smoke. "This could be critical, Rala. I need you to find out about her, everything about her. Use your..." he cleared his throat. "...connections and find out where she came from. Who her associates are. What she was doing before she showed up here. What she has done since she got here. Everything, do you understand?"

He nodded. "Yes, Uncle."

"This is important. A lot is riding on this. There is more going on than you could imagine. Just because of this very kind of thing I have limited your knowledge of our operations. Your lack of maturity and loose behavior have caused me to be cautious about bringing you into the center of things." Samel stood and began pacing in front of the window trailing a stream of smoke like a locomotive.

"It is time that you drop your frivolous pursuits. There are important matters at hand and you have a part to play. The drugs are just a mirage; a diversion. A way in. Americans are greedy and weak, easily manipulated by such things. There is a greater objective in sight. We have a responsibility, an old debt that must be paid. A blood oath." He shot a stream of smoke and a knowing glare at Rala. "Do I need to remind you why we are the only members of our family here?"

Rala closed his eyes. His hand went to a scar on the back of his head. "No, Uncle," nearly crying the words.

"She stands in the way of our retribution. Possibly, she could bring everything crashing down around us, depending on who and what she is. We cannot let this happen. We have plans that can broker no interference." Samel stared into the distance. The war-torn remains of his village filled his sight. A cold fire smoldered in his eyes. He spoke more to himself than Rala. "This will be our best opportunity to fulfill our obligation."

"But, how?"

"That is what you will find out when you return from completing this task."

"I'll find her ."

"No, that is not what you are to do. There are others who are looking for her. Let them take care of the finding. I need you to concentrate on the whys, whats, and the hows. When I talk to her, I want to already know the answers before I ask the questions. Whether she lies or tells the truth will tell us more than her answers will. That is your job. No more. No less. Do you understand?" Rala nodded.

"When you achieve this goal, I will bring you deeper into the fold." Samel released a fog of smoke that engulfed him. Like a god smiling down from the clouds he said. "You will not be disappointed."

6

The last light of day was melting away when Roger reached the city limits. The nightlife of the city was shaking itself awake. A lazy energy filled the air, subdued but vibrant. People had laid down the rush and hustle of the day. The anxious energy of the day calmed to a slow stroll. The world was relaxed and more inclined to laugh now that the lights were muted. The atmosphere seemed more at ease with the subtle glow of starlight than the focused glare of the day.

The fading scent of afternoon barbecues lingered in the air. Children played under waking streetlights. Overly anxious neon signs flickered to life, inviting the curious. Random music drifted on the air, mixing with the summer songs of Cicadas announcing their arrival after a 17-year sleep, a summer chorus of man and nature giving rhythm to the heartbeat of the city. The warmth of the summer evening seemed to say, "Come out and play before these times are gone never to return." Roger chose to take the streets instead of the freeway, slowly mazing his way through the cityscape, from the west side to the east side of the city.

Detroit, The Motor City, Gateway to Canada, home of the automobile, Motown music, and Vernor's Ginger Ale is a city that knew what it once was, but just can't make up its mind what it is now or what it wants to be in the future. On the national stage, it has at one time or another been the poster child for everything from the “Renaissance Comeback City” to the “murder capital of the world.” It seemed, at least to Detroiters, that the country needed a place to look down on. A place to be better than. Detroit seemed to always be the clear winner. Designated by other states and even some of its own citizens, as a dump, a lost cause, an unredeemable ghetto.

With the reports of blight and crime, Detroit had been crowned the armpit of America. No matter what happened in the city or any of its surrounding suburbs, if it is negative, even if it happened three hundred miles from Detroit, you could be sure the national news would always say "in the metro Detroit area," blaming Detroit for every unpleasant thing that happens in Michigan. Good news about the area was always specifically allotted to where it happened, anywhere, but Detroit. The suburbs could do no wrong. They were just the put upon victims of a decaying city. Detroiters, like an ugly stepchild, learned to live with it. Accepting the blows and knocks and asking, "Is that the best you got?" Everybody needs a fall guy from time to time, and Detroit had learned to play that role with an indifferent swagger. Remaining, sustaining and refusing to give in to premature pronouncements of its death.

"What do you do, Roger? I mean what kind of job do you have?" Na'Taya asked.

"I've got an MA in computer Science. I'm a tech guy, an IT specialist. I develop and install computer systems, set up networks, repair and service electronic equipment, that kind of thing. I love technology; electronics, computers, video games, you know. Growing up I spent a lot of time in front of my computers. I guess you can call me a certified nerd."

"I wish I had studied something as useful as that. I jumped around so much; Archeology, Sociology, Pharmacology, you name it. I even thought about being an engineer like my father, but my heart just wasn't in it. I was on my way to a degree in going to college."

"Eventually you would have figured it out." Roger cleared his throat. “What does "Lualua" mean?" He asked redirecting the conversation.

"What?"

"At the restaurant you said your father called you *Lualua*. I was just wondering what it meant."

Na'Taya laughed. "It's Arabic. It's pronounced "*Lualiwa*." I was born in June. It's the word for pearl, my birthstone. My father always called me his little *Lualiwa*. His little pearl."

"*Lualiwa*," he repeated. "That's nice. It fits you."

"Thanks." She blushed, twisting a sprig of hair around her finger and giggling to herself.

Roger slowed the car.

"If you don't mind. When we get to the apartment would you wait for me to go upstairs and get my things? After that, you can drop me off anywhere. I don't want to stay there anymore."

"What's wrong with your place?"

"Nothing really. Besides, it's not my place, anyway. It's Yvonne's apartment. I met her at one of the video shoots a couple of weeks ago." She twisted in her seat. "I'm just not comfortable with that situation anymore."

"Sure, I can wait. There's no place special I have to be tonight. Do you need help bringing down your things?"

"No. I don't have much. Just a duffel bag," she pointed. "Iroquois is coming up. Go down the next block. You can park on the side street next to the building. I'll go in the back door. I don't want to be seen moving out in the middle of the night. I'd like to make this as quick and quiet as possible. I shouldn't be long. It's only two flights up, apartment two-o-two, right by the stairs." She looked up and down the street. "I don't owe Yvonne any money or anything, so it shouldn't take me any more than ten or fifteen minutes. I'll hurry."

Roger watched her move to the rear door. *She should be in videos,* he thought. *The way she walks is like dancing. She's definitely got the looks. Bronze skin, smoky gray eyes and that bodacious butt. Man, there's no doubt she's got the goods.* He sighed. *She's probably out of my league, anyway. If it wasn't for her troubles she probably wouldn't give me the time of day.* She disappeared inside. *Too bad. Another time, another situation and who knows. I might have had a chance.* He shrugged. *A guy can dream.*

Na'Taya climbed the stairs. *He's really kinda sweet. Cute too. In that sad little boy way,* she thought. *Huh, A little sensitive, maybe, but that's not such bad a thing. Too bad he's leaving town.* She shook her head. *Girl, what are you thinking? You don't need any more complications. There's enough going on in your life without you dealing with a relationship, too. You have to get your butt from under this situation first.*

Reaching for her the keyhole she noticed the door was ajar. She pushed it open, "Yvonne, it's me, Na'Taya. I just came to get my things. I don't think I can stay..." She stopped when she saw the body crumpled in a ball in the middle of the room. "Oh, my God, Yvonne." Her hand went to her mouth, stifling a scream. Bending down, she poked the still warm body. "Yvonne..." She placed two fingers on her throat and felt for a pulse. Lifeless brown eyes and a circle of blood staining the carpet caused her to pull away. Na'Taya stood and wrapped her arms around herself. Frightened and confused she just stared at the lifeless corpse.

"Knock, knock. Na'Taya," Roger pushed opened the half-closed door and entered the apartment. "There you are. The door was open." He closed the door and crossed the room. "You were taking so long. I thought you might have more than you could handle." He stopped in midstride when he saw the body. "Na'Taya, what happened?" She didn't answer. He grabbed her shoulders and turned her to face him. "What the hell happened?"

She looked at him with eyes that resembled clouds ready to burst with rain. "I don't know. I came in and she was just lying there."

He bent toward the body.

"Don't bother. She's dead." Her voice was cold and definite.

"We've got to call the police," he stood and reached for his cell phone.

"No, no" she came out of her trance closing her hands over his. "You can't call the police."

"Why not? You didn't do this, did you?"

"No, I told you I didn't. I found her like this. It's just that I can't get involved with the police."

"Why not? What have you done?"

"Nothing. It's a long story. I just can't explain right now. Trust me, please. Just don't call the police right now. I'll get my things. We can leave and then we can call the police from somewhere else." She moved around the body, grabbed a duffel bag laying in the corner and began shoving things into it.

Roger stepped toward the door. "I don't know what you're involved in, but I don't want any part of this. Everything about you leads to something else."

"Roger, please!" She begged moving to his side. "I didn't have any part of this. I was with you, remember? I'll explain everything. Let's just get away from here. It's not safe."

"How do you know this? Who did this and why can't I call the police?" he demanded.

"I told you. I don't know who did this and why...oh let's leave. I'll tell you everything. I swear. Let's just go." Her duffel in one hand, Na'Taya reached for the door handle.

"Come on Disco. We'll wait in the apartment." A voice came from the other side of the door. The doorknob jiggled. "Did you lock the door?"

"Nope," Disco answered. "The wind must have shut it." The knob jiggled again.

"Damn it." Spade growled.

Na'Taya grabbed Roger's arm and pulled him back from the door. Walking around the body, she guided them toward the bedroom.

"What are we going to do?" Disco asked.

"Crack it. What else? I'm not going to stand in this hallway all night." Spade replied.

Just as the front door came bursting open, Na'Taya closed the bedroom door.

Disco stood over the dead girl wagging his shaved head. "You shouldn't have hit her so hard."

"I wouldn't have hit her at all if she would have told us where Na'Taya was. The boss wants to talk to her."

"What are we gonna do with her?" Disco asked.

"We'll wrap her up and drop her in a dumpster somewhere. Nobody will miss this one." He laughed. Spade flopped down on the sofa and put his feet on the coffee table.

"You might as well have a seat. This may take a while. We're not leaving until she shows up. Oh yeah, by the way, don't tell your brother about this. He's already a little pissed at me for this afternoon. We'll keep this part a secret between us, okay?"

"I don't know Spade. Calvin doesn't like it when I keep things from him."

"Look, I know he's family and all, but this isn't important. She'll be just another freak that went ghost. It won't matter, right?"

Disco's eyes bounced around in their sockets. "Alright, okay. I'll do it this time cause you're my buddy. But, you still shouldn't have hit her so hard."

"Yeah, I know. I'll do better next time. You'll see whenever Na'Taya shows up."

"What are we going to do? We're trapped. We can't stay here." Roger whispered. His eyes were as wide as dinner plates.

"I don't know," she answered desperately scanning the room, holding his arm like a grappling hook.

Roger pried her fingers from his arm and began tiptoeing around the room. Pale moonlight shown through the curtain less window, illuminating the small room. The dingy carpet was littered with half a dozen empty boxes and casually discarded clothes. A well-worn mattress slumped in the corner. Soiled bed linen laid crumpled on top, "We need a weapon."

"We can't fight them. They carry guns. Besides, you've seen how big Spade is. Disco is just as big. It would be like a rabbit fighting a tiger." She insisted showing no embarrassment at the comparison. Roger clamped his hands on top of his head, kneading at his scalp as if he could massage up an idea.

"Disco. See if she's got any beer in the fridge."

"The fire escape," Roger mouthed waving for Na'Taya to join him by the window.

"There's only one." Disco shouted from the kitchen.

"That's great. That's all I need." Spade answered with a laugh.

Roger unlocked the window and attempted to pull it up. "Help me" he whispered in her ear. "It's stuck." Together they strained, pushing and pulling at the old wooden frame, wobbling it back and forth trying to work past the years of dried paint.

The television blared on. "There's got to be a basketball game or something on somewhere. What channel is ESPN?" Spade asked. Disco shrugged. "How about wrestling? You like wrestling?"

"Yeah, I like wrestling. I'm not good at it, but I like it."

"Well I am. I tried to break into the big time when I left the service. But, it's like everything else. It's who you know and how much ass you are willing to kiss. Well. I ain't kissing no ass." He pounded on his chest. "They wanted me to fight these nickel and dime side card matches." He downed the last of the beer, crushing the can with one hands. "I'm not willing to get my ass kicked every night

playing the villain for chump change." The crushed can flew across the room.

"I bet you were a good wrestler."

"I was. I should be in those big Las Vegas matches where the real money is. Instead, I'm babysitting rappers from teenage girls."

The window gave a half-inch, then another half inch. "Stand back," he whispered. "I think I can get enough leverage on it now." Taking a deep breath and summoning up all his strength, Roger muscled the window half way up. "We can crawl out. You go first. Once you're on the grating head down the stairs and make for the ladder. I'll be right behind you." Na'Taya shook her head. It bounced on her neck like it was attached with rubber bands.

"How about another beer?"

"There was only one."

"You sure? Check anyway."

Disco obeyed lumbering back to the kitchen. "No more," he called out.

Na'Taya slid out the half-opened window and stood up on the fire escape. "Drop this over the side. We'll pick it up when we get down." She rubbernecked again. Roger forced the bag under the window and Na'Taya pulled it out. Lifting it in both hands, she hurled it over the railing.

The bag plummeted over the railing and side swiped a homeless drunk urinating under the fire escape. "Ow, hey. What the hell!" He yelled, crumbling to the ground. "What are you trying to do kill a man!" He yelled in a voice as grainy as sand. Rising from his knees, he staggered into the building, his pants sliding down his legs. He continued to shout at the top of his lungs. "God, damn it. You almost killed me."

"What was that?" Spade asked.

"Go, go." Roger insisted. "I'm right behind you."

Roger heard the heavy footsteps coming his way. He looked to the door. The knob started to turn. The door burst open. "Who the fuck is you?" Spade shouted charging for the window. Roger felt his hammering heart beating in double time. He dived out the window, landing on his side against the steel grating. He howled as the hard steel dug into his shoulder. Roger grimaced and scrambled to his feet.

Spade squeezed his hulk under the half-opened window. Stretching out his arms, clawing at Roger like a hungry lion. "Come here, you bastard. What are you doing here?" Roger pressed his back against the railing. He stared at the big man who looked like some monster emerging from a cocoon. Inching his way along the railing, making sure he stayed out of Spades powerful hands, Roger made his way to the stairs and headed for the ladder. Spade growled his anger. The veins in his neck bulged with blood. He pulled out of the tight opening and stood up. Grabbing the window, he slammed it up with minimal effort. The panes of glass shattered sending an explosion of glass shards firing back on him. A mosaic of small cuts and puncher marks dotted his face. Tiny spots of blood covered his face like measles. More glass rained down from between the grating falling on Roger, Na'Taya, and the half-naked drunk.

"Now, what the hell is this shit?" The drunk asked looking upward.

"Come on Roger. Hurry he's coming." Na'Taya yelled.

Roger jumped when he was half way down the ladder. Grabbing the bag and Na'Taya's hand, they took off running for the car. Spade stumbled out of the broken frame of the window. He roared and stomped his way down the iron stairs, dropping from the ladder after one rung. The complaining drunk was knocked back onto his knees again by Spade as he charged pass him in pursuit of the couple.

Disco followed behind shouting. "What's happening? What's going on?"

"Roger fumbled for the keys, remotely unlocking the car as they approached. "Hurry. Get in," he shouted. Tossing the bag in the back, he clumsily switched on the ignition; locking the doors. The car shifted into gear. Na'Taya screamed as Spade crashed into her side of the car. The car rocked like a boat on a choppy sea.

"Na'Taya, you bitch, get out of that car." Spade yanked on the door handle, threatening to rip it from its latches. He screamed. "You're not getting away this time." Flinging back his jacket, he reached for his gun.

Roger saw the gun. "Damn!" He screamed. The flood of adrenaline in his body burned like acid. His mind focused like a camera lens. It shouted. "Go, go!" Jamming his foot into the accelerator, the car lurked forward. The gun flew out of Spades' hand as the car jerked him off his feet. For a few moments, his body waved in the air like a paper streamer attached to the car. Na'Taya dropped her head down between her legs and screamed. She was lost in a nightmare scenario of ending up like Yvonne.

Roger pulled away from the curb dragging the big man with them. Spade held on to the door handle shouting and hammering on the window with his other hand. His legs dragged behind him. The pounding of his large fist caused the window to fan in and out as if it was breathing, balancing on the verge of shattering. Roger slammed on the brakes. Spade sprang like a rubber band and slammed into the side of the car. His grip on the handle released. He dropped like a leaf brushed away by the windshield wipers. Landing face first on the pavement, he struggled to remain conscious. Roger pressed his foot onto the gas pedal and raced down the street. Looking in the rearview mirror, he saw the Sherman tank roll over on to his back, with another tank was kneeling by his side.

Na'Taya continued to scream as they dashed away. Terror was in her eyes as she raised her head and looked around. She gasped and tried to speak. Roger raised a finger and cut her off. "Don't say a word." The ice in his voice stunned her silent.

7

Roger headed northwest, not stopping until he crossed Eight Mile Road, the demarcation line signaling you had left Detroit city limits. The heat of his anger radiated from his skin. The smell of it was pungent and intense as he sweated rage into the air. Roger lowered the window in an attempt to catch a breeze and cool off. He rode as if he were the only one in the car. Never once looking over at Na'Taya, not sure which one he was angrier with her, Spade, for trying to kill him or himself for getting involved with this growing disaster. Stopping at a twenty-four-hour drug store, he bought painkillers and first aid supplies. They drove to the Rock Crest Inn, a chain motel that was his home for the last week. Roger exited the car and marched to the street level entrance of his room. He entered, slammed the door shut, closed the curtains and sat in the dark.

Almost an hour later, Na'Taya knocked on the door. "Roger, can I talk to you? Please?" There was no reply. She closed her eyes and took a deep breath. Her cheeks were still flushed from their previous escapade. "I know I owe you an explanation." Her voice was soft and pleading. Still no reaction. "Please, Roger." The door swung open. Roger stood in the doorway, his chest heaving like an exhausted runner. His face molded into a combination of a sneer and a pout. He looked like a child who had just been told that candy no longer existed. Long moments of silence passed between them. He turned and walked back to his chair, leaving her standing outside the door, anxious and afraid.

Na'Taya stepped into the room and closed the door. The only light in the room came from the illuminated 10:33 pm on the digital clock at the bedside. Standing in the darkness, she felt small and vulnerable. It was as if all the light had been sucked out of the world and she was lost with no idea of which way to go. The sound of Roger's rapid breathing over ruled the faint sounds of traffic and the occasional footsteps from the other side of the door. Na'Taya stepped further into the room feeling like a defendant ascending the witness stand, preparing to plead her innocence to a biased jury. She swallowed and cleared her throat. Her nose itched and her knees locked as her emotions knotted up inside her. Roger never said a word. He only sat, wide-legged, gripping the arms of the chair. She couldn't even tell if he was looking at her or looking past her. The darkness pressed in on her. She took one final step and began to talk.

"I don't know, wait a minute. Let me start at the beginning. When my father died, I was lost and heart broken. I had a little money left from his insurance. I couldn't stay in New Orleans any longer, not without him there. So, I moved north. He always wanted me to go to the college he went to so, I went to Seattle and enrolled in the university. I met this guy." She spit out the word. "Salvador." Her face crunched into a ball. "We hit it off and eventually got a place together. Things were fine for a while. I got a part time job and continued to go to school. He worked construction. At least I thought he did. We talked about maybe someday getting married and building a life, you know, together." Unshed tears glassed over her eyes. "I thought he was an upright guy. It never occurred to me that he was doing anything..." She paused. "Wrong." Na'Taya wiped her nose with the back of her sleeve. Her voice became louder and harsher.

"That's not true. I didn't want to know. I was happy. At least I felt safe for the first time in a long time. At least that's what I told myself. I wasn't going to mess that up with questions I probably didn't want the answers to." Na'Taya spoke as if she were telling herself things she didn't know or at least didn't want to admit. "Turns out my happiness was a lying, stealing bastard who robbed everything from the money in my purse, to the bank around the corner. I found out what he was doing and I left. One of his robberies went badly and somebody died. I don't know why he did it, maybe to reduce his sentence. Or just out of spite. But he implicated me. I was scared. I didn't know what to do. I was at school when a friend who lived in our building called me and told me the police were at the building looking to arrest me. They were going to charge me as an accessory. I panicked and ran. That's how I ended up here. I...I" Her eyes darted around the room. She stopped and turned her head not wanting to meet the judgment in his eyes.

Roger shifted in his chair. His breathing eased from a hurricane to a steady breeze. In a voice straining against the anger he asked. "How does that take us to what happened earlier today and tonight? Why have I had to run for my life not once, but twice in one day? Why are there bullet holes in my car? Why was there a dead girl in that apartment? What the hell is going on? What are you really involved in?" Na'Taya moved closer to his chair. Roger tensed and gripped the chair tighter. She took a step back.

"I told you, Yvonne was somebody I just met, at the first video shoot I went too. I haven't known her but a couple of weeks. I don't know what she was involved in. I needed a place to stay and she needed someone to share the bills. I took the job and took her offer of the couch."

She bit at her lips and continued. "We'd been shooting most of the morning and I was starting to feel light headed from the heat of all those bright lights. I went to the back and took a seat under a window to get some fresh air." She dry washed her hands and steadied her legs. " Calvin Michaels and some guy were on the other side of the wall talking. I heard them through the window. It was something they didn't want anyone to hear. When they found out I heard them, Michaels went berserk. That's when that ape, Spade came after me."

She moved toward the door as if she were thinking about running away, but turned back to face him. "I don't know why they killed Yvonne. I didn't really hear anything important. I...I," She stopped.

"Na'Taya," Roger said rising and coming face to face with her. So close, each breathed in what the other breathed out. "I can tell you're not telling me the whole story. I don't know how I know that, but I can feel it. Stop holding back. Whatever it is, just tell me. I deserve to know."

She looked away. "I can't. Roger, I appreciate all you've done for me. But, I can't. You can't get involved any deeper in this. I'm going to leave. You'll be leaving in a couple of days. Just forget about all this and me. Do it for your own safety. I just wanted you to know that I'm sorry for the way things turned out. If circumstances had been different. well, we'll just leave it at that." She turned and headed for the door.

Roger reached out and grabbed her hand. "Why can't you just trust me?"

She opened her mouth, but nothing came out. Na'Taya closed her eyes and stepped to the door. Standing at the door, the knob in her hand, her back to Roger, tears in her voice. "I don't have any trust left. Everyone I've ever trusted or loved has..." She shook the words away.

"Wait," he pulled her back to him. "You can't go out like that. At least you can clean up a little before you go. Maybe take care of that bruise on your face."

She reached up and touched her cheek. "I forgot about that. I got that when I ran into a fence post trying to get away from Spade. It's alright. It doesn't hurt anymore."

Roger cupped her face. "It looks like it's fading, but it's still red. He ran his finger softly over it. She took in a deep breath. Allowing her head to fall onto his chest. He held her. She softly sobbed and allowed him to hold her. They stood in silence feeling each other's heart beat like dueling drums. The silence enclosed them and their heart slowed and began to beat as one.

A few awkward moments dominated the room. Roger released her and rotated his shoulder. "You must be sore and tired. I'm know

I'm aching and stiff from landing on that grating." He picked up a small plastic bag. "I bought some pain killers, alcohol and other stuff at the drug store. I even brought you a toothbrush. See it's pink. Why don't you go into the bathroom and clean yourself up?"

Na'Taya looked at him and looked to the bathroom. She hesitated. "I should go."

"Go on." He insisted. "I'll get your bag so you can change." He headed out the door.

Na'Taya sat on the bed and ran her hands through her ruffled hair. *I've got to get in touch with Martin,* she thought. *This has gone way too far. I don't know what to do. He's got to get me out of here. And Roger...*

"There should be clean towels in the bathroom." Roger said reentering the room. "While you're in the shower I'll go down the street and get us something to eat." He dropped the bag and hurried out the door before Na'Taya could respond.

When Na'Taya came out of the bathroom, Roger had moved the furniture around. Two chairs faced one another with a bedside table between them. An assortment of boxes filled with Chinese food and two paper plates sat on top of it. "I hope you like Chinese?" He asked smiling and holding out a bottle of water.

She took the bottle and eased in the chair, surveying the spread of food. A look of confusion and worry darkened her face.

"Why are you doing this? Ever since we met it's been nothing, but chaos and trouble. Why are you being so nice to me?"

Roger sat down the carton of almond chicken and looked at her.

"Truthfully, I'm not completely sure." He said with a mouth full of chicken. "I should be mad as hell at you. My normal instinct would be to run the other way when things start getting dicey. But, for some reason, I feel that you need me. I feel like I should be here. Something keeps holding me in place." He picked up an egg roll and waved it at her. "I know you haven't told me the whole truth. I know I'm getting involved in something I probably won't like, but I just feel it's right that I'm here." He chewed a couple of bites. "I truthfully don't know myself how I really feel about all this."

"That's crazy, Roger. You don't know me. You have no idea what you're getting yourself involved in. I don't have a choice, but you can walk away. I like you. I really do, so I'm asking you to please walk away. You've seen what can happen. You could get hurt or worse." She stood up. "Better yet. I'll leave."

Roger stood in front of her and guided her back down into her seat. He looked her solidly in the eyes.

"No can do." He passed her the carton of rice. "Let's just eat. We'll decide what to do tomorrow."

Na'Taya massaged her forehead. A fragile calm fell over the room. They ate in silence.

"I'm going to take a shower and pop a couple more of those pain killers. You can have the bed and I'll camp out in the chair tonight." She was silent. "Look Na'Taya, you're right. I don't know what's going on. I'm not even sure why I care, but if you got hurt. I wouldn't like that. This I know. You don't trust me enough to tell me everything, but that will change. And when you do everything will change." He went into the bathroom and closed the door. Roger took off his shirt. "Toothbrush," He thought. Cracking open the door he heard Na'Taya talking on her cell phone.

"Martin, this is Na'Taya. Things have gotten really crazy. There's something bigger than drugs going on. You have to get me out of here. They're trying to kill me. Yvonne is dead. They've killed her. I'm afraid I'm next. I'll call back tomorrow at noon. Please, be there. I'm really, really scared."

Roger closed the door and leaned against the sink. *What am I doing?*

8

"What the hell happened?" Calvin asked, leaning on his palms at his desk.

"You see, Mr. Michaels," Spade began.

"You, shut the hell up," he interrupted, staring Spade into a retreat. His expression was hard as stone. "I want Disco to tell me what happened." Disco lowered his head and tried to look invisible.

"You, get out of my sight before I do something you'll regret." He shouted at Spade, waving him away without looking at him. "Go and clean yourself up. I'll talk to you after I've spoken with my brother." Spade stood up and sulked toward the door. He looked to Disco for aid, but he wouldn't make eye contact with him.

Calvin sank down in his seat and threw his head back, letting out a long breath. "Okay, little brother. Tell me what happened and don't lie to me." His voice took on a parental tone.

Disco peeked up at him from a hunched over posture.

"It wasn't our fault." He sounded like a kid explaining a broken window. "We didn't know they was hiding in the bedroom."

"Hiding in the bedroom? Who was hiding in the bedroom?"

"Na'Taya and that guy."

"That guy? What guy?" Disco shrugged his shoulders. "You didn't know him?" He shook his head. "Was he clean shaven, short hair? Did he look like a fed?"

Disco shrugged again. "I don't know."

"I'm sick as hell of hearing about some guy." Calvin ran his hands through his hair. "What about Yvonne? What did she have to say? She knows who this mystery guy is, doesn't she?"

Disco melted further into his seat. His head darted about like a mouse looked for an escape hole.

"What did Yvonne say?" Calvin repeated.

Disco nearly fell on the floor, leaning forward onto the desk, in a pleading motion.

"He didn't mean to do it, Calvin. It was an accident. I swear. He hit her and she fell dead. He didn't mean to hit her so hard. She...she..."

"Spade?" Disco bobbed his head up and down like a jack in the box; his eyes full of fear. "Damn it. That heavy-handed psycho is going to get us all thrown in jail." Calvin said pounding on his desk. "Where is she now? Did you just leave her there?" Disco looked confused as if he didn't understand the question. "Yvonne, not Na'Taya. What did you do with her?"

"Oh, Oh, Spade wrapped her up in a rug and put her in a dumpster. He said that was the thing to do. I don't know where Na'Taya is."

Calvin closed his eyes and eased his breathing "Disco," he said. His voice calm and measured. " I shouldn't have sent you out with him. You're not equipped to deal with this him." He rose and moved behind Disco placing his hands on his shoulders. "There's a lot going on right now. Things are complicated. I think it would be a good idea if you went to Kansas City and stayed with Aunt Louise for a while."

Disco flinched. "Don't send me away, Calvin. I'll do better. I'll do whatever you want me to do. Just don't send me away again, please." His eyes teared up and he began sniffling.

"You promised daddy we would always stay together. Don't send me away. I'll be good. I promise."

"I don't want to send you away little brother, it's just that I don't want you to get hurt. Things are not good right now. Stuff is happening. There may be trouble coming our way. I want you to be out of harm's way. You can see that, can't you? Besides, Aunt Louise has been wanting to see you for a long time. You like her, don't you? You know she loves you."

"I don't want to go, Calvin. I want to stay here with you, together, the way daddy said we should be."

"It's not permanent. I promise. Don't worry; we'll be back together soon. Just right now I need you somewhere that I don't have to worry about you." Disco whimpered and shook his head. Calvin's face went flat and expressionless. He raised one brow and looked at his brother.

"Okay, maybe you can stay. There may be something only you can do."

"Anything you want, Calvin. Just tell me."

Calvin Michaels returned to his desk. He smiled like a used car salesman. "I need you to talk to Michelle. She's keeping something from me. I can tell. I can feel it. I don't know what it is, but I'm sure of it. I want you to spend a little time with her and tell me what she says and does. You know, who she talks to that kind of stuff."

"You want me to spy on Michelle? But, she's our friend?"

"Sure, she is, but you know Michelle. She sometimes gets these crazy ideas in her head. I just want to make sure that whatever she's up to won't back fire and get us in trouble. That's all. I'm just looking out for all of us. For our best interest; yours, mine and Michelle's."

"Michelle would never do anything to hurt us." His tears forgotten and curiosity taking their place. "Are you two going to get back together? Like you were when we were young?"

"No, Disco. We're not getting back together. I'm just taking care of her, the way I take care of you."

"Oh, but, is it right to spy on her."

"You're not really spying on her. I would never ask you to do something like that. You're just making sure that everything is all right with her. You know how sometimes I have to keep you from doing things, well it's the same thing. You'll spend some time with her and come back and tell me what she did and who she talked to. She'll like that anyway. Michelle has always had a soft spot for you. After all she's the one who gave you your name. Didn't she?"

Disco laughed. "Yeah, I was real little then. She said because I liked to dance so much she was going to call me Disco."

"That's right," He stared Disco directly in the eyes. "I need you to do this for me, little brother. You'll do it, won't you? I couldn't trust anybody else."

"She'll get mad. Won't she?"

"No, she won't be mad. Not if you keep it a secret between you and me, between brothers. She never has to know."

"Okay, Calvin. If you think it's alright."

"Sure, it is. Trust me. You'll be doing a good thing." He smiled like a fox with chicken feathers in his whiskers. "Now go on home. We'll talk more later."

"I can stay with you?"

"Of course, you can. We're a team, right?"

"Right, just like daddy said we are."

"Yep, just like daddy said we are. Now, go ahead home. I've got important business I need to take care of. I'll be there after a while."

Disco rose and headed for the door. "I can stay, right?" Calvin nodded.

"Knock, knock," Calvin opened his desk drawer. "Come in." Spade shuffled into the room, his face dotted with red spots like a pincushion. Calvin Michaels sized him up the way a mouse does a lump of his least favorite cheese. He nodded to a chair and sucked air through his teeth. Several long tense moments passed with Calvin stroking his mustache and staring at Spade.

"Are you stupid?" he finally asked. Spade was 12 years old again and heard the voice of his father. The same threat echoed in Calvin Michaels' voice. The same dangerous threat burned in his eyes. Spade shrank back into the chair. Calvin continued without waiting for an answer.

"You're supposed to be this big shot mercenary ex-marine and yet you've been punked by this little girl. Not once, but twice. Twice in one day. You shot at her and she got away. You killed the wrong person and she got away." Spade looked up from studying his shoes.

"Yes," Calvin nodded. "Disco told me. Unlike you, he's loyal and follows instructions." Spade tried to speak, but no words came out. He squirmed in the chair as if he was sitting on a ball of grease. Calvin tilted his head. "Are you sure you're not stupid?"

Calvin lifted up a gun and looked at it as he continued talking.

"There was a time when I would have cut your balls off and jammed them down your throat." He paused, raising his eyes from the gun and locking them on Spade.

"Failure has never been something I can accept easily." His eyes were dark, blank and empty like a new dug grave. "That was when I was young. Now that I have mellowed, I chose to go about things in a subtler way." He sighted down the barrel of the gun. Calvin sucked on his teeth.

"I must admit though, I still have an itch to return to the old ways. They were tried and true, so much simpler and straightforward. You have a problem. You get rid of the problem. Somebody falls short of expectations. You eliminate them and make room for somebody who can get the job done." Calvin aimed the 357 Magnum at Spade's head.

"Tell me why I shouldn't return to the old ways and blow your stupid ass head off?"

Spade's eyes went wide. He swallowed and lurked back scooting the chair away from the desk. His hands rose in surrender.

"Yes sir. I mean...I'm sorry Mr. Michaels. I don't know what happened. Somehow everything went upside down." He pressed his large frame deep into the curves of the chair.

Calvin cocked the trigger. "It's only because I don't want to have your worthless brains splattered on my walls that I don't put you out of my misery."

"Yes sir, Mr. Michaels," he said staring into the barrel of the gun, gulping down his fear, his head bobbing on his shoulders.

Calvin laid down the gun and replaced it with a cigar. Talking at the cigar, rolling it between his fingers.

"I'll tell you what you're going to do. You're going to leave this office and not come back until you find this slippery little bitch and bring her ass back to me. Damaged is okay, but alive is essential. I need to talk to her. I can't expect answers from a corpse. I don't care what you have to do, just get it done." He tapped the end of the cigar on the desk.

"If I see you again and she is not with you," he smiled. "You will find out what we used to call fire in the hole." Striking a wooden match, he stared at the flame and smiled.

"Now get the hell out of my sight."

9

Roger rubbed his eyes, squinting against the rays of morning light that poured through the thread worn drapes. The faint sounds of other guests going about their morning preparations rumbled through thin walls. Roger reacted to the movement of the figure half shrouded beneath the drab white sheets. Na'Taya had kicked off most of her covers and pushed the pillows into a mound beside the bed. She laid on her back, her knees creating mountain peaks. Breathing deep and heavy, her face was drawn into a frown. "I get first dibs on the bathroom," she said as one mountain collapsed, her eyes still closed.

"I didn't realize you were awake."

"Yeah," she groaned. "I've been awake for a while. I didn't want to disturb you, so I just lay here, thinking. I have a lot on my mind."

Yeah, like talking to Martin, Roger thought. "You can go first," he said standing and stretching. Smelling one of the cartons from last night's meal, he moved to clear away the table. "It's only 7:30. My appointment isn't until 10. We can get some breakfast and figure out what we're going to do about your situation."

"You need to make an appointment to see your brother?"

"No, of course not. I can see Henry whenever I want. My appointment is with the Patient Advocate. We have some decisions to make."

"You're going to sign over permanent care to the institution, aren't you?" Her voice was hurried and excited as she sat up and faced him.

Roger bristled at the accusation. A wave of guilt engulfed him causing him to turn away. "We just need to make some decisions about Henry's care. I want to make sure that he has the best of everything." Na'Taya eyes dulled as if she had switched off a light. She grabbed her bag and entered the bathroom avoiding looking at him.

Roger finished gathering up the empty cartons and dumped them in the trash. Then he repositioned the furniture. Thoughts of his mother ran through his mind. *You're the lucky one,* she'd say. Roger never understood how she could say that. At least Henry knew what his life would be like. It wasn't the best life, but at least he knew. While Roger had to worry and wonder if today would be the day it would strike him. Was today the day he would start to lose it and be like Henry? Was today the day his life would change forever? She never seemed to understand how hard it was for him to watch Henry day after day as he slowly declined and wonder if he was watching his future. *It will be up to you now to make the decisions. I know you'll do the right thing,* he heard her say. Roger eased down into the chair and rested his forehead in his palms. "I'm sorry, Mom. I know what you want me to do, but I can't. I've got to think of myself too. It's not wrong for me to want a life of my own. Don't I deserve some happiness? Don't I deserve some joy before it's too late? I've got to try and grab what life I can get before it comes to claim me. Please try to understand."

When Na'Taya emerged from the bathroom, she was bright eyed and fresh. The bruise on her cheek was just a faint impression. Dressed in a pair of skin tight jeans, pink sneakers and a thin pink hoodie, she looked like the average college co-ed. The silence between them screamed like a siren. Neither sure of what to say that wouldn't sound like condemnation on her part or an excuse on his.

Roger moved to the bathroom. Before he could close the door Na'Taya asked. "Can I go with you to see your brother?"

Roger turned toward her. "Why?"

"I don't know. Maybe he would like some new company?"

The words surprised him. "Henry won't know you and probably won't acknowledge you either. He may not even know who I am. There's no telling what condition he will be in."

"That's alright. I'd like to go and meet him anyway. Who knows what may happen."

Roger stared into her gray eyes. There was a sincerity in them that made him relax. Her partial smile was warm and innocent. "Okay, as long as I don't have to dodge bullets or run for my life." She ignored the dig.

As they got closer to the Wellington Long Term Care Facility (LTCF), Roger started to tense up. His foot began tapping the floorboard and he kept clearing his throat. Na'Taya noticed his unease and broke the silence.

"Roger, you never said what was wrong with Henry."

He bit his lip. "He has a variant of Huntington disease."

"What is that?"

"It's genetic. It's something you're born with."

"What does it do to you?"

Roger blinked his eyes closed, he sighed, and went into a practiced speech. "It's a neurodegenerative disorder. As it progresses you lose control of your muscles, your cognitive abilities..." Sarcasm crept into his voice. "...and your whole damn life." His words growing harsher as he spoke. "It usually doesn't rear its ugly head until you're in your thirties or later, but Henry has a rare juvenile variant that came on when he was very young. He's almost 21 now, but he has the mind of someone much younger. All through his childhood he was sick with something; pneumonia, falls, mood swings; everything. It was really hard for him being sick most of the time. It was hard for all of us. Henry's was one of those naturally happy people. I don't know how he did it, but he was always smiling and full of life, even when he was obviously in pain. Then the disease got bad. I always wondered how he did it. That is until he has what I call his demon moments. Then he's confused, angry and withdrawn. It's almost like he's several different people; Dr. Jekyll and Mr. Hyde in triplicate. My mother and I had to endure his episodes and watch him like a hawk. He was never allowed to be alone. He and I slept in the same room until he was sent to Wellington."

"What about your father?"

Roger chuckled. "What father? I don't really have any memories of him. After he dropped off the sperm, he hit the road. He came back and took one look at Henry, it was too much for the big man to handle. He took off again."

"I'm sorry..."

Roger jumped in. "Don't be sorry for us. From what I've learned about him, we were better off without him around. The only worthwhile thing he ever did in his life is he was a vet. He died in a knife fight shortly after Henry was born. His veteran survivor benefits kicked in. Thank God, at least he left us that. If we didn't have that, I don't know what we would have done. Treating Henry has been really expensive."

"It must have been really hard for your mother?"

"It was, especially toward the end; after she got cancer. She wanted to continue to look after Henry, but she was too sick to do it herself."

"I bet it was hard for you too."

"Growing up was difficult." He let out a held breath. "Mom and I helped each other get through it. That is until she got really sick. Then there were the two of them to look after. That's when we had to put Henry in the care facility. My mother couldn't help take care of him any longer. I couldn't do it alone. I had my hands full with her; going to doctors' appointments, getting tests, making sure she got her medication, and was eating and all that. Not to mention school. She fought it for 3 years. I spent all my time between hospitals and school."

"That's not much of a life."

"Huh, tell me about it. I considered dropping out, but Mom insisted I keep my schooling up. When I neglected my lessons, she would get so upset it would make her sicker. I would dive back in just to keep her calm. She didn't need anything else to stress about."

"When did she pass away?"

He swallowed. "Last year, about 9 months ago." His chest rose and fell in short pants. "She dissolved right before my eyes. The cancer ate her slowly. It started in her breast." He touched the left side of his chest. "And spread throughout her body. They cut her open and dug it out like she was a melon, first one breast, then the other, and then her liver. She was pumped full of drugs, but it only made her sicker. The radiation treatment made her weak, the chemo made her nauseated. All her hair fell out and she was exhausted all the time." Roger slumped like he was exhausted. "The pain killers didn't work anymore. They just stopped working." His eyes glassed over as he peered into the past.

"All their cures didn't stop it. It just spread. The cancer metastasized and was in so many places there was nothing left to do, but wait for the end. She was so weak and in so much agony. Sometimes she would be so out of it, she would talk nonsense about people and things I had no clue about. Reliving periods of her life over and over again. I don't know which was worse, watching her body die, or seeing her mind turn to jelly. God, it was awful. It was like I didn't know her. She died in so much pain." He stared straight ahead, his face sunken in like a fallen cake.

"I was holding her hand when she died. The pain rippled through her like sound waves. You could feel her shivering with it. I shivered with it."

His hand went to his mouth to stop himself from talking, but the words seeped out from between his fingers like water from a busted pipe.

"All the time she was going through her own ordeal she never worried about herself. Her every thought was about Henry. I tried to get her to concentrate on herself, on fighting to get better. 'Take care of yourself,' I would beg her. “Henry's in a good place.” But all she'd say in return was, “Take care of your brother. Take care of Henry.

Promise me you will make sure Henry is alright. You won't let him be alone."

Roger pressed his hand on top of his head, one-foot driving, the other tapping away faster and stronger; the words still fleeing from his mouth as if they were escaping a burning building.

"She was getting sicker and sicker. He was drifting deeper and deeper into his own world. There was nothing I could do for either of them. I watched them both moving away from me, each one drifting in a different direction. Further from each other and further from me. I kept reaching out, but it was like grasping at shadows. I couldn't pull them back. They were going places I couldn't follow. I kept trying to build bridges between us, but it was useless. The distance between us just kept getting larger and larger. I felt thin and strained like a string they were pulling too tight. I have never felt so small, so helpless, so alone."

Roger pulled the car to the curb and laid his head on the steering wheel. He sounded like he was offering an apology.

Na'Taya reached across the seat and squeezed his hand. "We've both been through things. It's hard to believe we've made it out the other side."

"We may have come out the other side, but not entirely whole. You're never complete again. You always leave something behind. Sometimes I feel I'm not all there. Like I'm just part of who I should be. Just a shadow of who I ought to be. I want to say don't look too closely, because, there are pieces of me missing. It's as if nothing remains in certain places like the broken glass missing in the windows of abandon buildings." She squeezed his hand harder.

Roger grunted, scared that if he spoke anymore it would come out as tears. He sat silently and tried to stuff back into place all those things he had let fall from their hiding place. Not used to exposing himself, or giving the world such an intimate look into his inner workings, embarrassment over came him. In one way he felt uneasy as if his skin had been peeled back and his fears and weaknesses had been identified, labeled and laid out for public inspection. Another part of him felt free and liberated and thankful.

The Wellington LTCF was located in Warren, Michigan, a north-east suburb of Detroit. The building sat at the end of a wooded cul-de-sac adjacent to an industrial park. Roger pulled into the parking lot.

"How long has Henry been here?" She asked.

"Almost two and a half years. That's when my mother first got really sick. I researched a lot of facilities. This was the best. They aren't afraid to thinking out of the box." Roger stared out the window at the building.

"The first year he was so depressed we weren't sure he'd make it. When our mother died, they had to medicate him for weeks. He broke down. He went crazy. I thought I had lost both of them. I was afraid he'd never come back."

Na'Taya looked at Roger with surprise. She asked cautiously. "If what Henry has is genetic. Does that mean that you have it to?"

"I don't know." He blurted out. His voice was weak and small; just above a whisper, but full of angry.

"They have tests that can tell you, don't they?"

"I don't want to know. If I have a time bomb inside me, I just don't want to know."

"But, there have got to be medicines that can help. If you don't know aren't you putting yourself at risk? Aren't you denying yourself any help they might be able to give you?"

"I don't care." He said harshly. "If it's going to happen, it's going to happen. I won't spend my life sitting around waiting on it to happen. Knowing won't make it easier. If it's going to happen it's going to happen." He twisted his mouth into a sarcastic scowl. "Let it be a surprise."

"Is that why you're leaving? Are you running away from it?" Roger turned his head away from her. "That's doesn't make any sense, Roger. No matter where you go you're taking it with you. Why are you running? You can't escape it. What are you running from? If not the illness, is it the responsibility?"

"I'm not running away from anything!" He shouted. "I'm trying to go to something. Something for me. To have the chance at something other than illness and death. To have a chance to be something. To find something to smile about for a change. Don't I deserve to have something for myself? I'm not going to just sit and wait for it to claim me. If it wants me, it'll have to track me down. I'm leaving." Roger forced open the door and stumbled out of the car. Slamming the door, he fell against the car, leaning his head on the roof.

Na'Taya got out and stood on her side of the car. The distance between them seemed like an ocean. Her eyes reached out to him like a life line to a drowning swimmer. He didn't reach out to take it. Nothing could reach him, he was too far at sea. "Everybody has their own crosses to bear. You can't find happiness shutting people out and running away. You won't find the peace you're looking for. Take it from someone who's tried it." She turned away and placed her back on the car. Taking a deep breath Na'Taya turned back to face Roger. Her voice was softer. Her expression, full of compassion.

"I'm sorry. I had no right to tell you what you should do. It's your life and your decision."

Roger straightened himself, finding his game face.

"I didn't mean to get so stupid about it. It's just that I've been living with this my whole life and it doesn't get easier. Watching Henry lose himself, little by little and knowing that's my future. Every time I got sick; a cold, a stomach ache, a freaking hang nail. I was terrified that it's here. That it found me. I'm tired of living in constant fear that I'm slipping into that damn illness." His voice dropped so low the words came out more as a thought than a statement. "I'm tired of being afraid."

Na'Taya looked toward the building. "You know Roger, there's always the chance you don't have it. You could just carry the gene and not have it yourself." She bobbed her head.

"It could happen." The lithe in her voice offered hope.

Roger didn't take the offering. He ignored her and walked toward the building.

10

Roger and Na'Taya entered the austere building. A cold fortress of white antiseptic stone surrounded them. The walls, floor, and ceiling were all part of a stark colorless shell. The air smelled like a bathroom medicine cabinet. All the sounds were muffled and hushed as if they were being heard from the other side of a pane of glass. Every whisper echoed down the halls like wind in a tunnel.

"Wow. This place is like something out of a 1950's B movie. Was this place built before they discovered color?"

"Now that you mention it the place is kind of boring. I never really noticed it before."

"How could you miss it? Boring would be an upgrade. This place is beyond depressing. This is the kind of place fun would come to retire."

"We were thinking about the care, not the décor."

"Obviously."

They stopped at the nurses' station and signed in. A vibrant red head with alert green eyes and a never-ending supply of smiles greeted them. "Good morning. It's good to see you, Mr. Beaufort. Henry will be so happy you've come. He's been doing exceptionally well lately. You won't even know him. I'm sure you'll be delighted with his condition."

Roger gave her a quick smile that fell away almost as soon as he formed it. "Is Ms. Scott here? We have a ten o'clock appointment."

"She's somewhere in the building. Just let me know when you want to see her and I'll page her for you."

He nodded and they moved down the hall toward Henry's room. Roger stepped slowly in a measured gait. Stopping outside the door and he leaned one hand on the wall. "I'm nervous. I feel like I'm going in there to break his heart. I don't want to do that. I don't want to set him back."

"He doesn't know you're leaving?"

"No," he admitted. "I haven't told him, yet. I wasn't sure if I should tell him at all. I thought I would talk it over with Ms. Scott. He doesn't really have to know. I'll be here whenever the doctors call for me. There's no need to burden him."

"You don't think he has the right to know?"

Roger didn't answer the question. He steeled himself and entered the room.

Henry didn't notice them enter. He was sitting cross legged, in the middle of his bed entranced by a music video. Rocking and swaying to the tempo of the music, he clumsily mouthed the words and drummed on his thigh. Henry had the same curious brown eyes as Roger. The same expression of surprise in them. The same up turned chin and small perky ears. The same pecan brown complexion. The same deep dimple on the right cheek. Except for the fact he was almost a foot shorter and lacked Roger's stubby facial hair and faded haircut, they looked more like twins than brothers separated by four years. Roger and Henry shared an aura of innocence about them, an easiness that comes from knowing total, unconditional love; a gift from their mother.

Roger walked up and tapped him on the shoulder. "What are you watching?"

Henry turned and sprang up like a surprised rabbit. "Roger!" he yelled, engulfing him in a smothering hug that forced them both to collapse on the bed. "I've missed you. Where have you been?" He rambled on, talking through the oversized smile on his face. "I've missed you. I got so much to tell you. The doctors and the nurses say I'm doing really, really good. I've been feeling really good, too. We went to the zoo. I fed the animals. Uhh, uhh, guess what. I'm going to the show on the bridge. I got choose Nurse Kelly!"

"Hey, Henry slow down. Don't you see we have company?'

Henry stopped and turned to see the young woman at the entrance. He knelt on the bed staring with his mouth hanging open, "Oh, she's pretty."

Extending her hand, she stepped closer. "Thank you, Henry. My name is Na'Taya. I've heard a lot about you. I'm very happy to meet you."

Henry looked from Na'Taya to Roger and back again before he took her hand. "Are you Roger's girlfriend?"

Roger groaned and turned his head to the ceiling. Na'Taya smiled. "No, Henry. We're just friends. I hope you and I can be friends too." Henry nodded yes without thinking, saying a word, or taking his eyes off her. Na'Taya blushed.

"Have you been behaving yourself?" Roger asked.

"Yes," Henry said sneaking looks at Na'Taya. "When can I come home, Roger?"

"I thought you liked it here? Aren't they nice to you?"

"They're o...kay, but I want to be with you. Like we used to."

Roger stood and faced him. "We talked about this, Henry. I can't take care of you the way they do here. What if you get sick or have a fall and I'm not around? Who would help you?"

"But, I'm better Roger. The doctors say so. I can take care of me. Just ask them."

"We'll talk about this another time, Henry. Let's not forget about our company."

"You always say something like that. You just don't want me to come home." He fell back onto the bed and buried his face in the pillow.

"Henry, stop that," Roger ordered like an irritated parent.

Na'Taya moved closer to the bed. She held up her hand, halting Roger's scolding. "Henry, would you tell me about your trip to the zoo. I'm new in town and haven't had a chance to visit there, yet." She laid her hand on his shoulder. Henry peeked at her from under his arm. "Did you see the polar bears and the penguins? Those are my two favorites."

Henry turned over on his back, a closed mouth grin on his face. He jiggled his head up and down. "The polar bears were all white and so big." He spread out his arms. Excitement entered his voice.

"Did you know they can swim? You wouldn't believe something so big could swim like that." He dog-paddled with his arms. "And they were good at it."

"I've only seen them on TV. I'd love to see them in person." She said.

Roger joined in. "Do you remember the time mom took us to the zoo? They didn't have the polar bears then." Roger laughed.

"Remember, you got the hiccups and scared the monkeys. They went up into the trees and wouldn't come down. They just stared at you like you were going to eat them or something." He laughed again. "We had so much fun that day."

"I didn't mean to scare them. I couldn't help it," Henry protested his innocence. All three laughed together. Henry frowned up at Roger.

"I really miss her.'

"Me too, little brother. Me too." Roger sat beside him putting his arm around his shoulder.

The redhead stuck her head in the door. "Mr. Beaufort, Ms. Scott is free and in her office. She's expecting you."

"Thank you. Tell her I'll be right there."

"Go ahead," said Na'Taya. "Henry and I will be all right. Won't we Henry? We have lots to talk about." She winked at him. Henry took her hand and tried to wink too, but only blinked opened and closed his eyes with the effort.

"Don't teach her any bad habits," Roger said walking to the door. "I'll be back soon as I can." They had their heads in a huddle giggling and didn't answer. Roger stopped at the door and looked back at them. A moment of doubt gripped him.

"Thank you for coming in Mr. Beaufort. You've seen Henry already I gather. I'm sure you can see how much better he is. He is doing rather well." Martha Scott said, spreading praise as if she were personally responsible for his condition. She was a stout woman with a matter of fact way about herself and a voice tuned to make announcements. Everything from her immaculate dress and her sparse office furnishings screamed order. A place for everything and everything in its place. Roger figured in another life she must have been a military officer or a sociopath.

"Yes, he's so lucid. I haven't seen him like this in a very long time. It's not what I expected. How is this possible?"

"It's not like he's cured. Unfortunately, the disease will continue to progress, but hopefully at a much-diminished rate. The new medications we have him on now have proven very effective. Henry has taken to them exceptionally well. His symptoms have been lessened and controlled to a point. We are still adjusting the doses, but we are very pleased with the results so far. The doctors will want to discuss this with you." He is very lucky. Most patients don't take to these experimental drugs so well." Her face lost its light and became stern and serious.

"I have to warn you. This is not a permanent strategy. The doctors will want to discuss other options and modifications with you." She said it as if it was an order rather than just information.

"Henry says that you have told him he could come home."

"Yes, why not? A more family friendly environment would be a positive. With Henry's naturally positive demeanor, I would say he would flourish. Now he will still need focused care, but we can manage around that."

"I don't think I can do that. I have been making plans to move out of state."

She craned her neck like a goose. "Oh, I see," she said taking on a pensive tone. "I didn't realize. I assumed you were here to modify Henry's living arrangements and arrange for home relocation. But, in reality what you're actually purposing is to institutionalize him on a more permanent basis?"

A wave of nausea washed over him. The idea and the word "institutionalize" made him feel sick to the stomach. Roger slouched in the chair.

"No...I mean...I'm just not quite sure. I mean..."

"Mr. Beaufort, as Henry's legal guardian, you have every right to determine what his disposition will be. If you are going to sign his permanent care over to the institution, we need to get the paper work started." She opened a drawer and began fumbling through papers.

Roger rose from his chair.

"Hold off on that for a few days while I decide what my actual situation will be. I'll contact you soon and we can move forward from there." He said as he hurried out the door.

"Don't hesitate, too long," she said sticking her head out the door of her office. "Dealing with the VA, the SSA, and all those other agencies can be a nightmare. If the paper work is not done properly and submitted in a timely manner, we could meet substantial delays."

"Yes, I'll remember that," Roger said rushing down the hall.

When he returned to Henry's room, Na'Taya was nowhere in sight and Henry was lying back yawning his self to sleep. "It can't be bedtime already?" he said aloud.

A nurse appeared from behind a screen. "It's the medication. Sometimes it revs the patient up and causes them to wear themselves out, putting them down for prolonged hours, Henry has been speeding on his own adrenaline since about 5 this morning." She gave him a reassuring smile.

"He'll be fine. It's just part of the process as his body becomes more accustom to the new drugs. It's time for him to regenerate. He'll probably sleep through the rest of the afternoon, wake up, eat and then sleep through the night. Why don't you sit with him till he falls off? It won't be long." She smiled as she left the room.

"Where's Na'Taya?" He asked.

"She had something important to do." Henry yawned slurring his words. "I really like her Roger. She's nice and very pretty."

"Yeah, she is." Roger sat on the edge of the bed. *"She's calling Martin,"* he thought.

"I'm glad you're doing so well, Henry. Mom would be happy too." Roger took his hand.

"Listen, I need to talk to you about something. I was thinking about going away for a while. Not forever, just for a little while. That would mean that you'd have to stay here where they could take care of you."

"But, I want to come live with you Roger. I'm better. I won't be any trouble." He insisted. His eyes trying to fan away sleep.

"I could go with you. It will be fun. You'll see. We'll be together just like we're supposed to be. Just like mom wanted." His eyes closed.

"Henry, I need to do this. It won't be long. I promise. I'll be back and then we can..." He realized that Henry was asleep and couldn't hear him. Roger squeezed his hand.

"Oh, little brother, what am I going to do with you? Huh, what am I going to do with me? I want to go. I feel the need to go, but I know I couldn't stomach thinking about you being institutionalized." He bristled at the word.

"I don't know what to do. I can't lock you away in this place to live among strangers. But, can I stay and not resent you for keeping me here?" Roger stood over him looking down at his peaceful face.

"Mom would have been so happy to see you so full of life again. Hell, I'm happy to see you so much better." Looking up at the ceiling, he sighed. "Okay Mrs. Beaufort. I guess you win. You know I can't leave him. I guess we'll try it your way."

11

Roger stepped outside the building, leaned against the wall and lit a cigarette. The early afternoon sun still hung high in the sky. He squinted against the light. Raising his head, he soaked in the warmth and exhaled his frustration. "Do I go back and get my old apartment or maybe find a house? My job? Will they take me back? Do I even want to go back there?" Questions swirled in his mind. He let them hang in the air until they drifted up and faded away like the smoke from his cigarette. "When do I get a life? Or is this to be my life?" Roger blew out one last long stream of smoke. Looking at the smoldering butt in his hand, he let it drop to the ground. A feeling of melancholy passed over him. He studied the discarded butt, lying abandoned at his feet. Tossed aside, used up, worthless; *Like my dreams,* he thought. Roger stepped on it, and walked to his car.

Na'Taya was slumped in the passenger seat. Her phone lay in her lap. Tears were zigzagging down her face.

"What's wrong?" She didn't answer.

"Na'Taya, what happened? Tell me. I want to help." She closed her eyes and shook her head. "Does it have something to do with

Martin?" Na'Taya turned to face him. Her eyes lit up with surprise at the mention of the name.

"I heard you on the phone last night. You said the name Martin and that you would call back today." He held up his hands in surrender. "I wasn't trying to eavesdrop. I swear. It was an accident. I wasn't going to say anything, but here you are sitting in the car crying. I can't help but wonder."

Na'Taya covered her face. A continuous flow of tears trickled down her arms. "I don't know what to do Roger. I'm scared," she mumbled from behind her mask of hands.

"About what?" he laid a hand on her shoulder. "Na'Taya, you have to be honest with me or I can't help you. Why don't you tell me the real story? Like who's Martin. And why are these people after you?" Roger let out a long breath. "Look, I'm trying to help you. I don't enjoy looking over my shoulder wondering if some giant is going to sneak up on me and unscrew my head from my shoulders. And I don't enjoy seeing you in so much pain. So, come on. Fess up."

Na'Taya lowered her hands and wiped her face with the sleeves of her hoodie. She took a deep breath and sat up straight. Turning strained red eyes to him she signaled her agreement.

"Martin is with the FBI." Her voice was barely above a whisper and still choked with tears. "The part I told you about Salvador was completely true. When I ran away from Seattle, they caught up with me in St. Louis. I know it was dumb to run, but I was alone and scared. I just reacted. Martin was the agent who chased me down. He offered me a deal. If I would come work for them they would make sure that I wasn't charged. I wouldn't have to go to jail. I'm innocent, but I couldn't prove it. So, it's either doing what they wanted or go to jail. I really didn't have a choice."

"You're working undercover for the FBI?" he asked, a hint of doubt in his voice.

"Yes," she nodded. "I'm supposed to be spying on Majestic Music and Calvin Michaels. They believe that he is a front for smuggling drugs from the Middle East. They believe the money is financing terrorists. Martin knows all about my background. That I'm half Egyptian and that I speak Arabic. I was perfect for them. My job is supposed to be to find out what I can about the operation and report back to him."

A whimper escaped her lips. "I'm scared, Roger. I don't want to go to jail. I don't want to do this either. But, there's nowhere for me to turn. I have to agree to do whatever he wants." Na'Taya held up a flip phone.

"Martin gave me this phone. He said it can't be traced. I'm supposed to use this to call him. To report to him." A snarl twisted her face. "I'd like to shove it down his smug throat." She snapped the flip phone closed and threw it to the floor.

"You've found out what they wanted to know, haven't you? Just tell them what you know and get from under this."

"You don't understand," she yelled pumping her fisted hands up and down. In her pink hoodie, she looked like a baby flamingo trying to fly.

"I told him what I heard. He said it's not enough. "Damn him." He wants specifics, names and dates and stuff like that. I don't have any of that."

"What did you tell him?"

"I told him what I heard. That drugs are just a cover. I told him Michaels and some guy were talking. I'm sure he's an Arab; I recognized the accent. After they talked, that woman, Michelle who Michaels works with, and the Arab guy were talking. He told her the FBI was distracted chasing down drugs and that allowed him plenty of time to move things in place."

"What does that mean? Time to move what things in place? That is kind of vague, don't you think. It's not much to go on."

"You sound like Martin." She frowned at him. "I don't know what it means. Like I told him, that's when Michaels saw me and I had to run for my life. I don't know what's going on, but it's bigger than drugs. I'm sure of it."

"Well, you have to make him understand."

"You're not listening! I tried!" she insisted. "He won't listen! He ordered me to go back. I told him they'd kill me like they did Yvonne." She shook her head. "He doesn't care.

HE SAID GO BACK or go to jail." In between sobs she continued. "I told him at the start I wouldn't be any good at this."

"I can't believe he would send you back in there, the bastard."

"What am I going to do, Roger? I can't go back there."

"Call him and let me talk to him. I'll make him understand."

"No!" she yelled. "I can't do that. I'm not supposed to tell anybody what I'm doing. He said if I did, our deal was over. You have to promise me you won't let him or anyone know I've told you this. Please Roger, promise me." She begged becoming more animated, jostling in her seat.

"Okay, okay. What can I do then? How can I help you?"

"You can't. I don't want to, but I have no choice. I either go back or I go to jail."

Roger gripped the steering wheel. "That's not fair. You can't go back there. They'll kill you."

"I have to," she whimpered. "I threatened to go to the press. He warned me that if I did, he would make sure I go to the worst prison for the longest time possible." The rain clouds increased in her eyes.

Roger snorted. His foot tapped the floorboard like a woodpecker assaulting a tree. "No, you won't." Ideas ricocheted around in his head. He stilled his leg with a slap. "I'll go."

"What? What are saying?"

"They don't know me. I can take your place. I'll go in and learn the rest of what you need to know. I'll tell you, you tell Martin, they arrest Michaels, you're free and clear; all this will be over."

"No," she said shaking her head. "It's too dangerous. Besides, it will never work. They don't need men for their videos. You're cute, but I don't think you'd look too good in a bikini and heels."

Roger gave her a '*that was not funny* look'. "Not in the videos. There's a lot of electronic equipment there, right? I'm an Electrical Engineer, an IT specialist. I'm sure they could use a good freelance IT guy. One who is branching out and starting his own business, somebody that can design, install and maintain systems while making upgrades, in-house." He beamed like a new father.

"I'm very good at what I do. And cheap, too. I know I could pull this off. It's what I was going to do in California; be a contract worker for firms in Silicon Valley. Maybe get in on the ground floor with a start up and make it big." His eyes shifted back and forth as if he was reading his ideas off a teleprompter.

"As the IT guy, I would be all over the building. On the roof, in crawl spaces, in the offices, the basement, you name it. They won't be able to hide anything from me. As a matter of fact, I could plant a few specialty items of my own." His mouth curled up in a smile.

"A few ears to pick up things when I'm not around. Maybe even an eye ball or two." His smile grew wider as the plan took shape.

"I couldn't ask you to do that. You would be putting yourself in danger. These people aren't playing around." She shook her head. "And what about Spade? He saw you."

"He only saw me up close once and it was dark. It'll be alright. I can do this. You tell me everything you know about the people and the place. That will give me an advantage. I'll know who and what to look out for. Once I find out enough to satisfy Martin, I'll get out of there. They won't even realize it was me who exposed them."

"You make it sound so easy. Do you really believe this could work?"

"Sure, I can make it work."

"You would do this for me?" She moved closer to him. Placing her hand on his chest.

Roger looked deep into her eyes.

"Yes. I think I'd do anything to make sure you're alright."

Roger pulled her closer to him. She didn't resist. Their lips met. He tasted the salt of her tears on her lips. The soothing warmth of her body as she pressed herself into him. Na'Taya looped her arms under his, resting her hands on his shoulders. The kiss was deep and long. When they separated, neither could look at the other in the face. Na'Taya rested her head on his chest.

"You don't have to feel that you're obligated to me," he said, forcing himself to speak.

"I don't," she said looking up at him. "I wanted you to kiss me. I wanted to kiss you."

Roger smiled. "Let's get out of here. We've got some plans to make."

12

Roger stopped the car on Cass Ave. in the Midtown District; just blocks from Wayne State University. The one-story brick building had iron bars on the windows and spotlights positioned on the walls like a prison. A neon sign with scarlet letters spelled out "Techno World."

Inside there was an electronics shop that catered to everyone from engineers to security firms, to high tech neophytes, to journeymen electrician, to teenaged hackers, and especially the college crowd that lived on a constant diet of electronic gadgetry.

"This place is great," Roger said, looking around like a kid at a circus. They've got things in here you wouldn't believe not just the usual video games and computers. Look at this," he rushed to a display case with penny-sized discs and waved her over.

"These are bugs, listening devices. They look like the head of a screw. Don't they? Put one of these babies on the corner of a shelf or cabinet and you wouldn't know it from the real thing. You could look right at it and not suspect a thing." Roger beamed.

"Check these out," he added. "Cameras with audio capabilities. Those others are strictly video." He added pointing to a line of silver buttons.

"You wouldn't believe the field of vision and resolution from something so small." His enthusiasm bubbled like boiling water.

Na'Taya looked around with apprehension. "Roger, this stuff must be expensive. I can't afford this. I've got a couple hundred dollars at best." She fluttered her hands like she was shaking them dry. "That won't buy one of these things."

"Don't worry about it. I know the owner. I 've done lots of business with him over the years. In my line of work, you learn to know who's got the good stuff. Besides, Ben and I are old friends. We have a history. His wife used to work with my mother. He's known me ever since I was a kid. Ben sells me lots of things at cost. Sometimes he gives me new arrivals to test for him. Those don't cost me a thing and I stay current on the latest and greatest."

"I don't know about this, Roger. What if somebody finds one of your little gadgets? They'll know you put it there. That could get you killed. And if you could convince them you didn't do it, they would wonder why you didn't find it." She shook her head and moved back from the display case. "No, the more I think about this, the more uneasy I get about it."

Roger grabbed her hand halting her retreat.

"I'm glad you're concerned about me, but don't worry. I can do this. Like I said, I'll be careful. Really, we can make this work."

A gaunt, gray-haired man with ice-blue eyes and a hint of mischief in his smile emerged from behind a black curtain.

"Roger, I haven't seen you in a while. You don't stop in as often as you used to." Ben Hartley said. "How's Henry doing? Better I hope." He moved in and took Rogers's hand; a sincere smile on his face.

"Who's your lovely friend?"

"Hey, Ben. Henry's fine. He's doing really well. I'll tell him that you asked about him. This is Na'Taya. Na'Taya, Ben." She gave him a smile that flopped back to a frown so quick it was as if her lips were attached to springs.

"Nice to meet you, young lady. Any friend of Roger's is welcome here." He turned back to business.

"I see you're looking at the surveillance equipment. They're a hot seller these days. Nobody trusts anybody anymore. Hell, I could get rid of the other stuff in the store and make a living just selling this stuff." He pointed to display case full of devices fit for a spy movie.

"Yeah, I bet." Roger said clearing his throat. "I'm doing a job for a client who wants to enhance his security. I need something to impress him. He's kind of paranoid about everything. He's a big tech guy and will be thrilled with this stuff."

"Corporate espionage?" Roger nodded smiling. "How extensive of a system?"

"Not CIA level. He doesn't have a CIA budget, but enough to monitor what's going on. A few ears, maybe an eye or two. I have to admit I have to keep an eye on cost."

Ben deflated.

"Okay, that's easy." He moved past the display case and headed to the other side of the store. His eyes brightened and a grin over took his face.

"Come over here. I want to show you something. I know that you'll enjoy this." In the far corner of the room, he unlocked a black metal cabinet and removed a small box. Inside were a dozen tiny cylinders about two inches long. They looked like sewing needles.

"I haven't had time to display these yet. They came in a couple of days ago. The latest, state of the art. Straight out of Q's laboratory." He chuckled.

"Ears?" Ben nodded. "Wow, these things are the size of a straight pin." He held out one in the palm of his hand to show Na'Taya.

"How sensitive?" Roger asked.

"They can hear a whisper at 75/100 feet away."

"You're kidding."

Ben smiled. "No, I'm not. Light absorbent so they blend into most any surface and become virtually invisible. There's an adhesive on one side that will adhere to any surface. Nano technology, it's amazing."

"What's the transmission range?"

"That's the major drawback. Its maximum range is give or take a couple of miles, maybe. But, that's under the best possible conditions.

Any substantial interference, thick concrete walls, bad weather, heavy electrical static and you are severely limited. These little guys are built for close range usage. Inside a single building or at least a couple of blocks. That's when you'd get the optimal performance."

"That means close monitoring." Ben nodded. "Yeah, that does limit their application."

"But, still it's a great achievement. If they keep improving like this, soon you'll be able to hear someone's thoughts before they think them." He laughed at his own joke.

"How much?"

"How many do you need?"

"Three, maybe four?"

"I'll tell you what. I think these are going to be very popular items. Because I've been a test market for Future Tech for a long time, they gave me these babies under cost. Seeing how you're one of my favorite people and favorite customers, it's only fair I pass them on to you at the same price."

"Thanks Ben. I really appreciate this."

"Hey, we're family. Aren't we? And besides the way your eyes light up when you get your hands on a new gadget makes it all worthwhile."

All the way to the hotel, Roger raved about his new toys. Na'Taya sat quietly listening, but not hearing his words, instead she studied his every move. She smiled at the sparkle in his eyes as he talked high tech and electronics. She watched the way the dimple in his cheek darted in and out as his jaws rose and fell with every word. She delighted in the hidden confidence he exuded as he laid out the details of their plan. Reaching across the seat, Na'Taya grasped his hand. The closer to the motel room, the more firmly, she held it.

In the room, she silenced him with a long passionate kiss. Slowly and methodically she undressed him, smiling to herself as she felt his nervous tremble. Pressing her body into his, she encouraged him to undress her. Slowly, never taking his eyes from hers, Roger peeled away her clothing, fumbling awkwardly the entire time. He kissed he neck, her shoulders, her breast. Enfolding her in his arms, they slowly sank onto the bed. They lay in each other's arms panting and sighing, gasping for breath. The heat of their bodies was igniting the air around them. A sticky layer of sweat glued them together. Folding into one another like pieces of a puzzle, they shared a night of tender passion.

13

Rala entered the club and pulled his new shades down, balancing them on the tip of his nose. Peering over the rims, he scanned the crowd. The closely packed bodies made it difficult to distinguish who was who. Dim lights and bone rattling music didn't help. Slithering through the undulating horde, he made his way to the bar. "A Corona."

"With lime?" The bartender asked.

"Naw, just make sure it's cold." Slapping the money on the bar, he melted back into the crowd making his way to a familiar corner.

"Rala, what's up my brother?"

Rala extended his fist. Like punching a mirror, the other fist met his knuckle for knuckle. "It's all good, man."

"Let the party start. I know you got some...?"

"I'm naked right now, Mac. Catch me up later, alright?" Rala took a swig of his beer. "Say, man have you seen Na'Taya lately?"

"That Arab chick?" Rala nodded. "Naw, bro. I ain't seen her since you yanked her out of here that night." He smiled. "I know you tore that up."

"You know it." Rala lied, gulping at his beer. "I lost her number. I'd like to hit that again. Do you know where she might be hanging out now?"

"Naw, can't say. I haven't been looking. I've got my hands full, hah hah," He pulled his female companion closer.

"Where'd she hangout before she came here?"

Mac hunched his shoulders. "Hell, I don't know, man. It's not like I asked her to fill out an application."

"Come on Mac. You checked her out, man. Where'd she come from?"

"Damn, she musta laid something wicked on you." He laughed. "Look, man. She's one of those college girls. You know the kind. They like to come into the city, get their freak on and then return to school and play the Virgin Mary."

"She goes to U of M?"

"She came with Eva. And Eva goes to Eastern in Ypsilanti. That's all I can tell you. Don't know no more."

"Alright, bro. I'm outta here." Rala sat down his empty bottle and headed for the exit.

"Damn," Mac said watching Rala disappear into the crowd. "Whipped after one lay. I thought he was smoother than that."

Rala sped down the highway. "When I find your ass, I'm gonna teach you that you're been fucking with the wrong one. I don't care what uncle says. Don't no female play me."

Two bars and twice as many beers later, Rala found Eva at the Raven's Nest, an off-campus pub frequented by co-eds, struggling artists, and want-to-be's.

"I've never seen you up this way before? What are you doing here? Expanding your territory, trolling for jail bait, or have you come just for the poetry?" Eva asked, a hint of sarcasm in her voice.

Rala looked around at the crowd of eclectic young patrons. His eyes settled on a young woman with pink hair and at least a dozen piercings.

"I like 'em young and eager, but I like 'em a bit closer to normal. Far as the poetry goes, it gives me a headache."

"And that other thing?" she asked. Rala gave her a hard stare. She raised her arms and dropped the subject. "Why are you here then?"

"It's a free country woman. I can go anywhere my money can take me." Eva gave his look back to him. "Okay, okay. I'm looking for Na'Taya. Have you seen her?"

"Na'Taya? She isn't up this way anymore. I heard she got hooked up working on music videos or some such shit down in the city."

"Yeah she was. I introduced her to the crew at Majestic and they put her ass in a bikini and yeah, whatever." He waved his hands spilling half his beer.

Eva leaned away, wiping at her arm. "Slow down, cowboy. I don't know what she did, but obviously, it's pissed you off."

"Say listen," he said lowering his voice to a whisper. "Where did she come from? Who were her peeps?"

Eva raised her brows. "What do you want to know that for? Are you in that deep?" She tilted her head. "Did she do something you're trying to get even for?"

"I have my reasons. I just need to know something about her."

"Can't really help you, slick. She came in and began to hang out... every night. Said she was staying at the Carlyle House."

"What's the Carlyle House?"

"It's a rooming house over on Evanston St. It's where college girls get supervised housing. You know one of those 'it's my first time away from home' female-only places. She said she was going to enroll and finish her degree. We kicked up a friendship and she came down to Detroit with me one night. End of story."

"Come on Eva. You girls talk. She must have said something more than that?"

"Maybe she did. I just wasn't listening that close. Hell, we were partying. I wasn't trying to sleep with her. What she said just wasn't that important."

"That's it?"

"I'll tell you one thing. Whatever she's doing seems to make her a very popular girl. There was this creepy guy here a few days ago asking about her too."

"And? That's it." He asked.

"I had nothing to tell him and he left." Eva tilted her head and held up her empty glass. He bought her a drink and left the club. Rala parked down the street from the Carlyle House. Several groups of young women traveled in and out. When the coming and going died down, he went to the front door. Through the large glass window and lace curtains, he saw a stout middle-aged woman sitting behind a counter, her face buried in a magazine.

Rala entered the lobby. A bell tinkled.

Before the ringing stopped, a stern commanding voice asked. "May I help you, young man?" Her expression was the opposite of her words.

Rala read the sign hanging over the door. "Admittance Restricted to Residents and Employees."

He smiled, cleared his throat and began talking with the heaviest accent he could fake. "I'm looking for my cousin. I am told she has room here." He sounded like he had stepped off the boat an hour ago.

Her cautious eyes looked him up and down. "What is your cousin's name?"

"Na'Taya." *Don't ask for her last name. Don't ask for her last name,* he silently prayed. "Black hair, grey eyes, very pretty." He smiled.

"Na'Taya what?"

Bitch, he fidgeted. "Ah, I'm not knowing if she use family name, Labib. Maybe she take American one. I do not know American one. If you call she will speech for me." He took a deep breath. *Damn, this is harder than speaking right,* he thought.

Her pinched lips drew a straight line. She moved her head sideways and looked at him with one eye. "We used to have a young woman named Na'Taya here, but she moved out weeks ago. I'm sorry. I cannot help you." Her eyes returned to her magazine, dismissing him with the gesture.

"Moved out? Can you tell me where she go? You have address or telephone number?"

She answered never raising her eyes from reading. "We do not give out personal information on our guests or former guests. Good night."

Rala insisted, "I have understanding, but I need talk with her. We not knowing where she be."

The woman raised her head and gave him a knowing grin. "If she is your cousin, why has she not gotten in touch with you?"

Rala shook his head. "That is..." The accent dropped away. "Fuck this" He pulled out his knife. The blade clicked as the sharpened steel extended itself. Faster than the stunned housemother could react he ran around the counter and placed the blade at her neck. "Look, old lady. I don't have much time and even less patience. I tried this the nice way. Now we're going to do this my way. We're going back into that room behind us and you're going to tell me everything you know about Na'Taya. If there are any problems, I'm going to slit your fat ass throat. Do you understand?"

His hot breath reeking of alcohol assaulted her face. Her eyes blinked rapidly as if they could create enough wind to blow him away. Afraid to move her head, she grunted a "yes." Rala guided the now timid woman through the door and slammed it shut.

Stopping at a gas station half way back to Detroit, Rala read the papers he had taken from the housemother. "Na'Taya Latten. One month's rent. Cash payment in advance. Present Status: Location unknown, no forwarding address, no further information.

Special notation: July 5th Inquiry made about her location by a private investigator. Reason unknown. Private investigator? I wonder if that's who Eva was talking about?"

Rala lit a cigarette. "There is more than one layer to you. It seems you have a few secrets little girl. I can't wait to find out the real deal on you."

Rala raised the paper and looked at the wet red stain on his leg. "Damn, bitch done ruined my favorite pants."

14

Roger extended one hand for shaking and the other to offer his business card; newly printed this morning at Kinko's™: "Roger Beaufort; Independent Contractor. Technology Consultant, Custom Electronics, Security and Computer Systems, 313 555-1196.

"Calvin Michaels. Can we make this quick? I have a dozen fires I need to put out." he asked, studying Roger with a suspicious eye.

"Mr. Michaels, I've come to offer my services. This business you're in requires good people with the skills and knowledge to navigate complicated systems. I..."

Michaels jumped in. "I already have the people I need. Everything that Audio Tech doesn't do, we take care of in house. Thank you for your time, but we won't be needing your services."

"You don't know yet what I'm offering." Roger responded.

"Calvin, we've got big problems." Kenny Taylor, the main sound engineers said bursting into the door. He was a pudgy middle-aged man with a scraggly beard and the eyes of an owl. "I just got off the phone with Audio Court. This guy they sent says he can't fix it. They're talking 20 grand to replace that part of the system, and that's going to take two weeks. We need that equipment, now, today. I'm already 2 days behind on the promos for the concert. And the remix on..."

"Bullshit!" Calvin shouted. "They sold us that piece of shit. Don't tell me they can't fix it." Calvin rose and headed out the door. "Where the hell is he?"

Taylor shuffled out of the way and followed close behind him. "He packed up his equipment. He's probably gone by now. We're screwed."

Calvin stomped into the sound room. "Get Audio Court back on the phone. I want his ass back here. He's going to fix this or else." He raised a foot to kick it, but held back.

"Do you mind if I take a look at it?"

"Who the hell is this?" Taylor asked, noticing Roger enter the room.

"This is expensive equipment, son. I don't have time for amateur hour." Calvin added.

Roger grinned. "I've done work for IBM, Cisco, Siemens, and most of the top 500. I personally have been responsible for multi-million-dollar systems. I was trained with the best on the best. I think I can handle a generic audio board," Roger boasted, raising his brows as if the question was ridiculous. He looked inside the cover.

"I can tell just by looking there isn't much if any, customization. Let me borrow a few tools and I'll see what I can do. It won't cost you a thing."

Calvin looked at him, taking him seriously for the first time. "All right kid. What did you say your name was?"

Roger pointed at the card Michaels was holding.

Calvin read, "Roger Beaufort. Alright, Roger Beaufort, go ahead. Show us your stuff. We're dead in the water any way." He turned away, but jerked back around to face him. "Don't fuck it up any worse than it already is."

"Keep an eye on this guy," he told Kenny. "Don't let him sink us any deeper in the hole. Help him out if you can. I'm going to give Audio Court a piece of my mind." Calvin walked away roaring for his secretary to get the tech company on the line.

"Don't give them too big a piece. You haven't got much to spare." Kenny laughed.

"Everything you should need will be in there." Taylor said to Roger, pointing to a tool box in the corner. "For sure we've got a couple of burnt out circuits. I don't see what you can do, but, good luck."

"There's usually a way around most problems." Roger said, retrieving the tool box. He rolled up his sleeves and bent over the board. "Yeah something is definitely burnt out. You can smell it. Let see if we can find a way around that."

"I'm going to get a cup of coffee. Call me if you need something," Kenny said as he glided out of the room.

Roger scanned the damage.

"This isn't so bad." He said to himself. "I only wish all my jobs were this straight forward. Audio Court is obviously milking some more money out of you, Mr. Michaels. A couple of burnt out rectifiers and a dead power supply wouldn't cost 20,000 dollars even if they were made of solid gold. That's the problem when you have no expertise of your own, you're at the mercy of every slick talking techie in town." He smiled.

"All I have to do is reroute these two circuits through the spare line on this auxiliary board, siphon some power form the panel light circuit, and adjust the feedback to balance out the impedance." Burying his head in the console, he snipped and soldiered.

"It's not pretty, but it'll work for now." Roger felt proud thinking of the endless hours he had spent dissecting and rebuilding systems as a kid. When most kids were playing with their GI-Joes, Roger was busy cozying up to a circuit board or a bunch of random components. He built his first computer at age 12, and by 16 was as familiar with tech as any MIT grad. "Who knew being a nerd would turn out to be so beneficial?" Straightening up, he looked around at the flashing lights on boards and panels. Testing the circuits, he grinned his approval. Most of the equipment was second rate and out dated.

Limited digital, he waved a disapproving finger. *I can't believe they're still using analog mixers? I wonder if that's on purpose or if he's just that cheap?*

No need showing off too much. I think I'll linger a few moments before I go find Kenny.

Calvin Michaels held the phone like he was strangling a snake. His face was turning an odd shade of red. The veins on his neck were beginning to bulge and pulsate.

"I demand to talk to McKay, right now. I don't give a damn if he's having a heart transplant at this very moment. You get his ass on this line or else." The sound of music blared down the hall. Michaels looked up from his tirade. Losing his train of thought, he slammed down the phone and ran to the recording booth.

Kenny was gyrating over the mixing board, giving the equipment and his hips a workout. Decked out in blue headphones decorated with stars that were lost in a forest of bushy hair, he dipped and swayed with the music. When he saw Michaels, he gave him a thumbs-up and a two-fingered drum roll that ended by pointing at Roger.

Michaels walked over and joined Roger, who was leaning against the wall enjoying his success.

"Good work kid. I see you found the problem. That good for nothing Audio Court. I knew they were just squeezing us to pad their commission."

"No, I'm afraid he was right about the burnt-out components and the failing equipment. I just reworked some of the circuitry to get you going. It's not a permanent fix. It will last for only a short while. A couple of months, a week or two, maybe. I wouldn't count on it for long-term use. You'll still have to make the proper repairs or you'll be right back where you were."

"20,000 thousand dollars' worth?" Michael's asked.

"No," Roger laughed. "The cost won't be anywhere near that. Maybe 5 to 6 hundred at the most. A new board, a couple of rectifiers, a new power supply, some soldier and the knowledge to use them properly."

"Can you do it?"

Roger grinned and tilted his head. "Are you offering me a job?"

"If you can guarantee me results like this. Hell yeah. Nothing would make me happier than to kick Audio Court to the curb. I always felt they were stacking the deck against us."

"I took the time to look around a bit. I am surprised how low tech you are here. I would think you'd have all the bells and whistles. Substandard audio and video, no interoffice communication, outdated low speed Internet. You could do much better."

Michaels raised his brows. "Hell, of a way to get a job, kid. Insulting your new boss. Bells and whistles don't come cheap. We aren't that successful, yet. I'm a businessman, the bottom line matters."

Roger shrugged his shoulders. "Quality and the proper equipment is not cheap either, but it's not as expensive as you think. I can design and install a system for you that I'm sure you'll be pleased with. I think you'll soon see the benefits of having a real in-house tech."

"Let's go back to my office and we'll iron out some details. I want to hear what you have in mind." Calvin held up a finger. "Remember, for now, there is always the issue of money."

"I'll have to warn you. I don't like to do things half way. Like I said, I'm not cheap. Neither is the equipment, but it will be well worth it to follow my recommendations. Besides," Roger added. "...I have a reputation to build and maintain."

Calvin took another look. "You talk with some authority like you know what you're doing?"

"About this? Yes, I do. I spent my childhood, my college time and the last few years learning this stuff. I know what I'm doing. I'm out to build a reputation and a following. I figure its time I used my talents to benefit me instead of some corporation. They say you never get rich working for somebody else. That's why I decided to branch out and start my own business. I won't let shoddy work ruin my name before I even establish one. I thought about moving to California and getting involved in Silicon Valley. Maybe find some start up to be a part of. Who knows, I could get in on the next Apple or Google," he shrugged and continued, "but there's so much building going on in Detroit right now, I figured I might as well take advantage of where I am and what I know."

"Smart man, there's a lot of opportunity right here. We need you young bucks to stick around and help us make Detroit what it used to be."

"Yeah," Roger said. "But, Detroit, though it's my home and I love it, doesn't have the best reputation around the world. I worry, it may be more advantageous in the long run to go where people look more favorably on the location."

"Bullshit," Michaels shouted. "People always need somebody to look down on, somebody to beat up on and Detroit is it. According to the media and the fancy magazines, we're the asshole of America. Problems, yeah we got problems by the boat load, but so does everywhere else." He started counting on his fingers. "We've got great people, world class culture, the Great Lakes, some of the best outdoors you can find, some of the best industry in the world, and the people here have more talent in their little calloused hands than all of those smooth skin intellectuals who sit back and bash us like we're lepers or some such shit."

"Are you running for tourist board president? That was quite a pep talk."

Michaels laughed. "Just don't get me started. I get tired of people looking down on us. We're better than that. I've been places. I'd put Detroit up against any of them. Yeah, we may not be the resort capital of the world, but we got a hellofva lot to offer." Roger nodded his agreement. Michaels gave him a sideways glance and stroked his goatee. "I've got a few things I'd like to run past you. This can be a cutthroat business and I may need some subtle ways to keep my eyes and ears on some things." His brows arched intensifying the statement.

Roger's hand fumbled in his pocket and cupped the gadget he nicknamed, "Ear Number 1". *This one is for you Mr. Michaels,* he thought.

"Sure Mr. Michaels anything you need."

15

"Disco," Michelle sang out as she answered the knock on her office door, spreading her arms wide. "Come here, baby, and give me some love." Pulling him close, she hugged him like a proud mother.

"I'm sorry I haven't seen much of you lately. There has been so much going on. The show is almost here and it's such a big deal. It's taken up all my time. How have you been?" She placed her hands on her hips and tilted her head.

"Has that brother of yours been treating you right? Because if he hasn't, you just let me know and you know I'll set him straight."

"Calvin's been good to me. He's always good to me."

"Loyal to a fault," she shook her head. "You wouldn't speak a word against that man if Jesus ordered you to."

"No, really. He looks after me good."

"I know, baby," she took him by the arm and led him to a chair, taking the one beside it. "What do you need from your big sis?"

"Nothing, I wanted to give you something."

"Oh, that's so sweet. Nobody thinks of me but you. That's one reason I've always loved you."

"I want to take you out to eat. We never spend any time together anymore like we used to."

"A lunch date with my special guy," she reached over and touched his hand. "I'm afraid I can't today. With the concert only days away, there is still so much to do."

Disco lowered his head. "Oh."

"Wait a minute," Michelle returned to her desk, shuffled some paper and jotted down a note. "How can I turn down my favorite fella? I'll have to reschedule a couple of things and delegate one or two others, but no problem. We're on for lunch. You get out of here and let me do my thing." Disco gave her a toothy smile.

"Okay, baby boy. You come back here about 11:30 and we'll go have ourselves a sumptuous lunch." Michelle kissed his cheek and shooed him out the door.

Michelle and Disco took their seats at a quiet table dressed with a crisp white tablecloth and fresh flowers. The West Tower, a French themed restaurant on Woodward Ave, the city's main through fare, was one of the many stylish new eateries that had opened in the last year. The minimalist décor, intimate ambience and health conscious cuisine made it an instant favorite of the area's gentrifiers.

"Good choice," she said. "Have you ever been here before?"

"No, but I thought you would like it. It's classy like you."

Michelle bowed her head. "That's sweet, Disco."

"It's true. You are the classiest lady I ever seen."

"Thank you, sweetie, but there is more to being classy then expensive outfits and a few bangles." She fluttered her fingers causing her substantial diamond ring to bounce light around like falling snow.

"Let's just say I put on a good show."

The waiter broke up their revelry with a pitcher of water, menus, and an attitude better suited for a truck stop. Through his forced smile he said,

"My name is Kennedy." His voice was nasal and dismissive. "I will be your server for today. Could I interest you in drinks and an appetizer?" He loomed over Disco, who looked at the menu with growing confusion.

Kennedy grunted. "Perhaps I should suggest something. Something simple and quick." His impatient posture and bored eyes added to Disco's visible discomfort.

Like a mother bear rushing to the protection of her cub, Michelle rose to the occasion. With the precision of a neurosurgeon and the coolness of an arctic breeze, she spoke. Her eyes never leaving the menu, her words cased in biting steel, her voice full of professional authority.

"Excuse me. Kennedy, was it?" She did not wait for him to answer. "We are here to have a pleasant meal. Your attitude is destroying that aura of joy. I would advise you to recalculate your presentation or retreat while that is still an option." She looked up at him and smiled liked a hungry lioness.

"*Nous apporter deux cokes,*" Michelle paused. Kennedy's eyes sprang open as if he had just been slapped.

"*Ne me teste pas,*" with the stare of an executioner, she sent him scurrying away.

Michelle looked to Disco. "Are you alright, baby? Don't let that prissy stuffed shirt upset you."

Disco nodded, pouting. "I'm sorry. I didn't mean to embarrass you."

"Don't you apologize to me. No matter what you do, you could never embarrass me. You did nothing wrong. Just because he is having a bad day does not give him license to take it out on you."

"Calvin says I have to be careful not to get in people's way. He says I have to try harder to be helpful. He was gonna send me to live with daddy's Aunt Louise. I promised I'd be good and he let me stay."

"How generous of him," she groaned, shaking her head.

Disco pouted and hung his head.

"Calvin doesn't mean to be mean. They don't understand him. He is just a very busy man. Lots of people depend on him. He's not like you. You was always good to me. You never treated me like I was dumb."

Michelle reached across the table laying her hand on his.

"I love you, baby. I don't care what anybody says you are not dumb. Don't let anybody tell you that you are. I have never known anybody with a kinder heart. Don't you let Calvin or anybody else push you around. If they mess with you, they mess with me."

Disco grinned and chuckled. "You sound like Aunt Louise."

"Is that old woman still kicking? I haven't seen her since...Well... That was about 15 years ago." She snickered.

"She was about 80 then. I have never met a stronger spirit. She is one tough old bird. I owe a lot to her. I don't think we would have made it without her. Thank God, we had that sanctuary to go to. After you and I got out of the hospital, I didn't want to go back to that house. I couldn't. So much had happened. Oh, the memories..." Michelle leaned on the table, her chin on her hand.

"She's the one who gave me the money to leave. She told me to go and not look back. Huh, it was hard, but it was the best thing that ever happened to me. She changed my life. I owe her."

"Where would I go Aunt Louise? My family don't want me anymore. I don't really know anybody else. Everything I've ever known is in Detroit."

Louise was a small, frail-looking woman with wrinkled sun-bleached skin and eyes like a pissed off alley cat. She spoke in puffs and wheezes, but with the conviction of a Baptist preacher. Louise crunched her face like a wadded-up newspaper and held her wrinkled fist in the air. She rocked forward in her chair. The floorboard of the porch protested. "Why would you go back to that situation? You've lost your baby and almost your life." Michelle winced and wrapped her arms around her stomach.

"Do you really think Calvin cares? How many children, by how many women, does he already have? If you go back, you'll be just another in that long line of forgotten conquests. Or end up bargaining away what dignity you have left for a few dollars. What else do you have, but your future? Do you want to throw that away on somebody who doesn't give a damn about you?"

"Calvin loves me," Michelle protested. "He will take care of me. He'll make sure nothing like this ever happens again. He has plans. He's going to make me a star. He..he..."

Louise closed her eyes and took in a deep breath. "Girl, don't be so stupid. You'll be his star whore." Michelle bristled.

"Calvin loves Calvin and what you can do for him. Listen to me. Calvin is a dreamer, a charmer, a user, and a selfish, heartless man. He is not worth your life. That boy is my nephew. God love him, because even his own mother didn't like him. He is his daddy's son. And he is my brother's boy, but I know the devil that's in them both. Just like he brought that gunfight to your house that killed your baby and damn near killed you and his brother, he will bring equal or worse to you again if you go back. You are just props he uses to get what Calvin wants."

"He didn't mean for this to happen."

"He never does, as if he cared at all. It doesn't matter, damn it." She slammed her fist onto her knee.

"It's who he is. That boy has had a black cloud over his head since the day he was born. He's got a mean streak in him that enjoys the evil he creates. His thoughts are only about what Calvin wants, what Calvin needs, what Calvin likes." She tilted her head and looked at her with one eye.

"Did he ask about the baby? Did he show any sadness about losing his child? Hell, no. Did he even come to the hospital to see you or his own brother? The answer is no. If your cousin Shirley hadn't called me and I told her to send you both to me, you'd be lying in some filthy hole somewhere. He'd be whipping on both of your asses because you were costing him and not serving him."

Michelle shoulders slumped. The dry wood of the porch quickly absorbed the tears that leaked from her eyes.

"Think about it. His brother gets shot and damn near dies. You, 8 months pregnant, get shot, lose your baby, and damn near die. Those two other boys did die and he comes out without a scratch. I hate to say it, he is my blood, but the devil rewards his own. God forgive me for saying it. His father, I watched that evil little bastard rain hell on everyone around him. The devil walked in his shadow. Like his son, he was handsome as a movie star, but deadly as nightshade. I watched him use them boys' mother up until poor Helen gave out from pure exhaustion. He broke her heart every way a heart could be broken. Calvin is his twin. Don't repeat her mistake."

"I can't leave. Where would I go? What would I do? Calvin would drag me back. And what about Disco? He needs someone. You'll need me to help with him."

"Girl, it's a big world. Getting lost is not impossible. Get you a bus ticket and ride until there ain't nowhere to ride to. Don't worry about Disco or me. I know with that bullet still stuck in his head, he'll never be quite right, but we'll manage. He's a sweet boy. Always has been and always will be. He got all the goodness and Calvin got all the rest. I wish I could keep him here with me, but he wants to go back and be with his brother. I won't be able to stop that. Big Calvin taught them boys to always stay together. Even that bullet in his head won't push that out of him."

Michelle stood up from her chair and leaned on the pillar. She looked toward the road cutting through the endless acres of corn, her eyes full of fear, and tears for what laid beyond.

"The doctors say I'll never be able to have children. The bullets tore me up too much inside me." She rubbed her middle.

"I feel like something besides my baby died in me. Like I lost some part of me. Like I..." Her voice trailed off to a whisper. "Calvin took that from me."

"Well, child," Louise interrupted. "Maybe your life was meant for something else. Get the hell out of here and find it. This is your chance. Take it. You'll be all right. You'll find your way. Wash Calvin out of your blood and make something of yourself. Don't end up old and alone, stuck in the middle of a corn field." Aunt Louise stared out into space. "Regretting what little life gave you instead of living the life you wanted. Don't end up being an old woman wishing you had made a different choice"

"That when you went and became a lawyer, wasn't it?" Disco asked.

"Yes, it was a long road, but..."

"I was so happy when you came back. Calvin was too. We were afraid we'd never see you again."

Kennedy delivered the drinks and took their order. He bubbled with enthusiasm as if he had been injected with sunshine. Michelle nodded her approval. Her phone rang. She looked at the caller ID and held up a finger to put Disco on hold.

"Yes. Alright, I'll be there." Her voice dropped.

"Are you alright, Samel? Good, see you later." She put away her phone and smiled with a half-hearted effort.

"Sorry about that. It was important business. I had to take it. But, now I'm all yours. Let's enjoy our meal." She held up her glass and offered a toast.

16

Spade took a seat at the bar. "Jack and a draft."

The bartender gave him the once over. "What happened to you?"

"I cut myself shaving," he growled.

"What were you shaving with an ice pick?"

"Are you a barber or a bartender? Give me the damn drink, and mind your own business." Spade drank and simmered, building up steam until he was about to burst like an over ripe grape.

"Na'Taya," he grumbled. "Make me look like an ass. When I get my hands on you and your boyfriend you're gonna regret messing with me. I'm gonna let you watch while I take your boyfriend apart; piece by piece."

He cranked his neck till it snapped like a cartridge clicking into the housing of a gun.

"Campbell," Spade laughed spraying a mouth full of beer across the bar. "...he learned what the price was for making me a laughing stock." Spade flexed the scared toe of his left foot.

"Taking your boots off Spade, is not a good idea." Campbell said. "Afghanistan is not a hospitable place, especially these mountains."

"My dogs are killing me, man." Spade complained massaging his feet. "We've been trekking through these lousy mountains for over two weeks. I'm gonna get at least one night of good sleep and that means with my boots off."

"Alright man, you've been warned. This isn't Chicago. There are things in this place that will eat you as easily as a dog will eat a bone."

"Fuck off," Spade said giving him the finger. "Ain't no Al-Qaeda in these God-forsaken mountains. The only things here are goats, camels, rats, and big ass flies." Spades' hatred for Campbell echoed through his words. Campbell had been promoted to squadron leader over Spade. *Because he kisses ass better than a whore at a Shriners' Convention.* Spade thought. He settled into a crevice in the cave. Dropping off, he snored like a washing machine. When he awoke a couple of 6-inch camel spiders were dining on his big toe.

"Aww," he screamed in a high pitch voice like a frightened girl when he noticed his uninvited guests.

"What the fuck," he yelled shaking them off and watching them scurry away up the wall. His eyes blared with terror like headlight in a fog. He screamed. "I've been bitten. I'm gonna die." Trying unsuccessful to get his foot to his mouth, he begged for help. "Suck the poison out."

"Not with your mother's mouth," Campbell laughed throwing him a first aid pack. "I didn't know those damn spiders liked dark chocolate."

"I don't need this shit." Spade shouted, chucking the pack against the cave wall. "I need something for the poison. Damn it. We've got to get back to the base infirmary." His chest was rising and falling like a race horse at full trot. A greasy layer of sweat covered him from head to toe. Fear reeked from him like the stench from a bog.

Campbell stood at the center of a crowd that had gathered around Spade. He led the laugh fest.

“No can do. We have orders, soldier. You've got to suck it up and take your lumps like a real marine." He waved off the situation.

"They aren't poisonous, idiot. At least not all of them, especially the big ones. They just stun you so you can't feel them dining on your ugly ass. If you die, it would probably be from infection." Displaying a satisfied grin, Campbell added. "If I were you I'd grab that med-pack and clean up those bites."

Spade crawled across the sandy floor of the cave and retrieved the first aid kit. His hatred grew in depth and intensity, as he fantasized about the countless way he would get even with Campbell. Spade vowed to himself that whatever it took, Campbell would pay for making him the fool. It only took two days before opportunity presented itself.

Spade, hobbled by on his sore foot, was bringing up the rear. Campbell constantly yelled at him. "Keep up. Stay in formation. Double time it, soldier." Spade grumbled to himself, but followed orders. The squadron searched a group of interconnected caves rumored to be the lair of an insurgent group. When they reassembled at the mouth of the labyrinth, Campbell was missing.

"Where's Campbell?" the captain asked. Everyone looked around in confusion. He called out, No response. "He went in with us, but didn't come out. Who was the last to see him?" No one answered. "Nobody heard anything?" Everyone shrugged their shoulders. "He must have gotten turned around in there. We've got to go get him men." He ordered leading the platoon back inside.

Campbell was found at the bottom of a chasm. It was assumed he had slipped, fallen, and broken his neck. The squad retrieved the body, buried it and GPS'd the location for later retrieval.

Downing another shot of Jack Daniels, Spade smiled at the memory. The joy of smashing his rifle butt into the base of Campbell's skull. The pleasing "crack" as his skull gave way. The satisfaction of watching his limp body tumble down to the bottom of the dark hole. It was almost too much to handle when he shined his light down and saw the camel spiders on the wall rushing down to their unexpected meal.

"A gift from me, you eight-legged freaks." The memory was always one of his favorites.

Taking a trek to the men's room, Spade stumbled into a blue haired hipster. He scared the skinny young guy so badly, he missed the urinal and peed on his leg. Like Godzilla storming through

Tokyo, Spade stomped back to his seat at the bar; reveling in his accomplishment.

"Hey, Spade." A hand rested on his shoulder. Spade shrugged it off and turned to see Spenser.

"What the hell are you doing here?"

"Ms. Hightower sent me in to get you. She's outside in the car."

"Why didn't she come in? She too good to be seen in public with me or something?"

Spenser looked around. "I'm just the driver. I don't ask questions."

"Suck ass," Spade mumbled under his breath. He drained his glass and belched like a bullfrog. Spenser turned and walked away shaking his head.

"I do not appreciate being kept waiting." Michelle said when Spade opened the door,

"Take a seat." She ordered. Spade fell into position. Michelle eyed the big man with the casualness used to scan junk mail.

"I won't try to guess how that happened." She drew a circle in the air denoting his face. "I'll just assume you haven't found the girl?"

"No, not yet." He replied, "I..."

Michelle interrupted him. "I have new instructions for you." She handed a business card to him. "When you locate the girl, detain her and call me. Never mind about Calvin. I will give you further instructions at that time."

"But, I have specific orders to bring..."

"Forget what you were told. Concentrate on your new directive. I will handle Calvin." She smiled. “I can imagine that he is rather upset with you. He never could deal with disappointment very well," she snickered. "You can thank me later."

"What's this all about? Why is this little piss ass girl so important?"

Michelle' voice lost all emotion. "It is not necessary for you to know that. If you feel you cannot do the job tell me now. I'll release you back into the loving arms of Calvin and you can ask him."

"No thanks," he smiled. "I'd much rather work with you." Spade slid over closer to her. Michelle gave him a look worthy of Medusa. He froze as if she possessed that ancient power and he was now a cursed block of granite. Every part of him, that is, but his mouth, which drooped like a soggy noodle.

"You aren't serious?" she asked looking him up and down.

"I don't know where you got the misbegotten notion that you could ever assume such a preposterous thing. Let me correct your incorrect assumptions." She raised one hand and rippled her fingers like the legs of a centipede.

"If there is ever anything that I want from you. I will come and take it. You can offer me nothing," Spade slid back against the door. Michelle leaned back in her seat and waited for a response.

"Good, we have an understanding. Now I would advise you to get about your job."

Spade backed out of the car. Embarrassed and confused, he stood on the curb watching the car speed away.

"Bitch," he mumbled. Gathering his senses, Spade headed for the liquor store. A fifth of Jack Daniels, a six-pack of beer and a loaded Glock rested on the passenger seat of his car. His search began.

17

Roger left the studio and walked the three blocks to the parking garage. Na'Taya was waiting in the car, scrunched down on the floor of the front seat. "Nobody is going to see you in here. I think you can sit in the seat."

"I didn't want to take any chances. We're pretty close to the studio."

Roger switched on the receiver for the electronics and scanned the frequencies for a signal. The radio offered only static.

Too much concrete, too much distance, he thought. *We'll have to get closer to the building,* he sighed.

"All I'm getting is static. Too many obstructions," Roger moved the car two blocks closer to the studio.

"Did you have any problems planting your little bug thingies?"

He laughed. "No problems planting my bug thingies. One's in Michaels' office, under the ledge of his desk, and another in Michelle's office in about the same place. It was easy. I just told him that I needed to see what systems they already had in place before I could draw up plans to upgrade. Michaels himself, took me on the grand tour all through the building, from the roof to the basement. I think he was scoping me out. Checking to see if I was legit. He asked all kind of technical questions. I dazzled him with

ANSWERS I'M sure he did not understand, even though he pretended he did. I can understand how trust in his world is hard to come by. I bet he's got his people in my old neighborhood asking all kinds of questions about me. No problem though, they'll find out I have nothing to hide. Not bad for my first day as a spy, huh?"

"This isn't funny, Roger. Don't get cocky." Na'Taya warned. "I've been sitting on pin and needles all day wondering if you were okay."

He winked. Roger pulled out a pack of cigarettes. "Do you mind?" Na'Taya scrunched her nose, but shook her head no. Roger lit a cigarette while he fiddled with the dials on the receiver.

"I guess he thought he was being clever. But, he was transparent as glass. Some of the questions he asked me had nothing to do with what I was there for."

"Like what?"

"Oh like, who was my favorite rapper. Where my people lived. Where did I hang out? Stuff like that."

"What did he think he would find out by asking you that?"

"He comes from the streets. On the streets where you go, who you go with, and what you do while you're there can tell a whole lot about your loyalties and intentions," Roger inched up the dial. The numbers on the LED wavered up and down. "Got it," he shouted. He pitched his cigarette out of the car and rolled up the window. They both leaned in over the receiver and listened intently.

Calvin Michaels voice came in loud and clear. "You two went to lunch," he asked.

"Yeah."

"Well, what happened? Did she meet with anyone else? Get any phone calls? Say anything that might tell us what she's up to?"

"We talked about Aunt Louise and the time we stayed there." He paused looking at the ceiling. "Oh yeah, her phone rang maybe three times she looked at it, but only answered it when Samel called. She said she'd see him later."

"Are you sure it was Samel?"

Disco wagged he head. "She said his name."

"Is that all?"

"The waiter was mean to us. At least to me."

Calvin ignored the answer and mumbled to himself.

"I knew they were up to something. I don't know what Samel and her have going on, but I don't trust the two of them together. There was something wonky about this deal from the beginning. The day she showed back up in town something told me there was bad weather coming."

He ran his tongue across his teeth and sucked in a whoosh of air. It squeaked a whistle like the air escaping a rubber duck.

"Stay close to her, Disco. Drop in on her a couple of times a day. Listen closely. I need to know what's going on. Those two are up to something. I know it. I can feel it in my bones."

A knock on Calvin's door, and the conversation became lost in a roar of music as the door opened.

"What do you think that was all about?" Na'Taya asked.

"I don't know. Maybe we're listening to the wrong somebody. You said that this Samel told Michelle about the FBI being distracted, right?" She nodded. "It sounds like Michelle and Samel are the ones we should be listening to. Calvin seems to be in the dark with what's going on if he has others trying to get information for him. It seems Mr. Michaels may be getting played." He paused for a moment. "We should turn our attention to Michelle." Roger sat back in his seat. "I wish we had some more information on this guy."

"I told you all I know."

"I got one more of our little friends. I'll have to get it on her somehow. That's the only way we'll be able to hear what she and Samel say to each other."

"How are you going to manage that?"

"I don't know, but I'll find a way. We just have to hope after I get it on her, she meets with him."

"Roger, I'm scared. This is getting way too complicated. Who knows what kind of danger you're putting yourself in."

He took her hand. "Don't worry. I told you I'd be extra careful. This will all work out. I promise. You'll see. It's important to me that you get free of this." He felt her relax.

"I don't know how to thank you for all you're doing. I've never had anyone risk so much for me."

"I think you're exaggerating things."

"No, I'm not. I don't know what I'd have done if you hadn't come along. You've saved my life in more than one way." She reached over and pressed her lips to his.

The music abruptly ended and Calvin's voice blared through the speakers. "I can get this Roger guy to come up with something that will make me a part of their conversation."

"Who's Roger?"

"Some smart-ass little nerd that I hired to handle some of our technology issues. Yeah, I'm sure I can get the little geek to do something. He may know tech stuff, but he doesn't seem to be very street savvy. I'm sure I can bend him the way I want him."

Roger and Na'Taya fell out of their kiss in a laugh. "Good to know he thinks so highly of me."

18

"Where's Na'Taya?" Henry asked, bobbing his head around Roger.

"What's wrong? Your brother isn't enough company for you?"

"It's not that. I just like her a lot. She's really fun. She said she would come back soon. I just thought," he pouted.

"There were things she had to do today, but she'll come next time. Oh, she did have a message for you. "Two eyeballs, a hunch back, two big toes, and a mud puddle. Whatever that means?"

Henry rolled on the bed laughing. The laughter was shaky. His head made small twitches he tried to hide.

"What does that mean?" Roger asked ignoring the sporadic movements. Don't acknowledge them and they might go away, as they sometimes did. It was an old strategy developed from years of practice. Then again, they might get worse.

"It's just a game we made up."

"You really like her, don't you?"

Henry nodded, "Yeah. Don't you?" he continued, before Roger could answer. "I know you do. I can tell."

"Yeah, I like her."

"A lot?" Henry added nodding his head.

Roger wagged his finger. "Don't you say anything to her about this. I care about her a lot," he paused and mumbled. "...plus, I think I may love her."

"Wow, are you going to marry her?" asked Henry.

"I don't know about all that. Let's not jump the gun. She may not feel the same way about me."

"She does. Yeah, I'm sure of it." Henry shook his head and agreed with himself. The twitches mixed with the shaking, hiding their presence.

"Really and when did you become such an expert on women?"

"I know lots of things. You're not the only smart one in the family."

"Oh yeah, Mr. Know-it-all. What brilliant thoughts have you had lately?"

"Well," he strained to sit up straight and look assured. "I know Na'Taya really likes you. I know that I'm not cured, but I'm getting better and I know..." He paused; the expression on his face became intense and serious.

"I know that you worry you'll end up like me." Roger snapped to attention. He tried to speak. His mouth moved, but only "ugh" came out. "Don't worry, Roger. I got all the sickness. You don't have to worry. You'll be alright."

"Why would you say something like that. I'm not worried about that or about me. I'm worried about you."

Henry tilted his head and looked at his brother sideways. A hint of anger entered his voice.

"I'm not blind. I'm not dumb, Roger. I know you're worried," his manner softened.

"It's alright I understand. I see the worry and fear in your eyes when you come around me, sometimes. Especially when I'm like this." He held up a trembling hand. They both stared at it till Henry grabbed it and stopped the shaking.

"I see it on your face. I hear it in your voice. It's been there all my life. I used to think you were mad at me, that you didn't like me. The way you stand back and stare at me when I have one of my spells. You look at me like one of those people in a scary movie when the monster is about to get them. I know you're scared of the sickness and not really scared of me, but it still hurts."

Roger added quickly. "No, I'm not. No, I don't. I'm not scared of you. I've never felt like you were a monster. I would never treat you like that."

"I know you don't mean to, but you do, Roger. Like right now, you act like you don't see me twitching and jerking," Roger shook his head no.

Henry reached out and took his hand. "It's okay, It's our way. Ignore it and it doesn't exist. It may go away. Admit it, and there's something to be scared of. Mom used to be the same way. That's where we get if from."

Roger hung his head. "All right, it does worry me a little. But, I'm more worried about you."

"Come on, Roger. I know. I used to ask mom why you hated me. She explained it to me. She said you didn't hate me. It was just that you were scared and scared people act like that. She and I used to talk about it all the time. At first, I was mad at you. But, I began to understand when I got older. Then it made me sad for you. Mom said that you were scared because you didn't know what the future was going to be like for you. If the disease would do to you what it's doing to me. If you would end up like me or be normal. She said she knew in her heart that you would be all right, so you could be around to look after me."

He twitched and smiled. "It's okay, Roger. I know you'll be alright. I can do this for both of us. I can carry it all. 'Cause I love you and know you'll always be there to look after me." Henry twitched and smiled again.

"You always thought I was moving away from you, but it was really you that was moving away from me. You can stop running now. Nothing is gonna happen to you. I got it. I got it like you've got me. I'm not a kid anymore, Roger. I know what's going on. I know what's going to happen. I can handle it." Henry stood face to face with his brother. "You don't have to worry about me. I'm stronger than you think."

Roger couldn't speak or hold back the flood of tears. A dark cloud lifted from over his head. A wall had been broken down, the feeling of relief was joyous, over whelming and shameful all at the same time. Roger stared at his brother and for the first time in his life saw someone other than a poor sick little boy. Falling forward, he smothered Henry in a hug.

"I'm sorry. I never meant to hurt you, little brother. I was so caught up in hiding from my own feelings. I didn't realize what it was doing to you." He hesitated. "I admit I was scared. I guess in a way I still am. I just didn't see what it was doing to you. Can you ever forgive me?"

"Don't worry Roger, we're brothers and brothers always forgive each other."

Roger wiped his eyes. "Of course, we do and we'll always be there to look after each other."

"I love you, Roger."

"I love you too, little brother. When you get out of here and we move into our new house things will be different. I promise."

"I know." Henry smiled and twitched. "I can't leave before I go to the concert on the bridge, though. I'm really, really excited about it."

"How did you manage to get a ticket? They were sold out the day they went on sale."

"I'm lucky, remember..." the twitching stopped.

19

"You and I need to talk." Calvin said, bursting into Michelle's office, his eyes focused as lasers.

"What has you in such a state?" Michelle asked, leaning back in her chair; the casualness in her tone was meant to irritate.

"You seem to have forgotten who's in charge around here. Lately you've been disregarding my orders and following your own agenda. I'm willing to give you some ground, but there can be only one chief and that is me."

"Calvin, be serious. There has been nothing that I have done that has not benefitted this enterprise. Don't tell me your ego is so fragile you're feeling threatened."

"That is not the point, Michelle. The decisions around here are made by me. Anyone who has a problem with that has no business in my world."

"Are you kicking me off the planet, Mr. Michaels?"

He stroked his goatee, threatening to rip out hairs. Keeping his voice measured, despite his irritation he said, "If you can't follow my lead then you should go your own way."

"Calvin, we've been through much together. To think that you could so cruelly toss me out the door without a second thought." A smirk crept across her face. "After all, who else would come to your rescue when you find yourself in another compromising position?"

The guard banged his club against the bars. There was a loud click and he pulled the heavy steel door open with a metallic squeak. "Your lawyer's here," he barked. The guard guided her into the cell and clanged the door closed. It locked with a deafening click. He stood outside the bars, ogling the backside of the tall attractive woman, smirked, and marched away.

Calvin Michaels remain unmoved, lying on his cot facing the wall.

"It's proper for a gentleman to stand when a lady enters the room."

Calvin turned at the sound of the voice, raised his head, and jumped to his feet when he recognized the face. His pupils expanded like he was looking at a ghost. "Michelle, is that you?" She answered with the lifting of her chin. "What the hell. What are you doing here?"

"Didn't you hear the man? I'm your lawyer." She smiled like a Halloween pumpkin.

"My lawyer?" he laughed.

Michelle raised a casual brow and held up a folded paper.

"Bond has been established. I will be waiting out front. She launched the paper at him like a paper airplane, turned, and signaled for the guard to return.

Calvin bent to pick the paper from the floor. "A lawyer, huh? You've been busy. I thought after you disappeared on me you might end up in some house, making a living studying the ceiling over some john's shoulders." The corner of his mouth rose in a snicker.

Michelle grunted a laugh. "If I had stayed with you that might have been a possibility." She spoke without turning around. "Luckily for me, I saw a different future. I've done well for myself. But, now I'm here to do something for you." Looking over her shoulder, she asked. "How's Disco?"

"Desperate to see you."

When Calvin exited the detention center, a man led him to a black limousine. He opened the door and directed him in. Michelle was reclining, crossed legged with a glass of wine. He sat down and the car began moving. Looking around, Calvin said, "Yes, you've done very well." He rubbed the smooth leather of the seats. She remained silent. "I had a feeling about you. After the...you know. It took guts to strike out on your own." He reached over and placed his hand on her knee.

"Yes," she said sitting down her glass. Picking up his hand with two fingers as if she were removing a soiled towel, she tossed it back at him. "I've reviewed your case. I don't think it will be too difficult to make this matter go away. After all, the witnesses are unreliable and there is no real physical evidence, just your history of questionable behavior." She gave him a lazy eyed look. "In the future, you will have to be more careful in your choice of associates. It's time to up your game." She wagged her head. "I'm sorry to see some things have not changed."

"How did all this happen?" he signaled to their surroundings.

"That is a long story. The reason I am really here is I have a proposition for you; a business proposition. I have an associate who is looking for a..." she paused and gave him the once over. "...looking for a facilitator. Someone who he can work with..." she added, "... discreetly. Someone smart, with a knowledge of the landscape."

"You're looking for a middle man?"

"In a manner of speaking."

"I'm nobody's second banana, Michelle. I don't do seconds. I'm the boss." He pounded a finger into his chest.

"Of course, you are Calvin," she said, holding back a laugh. "You misunderstand. My associate is willing to provide backing for your own enterprise with the understanding that the front of the house is yours and the back of the house is his, so to speak." Hurriedly, she added, "There will be a substantial cut for you of course."

"What enterprise and who is the benefactor?"

"You always wanted to be a music mogul. The next Barry Gordy. The founder of a music dynasty. Now is the chance. With the right backing, your personal skills, and the wealth of untapped talent in Detroit, you could make this happen. You could eclipse the success of

Motown and create a new musical legacy, right here. Your dream can come true."

Calvin leaned back in his seat and stared into the future.

"First, you and I must have an understanding. Then I will introduce you."

"What is your part in all this?"

"I work with you and act as a liaison between both parties. As far as the music goes, I'm in for a quarter, Disco is in for a quarter, and the rest is yours. You get thirty percent of the back house. As well, you get to call the shots of course; after all, you're the boss." She smiled and refilled her glass, but did not offer him one.

What is this sneaky bitch up to? Calvin gave her a wary look.

"You've got my attention." He reached for his own glass and filled it.

"Oh yes," Michelle said as an afterthought. "I told Spade to contact me when he found the girl."

"That's what I'm talking about," Calvin interrupted. "My people answer to me, not you."

"Calm down, Calvin. I only did that because your presence is needed elsewhere. In New York, as a matter of fact."

"What the hell would I be doing in New York?"

"I have arranged for you to be interviewed by Rachael Calloway on 'The World Today.' This will be a great promotion for the concert, for the company, and for you. You'll get a chance to cement yourself in the minds of the country." She waved her hands in front of her. "The man behind the music."

"Rachael Callaway?" He swallowed. "When?"

"Tomorrow evening. Shana is making your travel plans as we speak."

"When were you going to tell me this?"

"I just got confirmation. I wanted to make sure everything was set. I was coming to tell you this afternoon, but you jumped the gun and began raining all hell on me."

"The World Today," he patted his hair and felt his unshaven face.

"Don't worry, I have Shana making arrangements to get you to a barber, have your best suit cleaned, and to pick up and deliver you to and from the airport and the studio on both ends." Michelle smiled. "Give a dog a bone." She leaned forward and offered him some papers.

"There are some people I would like you to meet with. You know how important connections are. It is never wrong to expand your network. Not to mention, there is no better place to shop for a new suit or two. After all, there is the Performers Gala the night before the concert. Not to mention the press and the throngs of politicians, A-listers, and celebrities who will be at the concert wanting to be part of history, your history. Your image will be plastered all around the world. You will want to look your best." She spun her chair and nodded over her shoulders. "This is just the start Calvin, It's only up from here."

"I have to admit," he said. "You're a pain in the ass sometimes, but you do deliver." He straightened his tie and smoothed a hand through his hair. "I was beginning to be a little pissed. The press has interviewed the mayors of both Detroit and Windsor. They've also met with a lot of the performers, but nobody has made a move my way." He held up his chin like he was posing for a statue. "It's about time they recognize the man behind the scene, the driving force."

Good boy, Fido, Michelle thought. She smiled.

As Michelle left the office, Calvin grabbed his phone. "Shana, get me Harrison on the phone." He slammed down the receiver. *It won't be that easy Ms. Hightower. I know when I'm being led by the nose. We'll play along until I find out what you're up to.*

"Mr. Harrison on two," Shana beeped in.

"Harrison," Calvin yelled into the phone. "I need you to drop everything and get on this immediately. I don't care what you've got going. This is more important. Samel Nizam and Michelle Hightower, get everything you can on them, dig deep. I'm flying to New York. I'll be back tomorrow night. I'll call you when I'm about to land. Don't let me down. I'll take care of you."

20

"Will you take my place this weekend, Lucy?"

"What? You're giving up a weekend with the Shiners? You'd be giving up an easy two thousand dollars or more. Something important must be happening." Lucy spun around the trapeze pole, tossed her hair to one side, and shimmied down to a squat. She bent from the waist, presenting her rear end to the audience, and faced Michelle.

"I know. I hate to do it. I could really use the money, but I've got a really important exam first thing Monday morning and I have to spend the weekend studying and getting some sleep. This is one of the subjects I really struggle with. I have to give it more time," Michelle said.

"Okay honey. I'll take it for you. I was a little teed off I wasn't chosen to be one of the lucky girls, anyway."

Michelle sighed and started moving away, strutting across the stage. "Thanks, I owe you one."

"No, you don't!" yelled Lucy. "All the money I'll make more than makes up for it."

Michelle forced a smile. She bumped and grinded her way through the rest of her set, forcing herself to graciously accept the monetary tips for the free feels the men took. Making her way down from the stage, she headed for the dressing room, pulling money from every crack and crease of her body.

"Why do you do this to yourself?"

Michelle turned and came face to face with a balding, pudgy cheeked, sleepy-eyed man. He looked like a hairless chipmunk. "Excuse me?" she asked.

His voice was low and dignified, with a heavy eastern European accent. "I have been quietly watching you for weeks. It is obvious to even a blind man that you do not enjoy your work. So, I ask. Why do you do this to yourself?"

Michelle placed one hand on her hips and held out the other, rubbing her fingers together. "It's all about the money, honey. I can make more money grinding and shaking my way through one night here than I can busting tables or pounding on a cash register in a month. School is expensive and a minimum wage job just won't cut it."

"There are other ways."

"No, thanks. I don't flat back for nobody. Go find a nail if you want to pound something." She pivoted and started to move away.

"I am not trying to be your pimp or your john. I am offering you an opportunity to get and do all that you wish and not have to subject yourself to the hands of every overzealous drunkard with a dollar bill."

Michelle turned back to him, her hands planted firmly on her hips. "What, do you want me to be a kept woman? Your own personal call girl?"

"I don't ask you to do anything that you are not freely willing to do."

"What then? Why offer this to me?"

"I consider myself to be a good judge of quality. I see untapped potential in you."

Her curiosity peaked, she asked. "Give me some specifics. What exactly are you offering and what exactly do you want in return?"

"I offer you free reign of my home. I will pay all of your expenses and give you a generous stipend. All that I ask in return is your company and any kindness you wish to bestow on me."

"You want me to be a kept woman, your sex toy," she spit the words out.

"Since you wish to, how do you say, "cut to the chase," I ask nothing so crass as that. My days of sexual Olympics have passed. I do have certain," he searched for the right word, "needs, but not what you imagine. I am an old man, a lonely man. I seek only stimulating companionship." He smiled softly. "Let me introduce myself. I am Dumitru Gogean." He dipped his head and extended his hand. *"O onoare s ava intalnesc."*

Michelle stared at this strange little man. The idea was absurd, but it would solve so many of her problems. "I couldn't," she said. He tilted his head and eyed her. She took his hand and heard herself saying. "Maybe we can meet for lunch tomorrow and discuss this further?"

"That would be most acceptable." He cheerfully said. "Here is my card. Telephone me tomorrow when you are ready and I will send the car for you." He bowed again. "Until tomorrow, Ms. Hightower." A gentle smile and he left.

Two nights later, Michelle moved in. Over the next two months, Michelle went to classes in the day and nervously waited for Dumitru to come to her at night. He never did. One morning at breakfast, the butler sat a rectangle box in front of her. "What's this?" she asked.

"From the master," he answered bowing and leaving the room.

Inside the box, Michelle found a red leather riding crop resting on a black velvet lining. A braided loop extended from the handle and red leather straps fanned out from the top like a thick mane of hair. *What the hell,* she thought. *I don't ride.* She took it to her room, deposited it on a shelf in the closet and forgot about it.

Two weeks later another box arrived. This time a red studded dog collar. Two week later a black leather leash. Every two weeks for the next two months, a box would be delivered to her at breakfast. The schedule became so regular she began to expect them. Slowly the picture began to fill in like a drawing in a coloring book. The truth of what was happening at first caused her to wince and consider leaving. What was she becoming? What kind of life was she living? What had she agreed to? Did it even matter? Her apprehensions fell away and she embraced her new reality. One night six months after moving in, Michelle burst into Dimitru's bedroom. Clad from head to toe in black leather, sporting an eye mask and thigh high boots, she cracked the whip. The tendrils of the whip crackled in the air like electricity. Her mouth slashed with red lipstick. She radiated an intimidating sense of power.

Her pet wormed out of bed and crawled to her on his hands and knees. He knelt beside her, waiting to be collared.

Through her undergraduate, graduate, and law school days, Michelle fulfilled her role. Dumitru in turn exposed her to all the best things in life; art, books, music, languages, fashion, politics and everything her curious mind could absorb.

"Will you be free to attend a gala with me at the Saudi Arabian Embassy?" Dumitru asked. "There will no doubt be some valuable connections to be made. It is a launch party for some initiative or another."

Michelle looked up from her meal. "To whose ends? Mine or yours?"

"Yours, of course. My days of playing an active part in the politics of life are over. I have neither the energy nor the inclination. I am just an interested spectator in life's play. It gives me great pleasure to see you command the marionettes. You are such a good puppeteer."

Michelle nodded her consent.

21

"No sign of him, sir. We've covered every strip club, bar, and dance hall we could find. His last sighting was a couple of days ago."

Samel pressed his fingers into his temple. *Who knows what you've gotten yourself into. It was a mistake to send you out alone. I should have kept a closer watch on you.* Samel swiveled his chair around and stared out the window at the Windsor, Canada skyline. "Find him." He dismissed the men with a wave of his hand.

Samel rose from his seat and walked to the window. He stared down the banks of the Detroit River toward the bridge. The Ambassador Bridge, an international link between the United States and Canada; the busiest commercial bridge in the world loomed in the distance. On an average day, 10,000 commercial vehicles travel its 7,500-foot span. Billions of dollars of trade each year makes its way back and forth across the bridge. Just beyond the bridge, the new Gordie Howe International Bridge stood like a younger, more vibrant version of its aged predecessor. It gleamed like a shiny new silver medal.

Samel closed his eyes and pictured the broken remains of the Ambassador Bridge lying in the river. Hundreds, thousands of bodies floating, face down in the water. The tears of the nation sounded like music to his ears. "For you, Asilah and Badra, and you, Akram; my son."

In the early morning light, Samel stood with his son at his side, clutching his leg. "There are no enemies here. We are not combatants. We hide no one."

"Out of the way, raghead! We will see for ourselves!" The Marine captain shouted.

"I work with the UN," Samel insisted. He attempted to show his papers. The soldier brushed them aside. "This village has been designated as a safe haven. We have been cleared to be left in peace. We are a safe port for those fleeing the violence."

"That is a distinction we make, not the UN." The soldier pushed his way forward.

"No, you can go no further. We have women, children, and elderly to protect. You cannot violate their privacy like this. It is forbidden. It is unlawful."

"I don't know who this guy thinks he is, but I've had about enough of him." The captain said. He signaled with a nod. Another soldier standing behind Samel received the message. He said, "I never met a mule that didn't have an attitude." It was the last thing Samel heard before the butt of a weapon was smashed against the side of his head, knocking him unconscious. His prone body laid sprawled in the middle of the road. Little Akram, trembled, weeping at his feet. The soldiers began a systematic sweep through the village.

A disgruntled villager retrieved his Russian Kalashnikov and fired, bringing down the lead soldier. The village erupted in chaos. Firefights and pitched battles broke out throughout the town. The soldiers fired at anything that moved. The villagers fired antique weapons and hurled rocks or anything they could get their hands on. When the fighting ceased dozens of men, women and children were dead. It was a bloody rout. Even the animals were killed. Those who did not die in the battle wished they had. The soldiers, drunk on adrenaline and fueled with rage, raped and slashed their way through the rest. None survived. Every home and structure in the village was set ablaze and brought to ruin.

Just as night was cresting, Samel, bloody and disoriented, woke to a nightmare. His 8-year-old son laid dead at his feet, twisted in an odd angle, his skull bashed in. Samel, blinded by tears, picked up the broken body of his son and screamed to the heavens. Clutching the lifeless body tight, he pressed it to him as if he could force some of his life into him and bring him back. "Akram, my son!" He screamed. Running with the boy in his arms, he made his way through the horrific devastation. Wailing in pain as he passed numerous bodies, both young and old, littered the ground like fallen leaves. He waded through smoldering heaps that were once the homes of family and friends, the buildings smoking and crackling with dying fires.

When he reached his home, his heart stopped beating. His insides seized up and went cold. The roof of his house was reduced to ashes. The walls were piles of debris. Asilah, his wife, and Badra, his 12-year-old daughter, laid naked and mutilated in the front yard. Their bloody corpses had been tortured and violated. What was left of his sanity came apart. Samel fell to the ground in agony, still holding the cold dead body of his son. He wished for his own death. His entire family dead before is eyes. Hatred and rage throbbed in his heart. What was there to live for? The world had blinked and come to an end. This was not right. This was not fair. He cried to the heavens until his pleas became screams of curses for vengeance.

A groan and a whimper sounded between the hissing and crackling of the many dying fires. Tracking down the sound, Samel found his sister's son, his nephew, Rala, under a stack of fallen boxes. He was weak and wounded, but still alive. Taking the boy to a clear area, Samel dressed his wounds. A thorough search of the village found no one else alive. Cradling Rala's fragile and broken body, Samel rocked him and wept all thorough the night. Over the next few days, Samel took great care and buried every person in the village. The boy healed and regained his strength. When

Rala was strong enough for travel, the duo set off looking for a new life and for retribution.

22

Desperate hours of unsuccessful searching led Spade to the West River Towers. With two days of stubble and the lingering effects of a persistent hangover, he was surly and impatient. Stumbling off the elevator he confronted the guards. "Where's Rala?"

"Not here," the guard replied.

"Where the hell is he?"

"Couldn't tell you."

"Couldn't or wouldn't?" Spade asked, swaying on his feet.

"Try the tittie bars. That's where he likes to hang out."

"You're not very helpful, buddy. But then again, I've never met a mule that didn't have an attitude."

The door of the apartment swung open. Samel rushed out. "What did you say?" An anxious tension was in his voice.

"Sorry to disturb you, sir." The guard offered. This guy's looking for Rala. I told him he's not here."

"Not that," said Samel. "What did you just say?" he asked looking at Spade. "Something about a mule."

"Oh that. My father used to say that all the time. I guess it kind of stuck with me."

“Say it again!

“What?” Spade squinted in confusion. ”I never meet a mule that didn’t have an attitude.”

Samel reached out and steadied himself against the wall. "Who are you?"

"I'm Spade. I work for Calvin Michaels."

Samel studied him like an X-ray machine. "Have we ever met? I don't mean at the studio, but somewhere else." Spade shrugged. Samel narrowed his eyes on the big man's face. "Were you in the Middle East, in Afghanistan?"

Spade piped up, his face beamed. "I was a marine. I did two tours in Afghanistan, special ops. I don't remember meeting you." He chuckled. "Hell, I don't really remember half of what happened there."

Samel stared at him. His hand came up and rubbed the scar on the back of his head. "Rala is not here. I assume you're the one Michaels has looking for the girl?"

"Yeah, that's me."

Samel locked his gaze on him, trying to reconfigure his voice and face. With a suspicious sideways glance, he released him. "When you find the girl, I believe you will find Rala. It appears, against orders, he is seeking her whereabouts as well. Now if you will excuse me." Samel gave him one last evaluation before stepping back into the apartment and closing the door.

A cold wave ran through him. He placed both hands on the back of a chair and leaned heavily. *Is it him? Could he be the one who struck me?* The idea swirled around in his head. Try as he might, there was no image of the man behind him to recall. Only the voice and the words. *I never met a mule who didn't have an attitude.*

Those words that had haunted him all these years. They were words he could never forget; the last words he heard before his life forever changed. Now, here they were again for only the second time in his life. It's him. *It has to be him. There is no such thing as a coincidence. It was inevitable. All bridges lead home.*

Samel called Michelle. "I need you."

23

"With this system," Roger explained, "...we set up a network that allows all the computers to coordinate with each other. You won't need to email or even manually handle any documents. With a little twitching, we can even make everything video capable. This improves security because thing won't have to leave the building, as well, documents won't have to go through so many hands. Things will remain contained within your private network, subject to your personal wishes. You decide if you want them to be made accessible or not; you have complete control. It's a closed system. You couldn't be more secure."

"What else do you suggest?" Calvin asked eyeing the young man intently. "What about encryption?"

"I covered encryption in my report. Everything I suggested is in there, in detail. There are always things we can adjust depending on your own personal preferences. It just depends on what level you want to operate on."

"I wish we had some of this in place right now. I'm going out of town this afternoon and I'll be gone overnight, Things are moving very fast for us right now. I would like to be on top of what's going on around here, whether I'm here or not. The phone isn't good enough."

Calvin rested his elbows on his desk and laced his finger together. Cracking his knuckles, he grimaced. "I want you to be ready to put some special things in place the moment I get back. I want to be here to oversee the installation."

"No problem. I'll have the basics ready and we can refine it as we go. I need to make some more notes. I'll see you when you return." Roger left the office, walked around the building making notes and taking measurements.

"Come in," Michelle said, answering the knock on her door.

"Hello, Ms. Hightower. I'm Roger Beaufort, the new IT. I was wondering if I could look around, make some notes and take some measurements. Mr. Michaels has asked me to make some system changes and I need access to your space."

Michelle dropped her pen and leaned back in her chair eyeing him intently. "Exactly what kind of changes does Calvin have you making?"

"Basically, software updates for the computers. It's a complete network overhaul, increased encryption protection, that kind of thing. Improvements that will allow you to work more securely and more efficiently."

"Oh really. He never ran any of this by me."

"I wouldn't know anything about that. I'm just the hired help."

Her cell phone rang. Michelle looked at the screen and held up her hand to silence him. She swiveled her chair, placing her back to him and leaned into the phone. Her normal professional tone took on a soft pitch. "Yes. Samel."

Roger moved around the room, considering his options for planting the last of his bugs. *I don't think I can get close enough to plant it on her person. If I could, where would I put it?* His eyes settled on her expensive leather attaché case. Roger moved close to the desk and brushed against the case toppling it to the floor.

Michelle turned at the sound of the case hitting the floor. "Watch what you doing," she demanded.

"I'm sorry," apologized Roger bending to retrieve the case and its contents. "I didn't realize I was so close."

Michelle turned back to her conversation. "It's nothing," she said into the phone.

Roger scooped up the crop of paper, shoved them back into the case, and slid the bug into the accordion pleat on the inside of the case. "I apologize again. I've got all I need. I'm leaving now."

Michelle gave him a dismissive look over her shoulder and returned to her conversation.

24

With a piping-hot double chocolate latte and an apple walnut muffin, Na'Taya flipped up her hood and stepped out of the Starbucks™, heading back to the parking garage. A smiling Rala stepped up his pace and moved in beside her.

"You're a difficult lady to find." The words caught her by surprise, causing her to jerk to her left. Liquid splashed from the cup. Na'Taya tensed pressing her finger into the muffin. "Rala," she said, trying not to show her worry. "You startled me. What are you doing here?"

"I'm looking for you." He narrowed his eyes and bared his teeth like a grinning shark. "Spade is looking for you, too. Be glad I'm the one to find you. I don't think you'd be very happy if he found you first. I hear that psycho marine is looking to even a score with you."

One side of Na'Taya's mouth rose in a nervous smile. "What do you mean? What could you two want with me?"

"Ah, come on, Na'Taya, you're the most popular girl in Detroit. Calvin Michaels wants you, Spade wants you, my uncle Samel wants you, some private investigator wants you, and I want you too." Rala clicked open his knife and flashed the blade. The coffee and muffin fell from her hands. She started to scream.

"Don't do it," Rala warned with a headshake. He stepped on the muffin as he grabbed her by the arm. "This way," he said through a clenched tooth grin, shoving and directing her down an alleyway.

"Rala, why are you doing this?"

"Shut up. I'm asking the questions. You better have the answers I want." Forcing more than leading, he pushed her in the doorway of an abandoned building. The door creaked open and Na'Taya fell in, landing on her hands and knees. A cloud of chalky dust rose up from the broken plaster and cracked bricks that littered the floor. The room was dimly lit and dank. Dust particles danced in the dingy light that forced its way in through the partially boarded windows. The room smelled of urine and rot. The faint sound of dripping water could be heard in the distance.

"What do you want?" she asked turning over to face him.

"You set me up, didn't you?"

"Set you up? I don't know what you're talking about."

"You lying little bitch. It was no accident that we met at that club, was it? Who put you up to it? And why me? What the hell are you up to?" He moved in closer and stood over her. The stray beams of light bounced off the polished steel. The menacing blade held her attention. Na'Taya's heart pounded in her chest. Pictures of Yvonne's corpse scrolled through her brain, only the body in the picture had her face. Fear caused her to overheat and pant like a failing air conditioner. Excuses and inventive lies churned in her mind. Rala pointed the tip at her face. Na'Taya blinked at the knife and lost her train of thought, only to hurriedly begin running a new set of possibilities.

"Who the fuck got you to set me up?" he screamed.

"Nobody, I swear. I really don't know what you're talking about."

Rala grabbed her by the hair. "You embarrassed me in front of my uncle. Don't nobody do that to me, especially, no bitch."

Na'Taya twisted and squirmed trying to pull away. "Rala, please. I don't know what you're talking about. I didn't do anything."

"That's no way to treat a lady." A deep baritone voice said from over his shoulders.

Rala turned around to see a black clad stranger, a floppy Fedora pulled down over his eyes. "Who the hell are you? Get the hell out of here. This is none of your business."

"Salvador," Na'Taya whispered, amazement in her voice.

"Hello Taya," he said, looking past Rala.

"Hey, man," Rala said, moving toward him brandishing the knife. "Did you hear what I said? Get the hell outta here. I don't care if you do know her. Me and her have some personal business to conduct and it doesn't concern you." He waved the blade in Salvador's face. "Beat it."

Salvador raised his brows and peeked from under his hat. "You better be careful with that thing. Someone could get hurt."

"Yeah, like you if you don't get your ass out of here."

"Not without her," Salvador said with a wolfish smile.

Rala changed his hold on the knife. "There's plenty of blade to go around." he lunged forward.

Salvador jerked to the left; the blade missed his right shoulder by inches. He picked up a splintered 2 by 4 board. "Na'Taya get out of here. I'll meet you outside after I deal with your unpleasant friend."

"She ain't going nowhere," Rala said, moving toward her. Salvador cut him off and drove him back with a wide swing of the board.

"Go!" Salvador shouted. "This won't take long," he snickered, whipping off his hat and flinging it into a corner. His hair was pulled back in a single braid that whipped about his head like the tail of a scorpion. Na'Taya rose from the floor and started to speak. She looked at the two men staring each other down and headed out the door, slapping the dust from her clothes.

"You've stuck your ass in it now, boy. I'm gonna have to teach you a lesson. I've been hunting for her for days. Now I have to start all over again. You're gonna to pay big time." Rala said, kicking up a dust storm as he shuffled around the room. Raising his bladed hand, he surged forward. Salvador swung the board. Rala ducked and sprung up at him like a jackrabbit. Salvador pivoted and met his shoulder with a solid slam from the board. Rala screamed and dropped the knife. Salvador spun around on one foot and hit him again with the force of both hands holding the board. A loud crunch sounded as the board made contact with the back of his head. Rala whimpered, shook, and dropped like a brick tossed out of window. Salvador stood over him, panting and heaving. The cloud of dust they had stirred up began settling on the still body like dirty snow. A bright red smear of blood stained the board. A puddle of blood began to pool around his head.

Salvador dusted himself off, retrieved his hat, regripped the board, turned, and started for the door. The pearl handled knife lying by Rala's open hand caught his attention. "Nice blade," he said, picking it up and bouncing it in his hand. He hunched his shoulders. "Guess you won't be needing this."

He flipped it closed, slid it in his pocket, and headed out the door. Moving down the alley he pitched the bloody weapon into a dumpster. Na'Taya was waiting at the corner of the alley, peeking around the building.

"Where's Rala?"

"He's sleeping off a headache." He took her arm. "Let's get out of here."

Na'Taya pulled away from him. "No, I'm not going anywhere with you. What the hell are you doing here? How did you find me? Don't they put bank robbers in jail anymore?" Her grey eyes were as sharp as her words were harsh.

"After the situation I just rescued you from I would think you'd be a little happier to see me." She wouldn't move. Salvador's voice became stern and pointed. "Do you really want to have this conversation right here, right now, out in public?"

Na'Taya looked around, raised her hood and stomped off toward the parking garage. Salvador slapped his hat against his leg and trailed off after her. Na'Taya stepped inside the parking structure and turned. "What are you doing here?" Her voice was rough as the concrete that surrounded her.

"I've been looking for you."

"Why aren't you in jail where you belong?"

He smiled and looped his thumbs in his waistband. "It turns out the Feds jumped the gun. The videotape from the bank was corrupted. No positive ID. Nobody in the bank could positively identify anyone. Besides I've got half a dozen eyewitnesses who will swear I was on the other side of town at the time." His face wore the smirk of a kid who had got away with pranking the teacher.

"You mean there are no charges against you?"

"Nope, not a one. I'm free and clear."

"The FBI knows this?"

"They're not happy, but yes. They're the ones who released me with a stern warning they're watching me." He wagged his finger and smiled.

"You mean they've been using me? Lying to me all this time? Threatening me with jail time, and they never had anything against me?" Na'Taya said, more as a thought than a statement.

"Why would they have something against you?"

Na'Taya raised her fist and screamed. Her knees wobbled and she felt sick to the stomach. "You told them I was part of your gang. You used me. They came after me. Threatened to lock me up and throw away the key."

She fell against the wall. Droplets formed in the corner of her eyes. She stifled a whimper. "Martin, you black hearted bastard," she whispered.

"I didn't implicate you. I would never do that. Why I never even mentioned your name. And who's Martin?"

"What do you want?" she snapped.

"I want you," he continued, before she could reply. "I know I was wrong. I want to make it up to you. I want us back. I convinced Gloria in Seattle to tell me where you went. She led me to St. Louis where I had to go to nearly every Starbucks in town. I know how much you love your lattes. I showed your picture around before I got a lead that steered me here. That Pakistani girl, Leia, that you kicked up a friendship with told me you were coming here. She could see true love and extended a little pity to me."

"True love?" Na'Taya laughed. "What do you know about love? True or otherwise. You're just like everyone else. All you want to do is use and deceive people."

The smirk faded from his face. His dark brown eyes softened. He reached out his hand to take hers. "No, Taya. When I was sitting in jail all I could do was think about you. The realization hit me. More than my freedom, more than beating the charges, more than anything; I was missing you. I felt ashamed of the way I had lied to you and let you down. Now all I want to do is make amends. To be the kind of man I should have been. The kind of man you thought I was," he swallowed. "If you'll let me?"

Na'Taya stepped away. "What game are you playing? You never really cared for me. Are you in this with Martin? Did he make some kind of deal with you to let you out so you could come and put pressure to me?"

"What are you saying? Who the hell is this Martin you keep asking about? I don't know a Martin. I don't know what you're talking about." He moved in close and took her hand. Her skin was hot. Her hands were trembling. His voice dropped to a whisper. "I came looking for you because I love you."

Tears flared up like a fire in the wind. Na'Taya shook her head. She mouthed the word "No," and began to move away. Running in a way that looked more like falling, she disappeared into the maze of cars.

25

Na'Taya fled back to the car. Falling into the passenger seat, she knelt on the floor and buried her face in her hands. A storm of tears gushed from her eyes. Every hurt, every betrayal, every harm, and heartbreak rose up inside her. Trembling fingers danced against her chest. Everything was a lie. Everything she had been told was untrue. Everything and everyone she had believed in had turned out to be false. No matter where she looked or what she tried to do everything always ended in pain and disappointment. The one constant thing was disappointment. The one sure thing was regret. No matter the effort or belief, the only reward, the only outcome was pain and disappointment.

As the tears gushed out of her, the sorrow inside began to morph and change. Like the bed of a river drained of water, something was hardening inside her; everything dried up. Tired of the pain. Tired of the lies. Tired of the disappointment. Tired of being used and let down. Na'Taya raised her head, her chin rising a little higher than it had before. The intensity of her resolve grew in strength. Sadness was replaced by a controlled rage; self-pity was changed into smoldering determination. A bittersweet sense of independence began to take shape. Na'Taya sat up in the seat and pulled out Martin's phone. *First things first,* she thought and dialed.

"Yes," the voice said.

"You lying piece of shit," she calmly said into the phone, holding it in front of herself as if she were looking down into his face. "You used me. You lied to me and tricked me. You lousy piece of filth. You made me believe I was going to jail so you could scare me into doing your dirty work. I hate you."

"Na'Taya? Is that you? What are you talking about?" A never-heard-before hint of panic was in his voice.

"You know exactly what I'm talking about. Salvador's not in jail. You don't have him. You don't have anything on him. You don't have anything on me. Nothing to hold over my head. You never had anything on me. You knew I was innocent, but, you lied. You used me and put me in danger anyway. I begged you to let me go, but..."

"You don't understand," he pleaded. "I didn't know he was released until a few days ago. I was going to tell you ."

"But what?" she interrupted. "You were going to tell me what?" She laughed. "That you're a lying sack of shit? Tell me that you're a good for nothing bastard?" She laughed again.

"Don't bother, Mr. FBI man. I know already. You don't have to worry about letting me off the hook. I'm letting my own damn self, off the hook and you...you bastard, you can go straight to the deepest part of hell." She yelled into the phone. Kicking the car door open, she hurled the phone at the concrete wall.

Martin shouted, "Na'Taya, we need you..." The phone broke into two pieces and fell to the ground. Na'Taya leapt from the car and stomped the remains until the parts were so small you couldn't tell what they once were. She pounded the ground until the heels of her feet began to ache. Standing in the crumbs of the destroyed gadget, she puffed and panted like a bull looking for something to charge at.

Slowly breathing calmer, Na'Taya fell back into her seat. The red-hot heat of her anger started to cool. She closed her eyes and leaned back into the seat. *I can leave this place,* she thought. *I can have my life back. I can be free.* A small smile mixed with bitter tears on her face.

Na'Taya never noticed the black Fedora behind the pillar. Salvador had witnessed the whole scene and heard her confrontation. He fell back against the stone structure and tried to put the pieces together. The one side of the conversation he heard began to make sense. Returning to his car, he moved it and parked on the same level, watching, waiting, and thinking.

"Hello beautiful," Roger said climbing into the car. He bent over to give her a kiss. She turned her head and he planted one on her cheek. "Did I wake you?"

Na'Taya didn't answer just shook her head.

"I did it." His voice was full of optimism and confidence. "I got the last bug on Michelle. Well, not <u>on</u> her, but in her attaché case. She was actually talking to Samel. I wish I could have bugged her phone. I think they were making plans to meet up. All we have to do is wait for her to leave and follow. We'll not only be able to hear her and Samel, but we'll also know where to find him. That should be enough for our old friend agent Martin. You'll be free of all this in no time." Roger noticed her lack of enthusiasm.

"What's wrong? I thought you'd be happier. Isn't that what we wanted?"

"Yes, of course," her words and expression were stifled and hesitant. "Roger, we need to talk. Something's happened."

"I know what you're going to say. You worry too much. I got this. You'll see." He smiled at her. "Don't worry. We'll talk later, okay. We need to get within sight of Michelle's car. I don't want her to leave without us. The range on those bugs means that we have to stay close or all our efforts are for nothing." Roger pulled the car out of the garage and parked a block away from the studios, providing them with a direct sight line of Michelle's midnight blue Lexus LS.

Na'Taya scrunched down in the seat, fearing someone would walk by and recognize her. Roger put on a baseball cap and lowered the brim to obscure his face in case someone from the studio might see him.

Half a block behind them, Salvador sat in his car, watching and waiting, trying to understand what was going on.

Huh, it's no surprise she's found a new guy. Women like her attract them like flies to rotting meat. But, the FBI? What the hell did they tell her and what were they making her do?

Images of Rala popped into his head. *Too bad that young punk made me do it. He probably could have filled in some of the missing pieces.*

Roger took Na'Taya's hand. It was cool and clammy. A slight shutter rippled through her. "It'll be alright. I promise," he reassured her.

"We need to talk, Roger. There is something I need to tell you."

"There she is," he said, throwing the car into gear.

"Roger," Na'Taya insisted.

"Later, please. We've got to concentrate on her and Samel. This could be it. We have to stay focused."

Na'Taya fell deflated back into her seat.

Michelle slid behind the wheel and maneuvered the sleek blue Lexus into traffic. Turning south, she headed toward the downtown area. Roger, a half a block behind, kept pace and matched her turn for turn. Growing more and more confused, but more intrigued, Salvador, followed a few car lengths' behind Roger and Na'Taya.

Michelle pulled into the parking structure of the West River Towers, an exclusive riverfront apartment complex. Roger slowed down and let her enter. As she advanced, he followed. Salvador matched Rogers' maneuver, managing to keep his distance without drawing attention to himself.

Michelle parked on the top floor of the parking structure. Roger parked on the same level, a couple of lane behind her. Salvador did the same. Michelle slid out of her car and moved to the elevator.

"Damn," said Roger. "She doesn't have the attaché case with her. We'll never know what they have to say without it." His foot began tapping the floorboard. "Damn it. I know she has it. Didn't she have it when she got in the car?" he groaned, smacking the steering wheel. Na'Taya shrugged nonchalantly.

Michelle looked up at the descending floor numbers, pivoted on her heels and returned to her car. Retrieving the attaché, she walked back to the waiting elevator and disappeared behind its door.

"Yes!" cheered Roger as if his team had just scored a touchdown. He began fiddling with the dials. "We'll give her a few minutes to get where she's going and then we'll see what we can get." He smiled at Na'Taya, caught up in his adrenaline rush. His enthusiasm proved to be enough for both of them. She sat quiet and morose.

"What's the matter? Are you sick or something? What's got you so down in the dumps? I would have thought you'd be on pin and needles, more excited than I am."

"I want this to be over with. Roger, I need to tell you what happened." Na'Taya stared at Roger. He hadn't heard a word she said. He was totally engrossed in his gadgets. His ears tuned to the erratic crackling coming from the speakers.

26

Samel paced in front of the window like an anxious tiger. A dark mask of disbelief, astonishment, and anger colored his face. Stepping with ever-increasing force, Samel would stop and stare blankly into the distant; a shake of his head, a few mumbled words, and he'd march back the other way.

Michelle entered the room and immediately moved to intersect his path. "Samel, are you alright? Has something gone wrong? You sounded so unsettled when you called." He looked at her with unfocused eyes. "Tell me what's going on," she pleaded, grabbing his shoulders.

His voice came out deep and resonant as if it were being broadcasted form a deep hole. "It's him. He was there. He was one of them." He cupped the back of his head where he was struck. A wave of anger rippled through him. Michelle withdrew her hands as the heat of his fury sent out tangible waves. She stepped away from him unsure of what he meant. Without intent or purpose, he swung his arms out in an arch. On one side, a fist-sized indention marred the wall. On the other side, a statuette was swept from a side table and smashed to pieces when it hit the floor. Plaster exploded into a cloud of chalky white dust. Samel planted his legs in a wide stanch, squeezed his face into a ball, threw back his head and roared like a wounded lion. He wheezed and panted as only a dying motor can.

Michelle moved to his side and whispered in his ear. She massaged his shoulders and neck. "It'll be all right. Tell me what happened." Her words were measured and practiced. She displayed the patience and steady manners of someone who had seen this before. Her mind replayed the memories of the numerous nights Samel woke up in a cold sweat, begging the solider to let them be, then scream the names of his dead family, and end with a blood-curdling howl before dissolving into a weeping puddle. "Who was there? Who was one of them?" she asked in a gentle voice.

"Him," he paused. "Spade."

"Spade? What does Spade have to do with your family?"

"It was him. His words were the last thing I heard before I was knocked unconscious." He repeated the phase that had haunted him for years.

"That doesn't make sense. He has nothing to do with you. And even if were possibly right, how can you be sure?" she asked slowly, petting him like a dog.

"It was him. He was there. I'm sure it was him. His voice. His words, linger in my mind like a foul stench." Samel's knuckles burned crimson as he clenched his fist tighter and tighter. "I will kill him." His voice was cold and hollow like the winter wind blowing through barren branches. "I will kill him. Through some grand plan a bridge has been built to the past, so that I can avenge my family. I will see him dead." His eyes were like burning embers; his voice was cold and sharp as broken glass.

The worry shifted from Michelle's eyes to her voice. "Samel, we are too close to our goal to lose sight of it now. Spade, if he is the one..."

"He is!" Samel shouted.

"Okay, he is," she conceded. "He will be dealt with, but there are other considerations that are more important at the moment."

Samel turned to face her. He moved like a mechanical man on a turntable. Only his upper torso pivoted the rest of him remained planted like a cement pillar. He spoke with the demeanor of a computer program written to understand only one command. "There is nothing more important than his death." There was a definite finality in his voice that made Michelle draw back.

She backed away from the brooding man, her body rigid with disapproval. "Your obsession with the past is clouding your judgment." The chastising tone of an irritated nanny sharpened her voice. "You have lost your focus. The bridge, Samel. The bridge must be our main business at this time. There will be time later to settle old scores and revisit past indiscretions. I need you in the moment, dedicated to the situation at hand. We have made commitments and promises. Our future success is at stake here. There is no time now for past maybes. If we fail to deliver as we promised everything is forfeited, even up to and including our lives. Remember we made a deal. There are consequences for breaking our word."

Samel's face went from sad contemplation to indignation. He rose slowly from his chair. "No time for the past?" he shouted. "Committed to the situation at hand? Revisit past indiscretions?" He growled a manic laughter.

Moving from behind his desk, he began circling Michelle like a skeptical buyer eyeing a used rusty car on cinder blocks, a sour expression painted on his face.

"You seem to forget the real reason you are here is the past, to destroy Michaels. To pay him back for..." he emphasized the words. "...past indiscretions." Sarcasm dripped from his words. He snorted a grunt. Michelle opened her mouth, but nothing came out. Samel continued.

"You and I are black holes; orbiting each other; feeding off each other's misery. Sucking in and exchanging anger and hate that emanates from us like fumes from a stink hole. Neither one of us gives a damn about anyone, anything or..." he stressed the words," each other. Not even... Our lives. Our only motive, our true passion is vengeance; to see others suffer as we have. To pay back a world that has trampled on our hearts, removed our reasons for living, and left us with this pathetic emptiness we call a life.

"The bridge," he said, "The bridge will fall because, it feeds our hunger. Because that black heart the sits in the center of that empty black hole demands it. The death and destruction mean nothing to us. We will fulfill our contract. The fanatics will have their disaster. The world will have its spectacle. We will get our payment for pulling it off. You will have the satisfaction of seeing Michaels twist in the wind as blame hangs over his head and I ." He laughed, falling back against the wall and staring at the floor. "I will be able to lift this shroud that has darkened my life for so many years. Maybe after all this is over we will be able to feel something again. Something real, something other than this purgatory."

Samel stood erect. He stared at Michelle. A fire burned in his eyes. His voice boomed like a foghorn. "Never walk between a man and his passion. You will be crushed." He turned and walked away. The sound of the bedroom door slamming echoed through the silence.

Michelle braced herself against the back of the chair. She closed her eyes; a shutter reverberated through her. Reality weighed her down like iron blocks hanging from her shoulder.

"There it is," Roger said, his voice full of excitement. The crackling static began to dissipate and faint voices became clear.

"What will you do?" Michelle asked.

"When Rala is located," Samel said, composed and resolute. "together he and I will do what must be done. He has a stake in this as well. I will not deny him his vengeance."

"Samel, please. One thing at a time. First the bridge and then Spade. It will be better when you can devote your undivided attention to him."

Samel clenched his jaws, but did not respond.

Na'Taya grimaced at the mention of Rala's name. *He's still missing? Is he still looking for me? Did Salvador do something more to him than give him a headache?* Thoughts of Rala, Salvador, Martin and the phone threatened to burst out of her. Na'Taya squirmed uncomfortably in her seat. *I have to tell him. Maybe if he knows we can just leave and forget all this.*

She took a deep breath and faced him. "Roger listen,"

"Quiet," he said never taking his eyes off the controls. "The reception is very faint. I can't make out what they're saying if you keep making noise. Stay quiet. This is the pay off. This is what we've been shooting for."

Na'Taya opened her mouth to protest.

"Quiet, you'll make us miss something."

"I..." the words caught in her throat.

Samel stood basking in his fury. With an eye on distracting him, Michelle redirected the conversation. "What about the final report from Ayham?"

Returning to the moment, Samel shook his head and stared at her. His body relaxed, his breathing eased. Blowing out a calming breath he replied. "He will be here soon. You can hear it for yourself," he snapped and took a command position behind his desk.

Michelle fixed herself a tall highball and slammed a glass half full of scotch down in front of Samel. She retreated to a seat in front of the window and turned her back to him.

A guard opened the door and signaled. Samel nodded. Michelle started to speak. He silenced her with an upturned hand. A moment later a stooped little man entered the room. He wore an oversized suit that made him look even smaller and thinner than he was. Dipping his head, he inched toward the desk in a shuffle that was two steps with the right foot and one with the left. Lying down a stack of papers and a finger-sized box, he took two steps back and became a statue.

Samel scanned the papers and tossed them aside. "You have worked out the sensitivity problems?" he asked, leaning back in his chair until it squeaked. "I don't want to image things going off ahead of schedule."

"I think so," said Ayham.

"You think so?" his voice banged off the walls with the authority of someone who was used to giving orders. "There is no room for ambiguity. You either have or you have not."

Ayham took a step back. His eyes widened as if he had just been slapped awake.

"The deadline is too near not to be absolutely certain. Much is dependent on everything going off as planned." Samel said.

"Yes, yes. It will work," Ayham added quickly. "I have no doubt about it." He began pacing and massaging his temple. His feet brushed the floor as if he was walking in tall grass.

"To keep from causing the explosions to happen prematurely, I was forced to make some rather complicated modifications. We basically re-engineered the compounds." The short balding man talked absent-mindedly as if his every thought was new and fascinating. Deep-set sleepy eyes moved constantly from side to side reading from imaginary notes held in front of him. His hands poised ready to erase and recalculate any perceived errors.

"Such as?" Samel asked, a growing irritation in his voice.

"In order to bring down such a large structure as the Ambassador Bridge, the explosion will have to be powerful and precisely focused. Because of the need for stealth, it is impossible to do the job in one large explosion. Besides, it would take an exorbitant amount of combustion. So, it will happen in three coordinated stages. Not one big blast, but a series of smaller, but highly effective explosions."

"That's a lot of moving parts?"

"It is necessary, Rayiysi. This is a very complicated task you have given me. The Ambassador Bridge is a formidable structure." His head sank showing a measure of deference.

"Explain."

Ayham cleared his throat and began counting on his fingers. "The first stage is the paint, the ammonium nitrogen triodide. We had to stabilize the volatility of the compound. It is highly sensitive and unstable. If not properly formulated a strong gush of wind, a random vibration, even a sudden change in the temperature could set it off. There was also the problem of making it viable when exposed to moisture since the supporting structures are near water. Its natural tendency is to become inert when wet. As well, I wanted to increase the potency of the reaction. To ensure destruction and not just superficial damage. I am happy to report my team has accomplished all these things. That element is already in place. We have painted the supporting towers and the beams that extend the total length of the bridge. Really, choosing the right shade of color was the hardest part of that." He attempted a laugh. The effect failed. He apologized with a bow.

"How were you able to conceal the alteration to the paint?"

"We used an aging solution to mask the iodine crystals, along with radiating it with phosphorescent particles. The paint appears to be a thick rust-resistant mixture necessary for metal that is in close proximity or will be exposed to moisture. The day glow effect of the phosphorescence disrupts detection of any hidden ingredients. The paint was inspected and cleared with no problems. It will take a couple of weeks before the iodine crystals penetrate and fully adhere to the surface of the metal. It has been 13 days since the painting was complete. By the scheduled time all will be viable."

Na'Taya screeched and shook her head. Roger gave her a look that screamed "silence." He focused on the receiver as if it was an alien introducing itself to humanity.

They both leaned in closer, not believing what they were hearing.

Ayham tugged at his scraggly beard. "The second part is the acid. Simple hydrofluoric acid, but highly concentrated. It will weaken the metal. It's in the form of a thin powdery film coated inside of the balloons. The balloons are in quadruple spirals wrapped all along the girders, the support cables, and all beams, including the towers. The acid, when released, will react with the moisture in the air and then the steel. It will eat into the metal and compromise its integrity, weakening it and making success easier to achieve. We hid it in balloons because the acid is harmless to the kind of plastic the balloons are made of. The balloons are opaque, so the inner coating looks perfectly normal.

"Lastly, and most critically is the use of sound. A high-pitched sound wave to be exact. One that is in a range inaudible to humans. The pitch and frequency are so high it would take specialized equipment to detect it. Our theater of operations is so very close to the bridge there will be no problem directing the sound wave. When activated, it will create a sympathetic vibration that will burst the fabric of the balloons and cause the acid to be dispersed on to the metal and begin weakening the structure. We have the added benefit of the acid and the triodine reacting to each other. The resulting compound becomes highly unstable. A moment or two later and another higher frequency sound wave will be activated. The iodine crystals will be excited to a critical stage. The crystals will begin to vibrate and expand. Once the crystals have been activated, the instability of the compound produces a chain reaction that will end not with a large explosion, but with a cascading series of small, but deadly explosions that cannot be stopped."

He added, "The bridge will fall." He paused and stood erect for the first time. "You will only need to initiate the process with that remote." Samel held up the small box. Ayham nodded.

"Once the sequence has been initiated the process will proceed automatically. It cannot be stopped.

"I am explaining these things in simplistic terms. Oh," his eyes opened wide when his words registered to his own ears. "No insult intended. I am trying to keep the scientific terms to a minimum."

"Understood," nodded Samel. "I take no offense."

Samel sat with his fingers knitted together. A movie of the destruction played in his mind eye. The corners of his mouth rose in applause. "What about the other bridge?"

"Unfortunately, the other bridge is too far away to suffer any damage. We can only hope that the subsequent vibrations through the ground can maybe unsettle its foundation a bit, but I am afraid it may not be affected at all."

"Unfortunate." Samel nodded. "Very good, Ayham. You have done well. There is just enough artistry and drama in this plan to produce the desired effect. Much glory will be in this for you." Samel stood and placed the remote in his pocket.

"Thank you, Rayiysi," he mumbled, shifting from one foot to the other. "There is still much to do. I must be getting back." He dipped his head even lower than his stooped posture already held it and scurried out of the door.

Roger and Na'Taya stared at each other. The air between them felt cold and stilted. Afraid to speak, fearing words would make what they just heard more real than it was, each consumed by their state of disbelief and horror. Their emotions knew no words. One would try to speak and the expression on the others face would kill their sound.

"A truly nervous little man, isn't he?" Michelle stated. "I'm not sure I'd trust him to carry a cup of coffee. The thought of him with explosives doesn't give me confidence."

"Yes, he is not the most assertive and stable individual, but he is brilliant. I am not sure if we will be able to keep him around after this is over. It has been my experience that the nervous ones break and run even when there is nothing chasing them."

"It would be a shame to lose such a valuable asset."

"I agree, but loyalty, commitment, and a solid set of balls are crucial to our success. A mouse cannot live among lions. If we have a weak link it is necessary to remove it. In order to build and maintain this organization, we must be able to depend on every member. There is no room for doubts."

"You cannot appeal to his sense of devotion? His duty to God or some such nonsense as that?" she asked.

"A person who cannot be bought is a dangerous person. There is no worst foe than the true believer. Despite logic or truth or even superior odds, the true believer will press on believing that sacrifice is noble and required, instead of the foolish waste that it is. No, unfortunately, his usefulness will be singular. We bring the bridge down during the concert and his worth will have been exhausted."

27

"Oh God. I don't believe it. This can't be happening. I knew they were up to something else. But this. They're going to do this during the concert. All those people...no... Oh God." Na'Taya folded her legs against her chest and wrapped her arms around them. Burying her face, she muttered "God, no..." ...over and over again.

Roger sat paralyzed, his eyes darted about searching inside his head for his lost thoughts. He gasped for air as if he'd forgotten how to breathe. "This can't be real. This is crazy. We must have heard them wrong or something." He whispered to himself. "People don't do this to each other."

Everything was upside down. Nothing made any sense. Everything seemed to have come to an abrupt stop. It was as if time itself had slammed on the brakes, making everything and everyone stand still and take notice. Roger's mouth began moving before his mind had found words. Cradling his forehead, his words finally found sound.

"We...we have to tell somebody. We've got to do something." His foot began tapping the floorboard. "They're going to kill all those people. We have to stop them." The pitch of his voice rose as his anxieties grew. He began to sound like a child's toy that squeaked when you squeezed it. Scenes of mass destruction played before him, fires, explosions, death. He closed his eyes against the images.

"MARTIN," he yelled. "This must be what he's been searching for. Call Martin. The FBI can handle this. They can stop them. This is too big for us." He shook his head up and down prompting her to agree.

Na'Taya raised her head. Her eyes were wild with despair. She whispered, "I can't call Martin."

"Huh, what do you mean you can't call Martin? Of course, you can. Why not? This is what he demanded of you. This is your ticket out. You can blow this thing wide open and save a bunch of lives. You'll be a hero."

"I can't," her voice was thin and weak. "The phone I found out things. Martin and I argued. He made me so angry. I cursed him out and broke off all ties with him."

She lowered her head and looked away. "Then I...I destroyed the phone."

"You did what?" Roger yelled. "Tell me you didn't do that?" He asked shaking his head. A look of utter disgust took over his face. Na'Taya just stared at him. "That was the most incredibly stupid thing you could have done. How could you? What are we supposed to do now? We can't just call up the FBI and say, "Hey, they're going to blow up the Ambassador bridge. We just happened to hear about it while listening to some illegal bugs. They'll think we're crazy. Nobody is going to believe us. We'll be locked up for making false reports and then when it happens they'll claim we were in on it." Roger buried his face into his hands.

"You don't understand." She pleaded. "I found out things and..."

"Found out what? That you've made the dumbest move ever?" Roger threw his hands up in the air. "What the hell were you thinking?"

Na'Taya drew back, pressing herself against the door. She placed her hand to her face as if she were soothing a slapped cheek.

"If you would have stopped playing James Bond and listened to me, you'd know. You'd understand I've been trying to tell you what happen ever since you got in the car, but you've been too busy congratulating yourself on being a super spy to listen."

"Excuse me for trying to keep your ass out of jail, Ok? Go ahead. I'm listening." His tone was condescending and bitter. "Go ahead and explain how you screwed us both and thousands of innocent people who are going to die because you decided to throw a tantrum. You seem to have forgotten that we're doing this whole thing because of you. Because of your screwed-up life."

Na'Taya's face turned colors like a traffic light. Her mouth went slack until it sagged like a damp towel. Her skin went ashen as the blood drained from her face. The twinkling grays that were her eyes faded out like dying embers. Na'Taya blinked slowly, lowered her head and trembled, gulping a mouthful of air. When she looked up, she was a thunderstorm, full of fury and rage. Na'Taya erupted. Springing forward, she came face to face with Roger. So close; the breath of her words struck him like a wooden club.

"I never asked you to do this, Roger. I didn't want you to do this. I tried to leave. You wouldn't let me. You insisted. You wanted to play the big hero, remember?" Her teeth pressed into a snarl.

"I never thought that you would sabotage us!" He shot back. "I should have listened to my instincts and..."

"And what? Thrown me out of the car and let Spade have me? Left me at that rest stop?" There was a smirk to her snarl.

"Maybe you should have. No doubt we both would have been better off." She pushed open the car door and jumped from the car. "You won't have to worry about being stuck with someone so stupid." She spit out the word, “Roger”.

"I don't need your help. I don't want your help. I don't need you. I don't need anybody. I won't sit here and listen to this." Na'Taya slammed the door and stomped away.

"What the hell? What about the bridge?" Roger looked at Na'Taya marching away then to the crackling receiver and back again. His hand went to the door handle. His reflection in the mirror stopped him cold. *Don't chase her. What is she mad at you for? You didn't mess up. She did. Besides..."* his reflection said. *There are more important things going on.*

Na'Taya pounded her way down the ramp of the parking structure. Her cheeks so tight with anger they looked as if they would burst. "Here I was starting to have feelings for that self-righteous blow hard."

Salvador sat unnoticed in his car, taking in the whole scene. After Na'Taya stormed past his car, he started the engine. *Whoa, whoa,* he thought. *Maybe I should just let her cool off first. I don't want her taking it out on me. It may be better if I just eliminate the competition first.* Salvador turned off the ignition and focused on the occupant in the black Fusion with the two bullet holes in the trunk.

Her anger in full bloom, the blocks fell away. Na'Taya marched over the streets like an invading army. The thought of the bridge started to shave away more and more of her anger. Horrific pictures of bloody bodies and twisted metal beams began to over whelm her.

How am I going to get in touch with that bastard Martin, she thought. *Just when I thought I was free; I'm pulled back in.* Na'Taya slowed her march. Her face darkened as if a cloud had blocked out the sun.

"How could he talk to me like that? I thought he cared about me. I thought we..." The words faded without taking hold. Her eyes moistened with tears, she didn't notice the set of satisfied eyes that were following her. When she approached a cloistered intersection, a pickup truck pulled up short and stopped in front of her. The squealing brakes caused her to jolt to a stop and look up. The door of the truck sprang open and a shiny silver revolver greeted her.

"Get in." The voice was cold and ominous. "If you try to run or scream, I'll drop you where you stand."

Na'Taya looked into Spade's pot-marked face. He was smiling like a hyena hiding in tall grass. Her knees went soft and shook like Jell-O. All the strength seemed to drain from her body. She grabbed the door to keep from falling to the ground. He restated the demand with a grunt and the wave of the gun. Na'Taya fell into the seat, her heart beating as fast as the wings of a hummingbird. She let out a small whimper. Spade smiled and slammed his arm across her chest forcing the air from her lungs and causing her to crumple, folding over his massive arm. He grabbed the buckle of the seat belt and handed it to her. "Fasten your seat belt. I wouldn't want you to get hurt. Remember, safety first," he laughed, slowly dragging his arm back across her breast, and allowing his hands to stop and painfully press against them.

28

Roger stood outside the car. He watched Na'Taya disappear down the ramp and out of the garage. He fought the urge to run after her. His anger held him locked in place, though his heart threatened to mutiny against his head and force him to chase her down. A black-clad stranger emerged from a sedan parked fifty feet away. Roger tensed as he realized the focus of the man was directed at him. The stranger stared intently as he approached. He had the confident gait of a predator and a lopsided smirk of someone who knew something Roger didn't. He radiated a physicality that was both menacing and impressive. Roger considered jumping in his car and speeding away, but something inside him was tired of running. Tired of feeling like the prey, the victim. In the past couple of days, he had run for his life more than once. He felt he had enough of that. It was time to take a stand. Time to say no. He stood his ground.

"Hello, Roger," the stranger said, stopping a dozen feet from the car.

Roger felt uneasy at the sound of his name. This stranger said his name as if it was a four-letter word. "Do I know you?"

"Not really, but I know you. I do have a feeling you've heard of me." He smiled and paused for effect. "My name is Salvador Trovao." He tilted his head, lightly touching the brim of his Fedora.

"Salvador? But, aren't you supposed to be in...?"

"In jail? I see Taya did not inform you?"

"Inform me of what?" Roger snapped.

"Of my innocence, of course." Salvador looped his thumb in his waistband and leaned back as if he were resting against a tree.

"All the charges were dismissed. The whole thing was a big unhappy misunderstanding." He smiled like a turkey the day after Thanksgiving.

Roger couldn't hold back the look of surprise that claimed his face. "But, Martin and the FBI and the whole threatening her with that jail thing and..." a hint of anger entered his voice.

Salvador sensed an opportunity and wedged himself into Roger's confusion. Offering sympathetic eyes, he added wet kindling to the smoldering fire; meant to create smoke and cloud thing up.

"Taya and I were together earlier and we talked things over. You know, resolved our issues. I thought she would explain things to you."

"She didn't mention any of that." Roger admitted.

"I suppose she didn't want to...well, add any more pain than she had to. After all, we will probably be leaving here soon and..."

"But, the bridge. We just found out about the bridge. She can't leave. We have to find Martin and warn him about the bridge."

"Bridge, I don't know about any bridge? I'm afraid that's your problem."

"No, you don't understand." Roger pounded on the roof of the car. "We just found out about the bridge. They're going to blow up the Ambassador Bridge and kill all those people."

"Who's going to do that? That's crazy. Do you know what it would take to bring down that thing?" Salvador said dismissing the idea.

"Na'Taya knows what going on. She must want to stop this as much as I do."

"Are you sure?" He faked a look around. "Why isn't she here with you finding a way to solve your little problem?"

Roger stuttered. "She...she ."

"Huh, I saw you and I heard you. You don't understand her at all. You don't get her. I'd say you really pissed her off. If I know Taya," he paused. "And I do." There was a laugh in his voice. He raised his brows and flashed a grin. "She isn't coming back. Your little bridge thing is just that, your little bridge thing."

"I don't believe that. Na'Taya wouldn't just walk away from this. She's mad at me, yes. But, she'll be back. I know it." Feeling a bit surer of himself, Roger went on the attack.

"If things are so good between you two, why were you hiding? And why didn't Na'Taya come looking for you, instead of walking right past you?"

Salvador chuckled. "Try and rationalize it all you want to, Roger. But the facts are she didn't tell you about me. She didn't tell you about Martin or why she was really here until she had to. Did she? She didn't tell you about Rala either, I bet."

"Rala?"

"Yes, Rala. We had a little encounter with him earlier today." He smiled. "Face it, Roger, my man, Taya is back where she belongs; with me." He poked his finger into his chest as if he was pointing out the obvious winner.

"Save yourself the trouble." He added with a smirk.

Roger thought about Na'Taya and immediately regretted that he hadn't gone after her. He remembered her asking to talk to him and him putting her off. *What was I thinking? What was so important I couldn't listen for a few minutes? Roger bit his lip. Why did I attack her like that? Was I really so busy, so caught up with patting myself on the back that I became a total asshole? Or was I looking for some way to push her away?*

Pictures of Na'Taya smiling, Na'Taya laughing, Na'Taya crying, and talking with Henry; Na'Taya in the car, pictures of her laying naked in his arms rushed through his mind with such intensity he had to lock his knees to keep from falling. A dark feeling of loss engulfed him and he gnashed his teeth to keep from screaming out her name.

Images of the bridge, its beams and girders mangled and

twisted juxtaposed themselves with scenes of thousands of bloodied bodies, burned, and broken, floating on the water and lying on the shore. The horrors of the image made him shut his eyes and gasp for air. The voices of Samel and Michelle echoed through his mind, taunting him with laughter and pitying excuses at his failed attempt to stop them. Roger steadied himself against the car. He looked at Salvador's smirking face and knew he had to find Na'Taya.

"I've got to go."

"Sure, Roger. You just mosey along and take care of your bridge thing. Taya and I will be just fine."

Roger gave him a cutting look out of the corner of his eyes.

"Ring, ring." The sound came over the speakers from the receiver in the car. Roger bent down and surveyed the readout. "Ring, ring."

She must have her phone in her attaché, Roger thought. *It sounds like the phone is right on top of the bug.* He reached into the car and increased the volume.

Michelle's voice drew him in. "Hightower," she said.

"Listen, Roger," Salvador said.

"Quiet," Roger demanded. "This could be important."

"Not half as important," Salvador said. Roger waved him off and increased the volume.

"This is Spade." The other voice said. "I've got the girl. What do you want me to do with her?"

"She is alive and unharmed?"

"For now," he laughed scratching his stubble with the gun, making a noise that sounded like radio static.

"Good, keep her that way. Bring her to the warehouse, Springhill and 14th. We will meet you there."

"Yeah, I know the place. We'll be there soon."

Roger stared up at Salvador. In a shaky voice, he said. "They've got Na'Taya."

"They could be talking about anyone. How do you know they're talking about Na'Taya?"

"Are you kidding? They've been chasing her for days. Why the hell do you think we've been doing this?" Roger gave him a look of utter disbelief.

"It seems like I'm not the only one Na'Taya has been keeping secrets from. If you knew as much as you claimed you did, you'd know that Spade tried to kill her. He tried to kill us both, twice." Roger looked over the roof of the car and gave Salvador a head-to-toe evaluation. Grunting his disapproval, he ducked down into the car and slammed his door.

Salvador rushed over and jumped into the passenger seat.

"What the hell do you think you're doing?" Roger demanded.

"Na'Taya's my girl. If she's in trouble, then I'll be there."

"She's been in trouble and you weren't there. As a matter of fact, aren't you the reason she was in trouble in the first place? Seems to me, none of this would be happening if it wasn't for you." He glowered at him. "Besides I don't need your help."

"The hell you don't," Salvador shrugged. "Whether you want it or not, you've got it. So, are we going to keep bumping chests or are we going to rescue my girl?"

Roger scowled at him before starting the car. "She's not your girl anymore," he muttered.

"We'll see about that," Salvador mumbled back.

Reluctantly, Roger started the car and pulled out of the garage. He kept adjusting the controls trying to pick up some more conversations, all the time exchanging dirty looks with his passenger. Only static and the occasional muffled couple of words came through. As they wove their way toward the warehouse, Roger reluctantly explained the particulars to Salvador filling him in on all they knew. "They're some kind of terrorists. They plan on bringing down the bridge during the concert. That's what we heard on the receiver just before..." He stopped and swallowed. "Na'Taya left."

"That's crazy. Why would they want to do that?"

"I don't know, man. They're terrorists, that's what they do. The hell with them. Why would Martin do that to her? Why didn't you do something to protect her?"

"I'm not to blame for what the Feds did." He glared at Roger.

"They saw a situation they could use and they took advantage. I had nothing to do with it."

Roger returned the glower with one of his own. "All I know is we have to get in touch with Martin. He's the only one who knows enough about all this to believe what we heard. If we can't convince him or somebody else in the government, thousands of people are going to die."

"I don't know who this Martin is, if he's with the FBI, maybe I can get Foster; he's the agent who arrested me," Salvador cocked a half smile. "the one who tried to put me away. Maybe he can put us in touch with this Martin," He laughed.

"This should put a shine on Foster's bald head. Yeah, this should make his day. I know his kind. He'll want in. I don't doubt he'll be all over this. Maybe I should say all over me. He'll believe I have something to do with this. The guy has a hard on for me. He feels he owes me, huh."

"Whatever, man. The hell with your bromance. It's Na'Taya and the people on the bridge we should be thinking about. Just get in touch with somebody."

Salvador opened his mouth to complain, but only heated breath came out. He cut Roger a hard stare and whipped out a cell phone. Scrolling through his contacts, he muttered under his breath.

29

Spade crept slowly through the city, gulping beer after beer, leaving a trail of discarded cans as he casually tossed them out of the window. "I owe you. You made me look like a fool," he belched, "and incompetent. You caused me a lot of problems." His speech was slow and slurred. "I owe you for that." He gripped her knee and pressed. His hands felt like a vise. A tiny whelp escaped her trembling lips.

"When they are done with you, it's my turn," he smiled and nodded.

Na'Taya cried inside. Clutching the sides of her seat, her chest seized up with panic. Terrified eyes darted about searching for a way to escape. Biting the inside of her cheek, she thought of Roger and of Salvador and wished at least one of them knew where she was.

Spade pulled up to the warehouse. Michelle's Lexus was parked near the door. One of Samel's men stood guard at the entrance. Spade grabbed her by the shoulder and dragged her from the car. Ignoring the guard, he pushed her into the building. Once inside, Samel forced himself to look at her and not Spade, as he pointed to a chair. Spade forced Na'Taya into the seat in the middle of the room.

The guard inside the building tossed Spade a rope and he tied her to the chair.

The large room was silent and dimly lit. A single rusty fluorescent fixer hung crookedly from the ceiling. Samel paced around the chair, walking in and out of shadows. The clink, clink of his heels echoed off the walls. Na'Taya's frantic breathing sounded like a struggling air conditioner. Michelle sat in one corner, shrouded in partial light. Cigarette smoke billowed around her, sending anxious clouds zig-zagging into the air. She clicked her nails against the plastic of the chair. Spade leaned against the wall in another corner. Abruptly he began smacking his fist against the wall like a hammer hitting a nail, the muffled booming reverberating through the wall.

Na'Taya shivered as if she had been stripped naked. Every nerve ending in her body was turned up to ten. The sound of Spade's hand striking the wall rang in her ears. She winched imaging those fists hitting her face. The pungent smell of Michelle's cigarette assaulted her nostrils as if she were blowing the smoke in her face. Samel's footsteps sounded like balls of hail crashing against a tin roof. The clink of each step grew more ominous with each pass, pounding inside her head, increasing her fear.

"Who are you working for?" he demanded.

Na'Taya batted her eyes and shook her head as if the language was foreign to her.

Samel stopped pacing, walked to her and slapped her. Na'Taya's head snapped to the side. When she turned back to look at him, a tickle of blood ran from the corner of her mouth. He crossed his hands in front of himself, leaned back, and scowled at her.

"Tell me what I wish to know. I will not tolerate lies and delays. Who are you working for?" Na'Taya, frozen with fear, shook her head and lowered her face. He stomped his foot and she jumped, expecting another blow.

"I do not have time to waste and even less patience. You will answer my questions one way or another." She saw Rala's angry stare duplicated in his uncle's eyes.

"No one," Na'Taya whimpered.

"Na'Taya, is it?" he made a half turn and looked at her out of one eye. "Another question then. Rala, where is he?"

Na'Taya visibly tensed, shifting in her chair.

"A reaction, good. So, you have seen him. Lately, no doubt? Where is he now? Is he with your friends?" Na'Taya remained still.

"Come, come Na'Taya. Playing the unfortunate innocent will not work. You, my dear, are in too deep." His eyes shifted to Spade as he spoke. "There are too many bridges that lead to you for this to be a coincidence. Our actions have consequences that we must answer for."

Michelle leaned out of her seat in reaction to the exchange. A spark of worry pulsed through her mind. The look, the implications of Samel's words meant nothing to Spade. His mind was fixated on what he would do to Na'Taya once he got his turn with her. The words went over his head. But she caught their meaning. Samel's obsession worried her. He was a passionate man and could be unpredictable. Too much was at stake to allow him to lose focus. She started to remind him of the black-tie gala being held tonight before the concert, but she realized it would have been a waste of time.

Samel returned to Na'Taya. "Shall I allow him," he pointed to Spade resisting looking his way, "to have his turn in conversation with you, first?" Samel smiled. "*Kunt sawf yuqaddim.*"

Na'Taya head shot up. She heard Old Mother saying, “You will submit.” An old anger sieged her heart.

Na'Taya stared up into the face of parched skin, rutted with age, and the pair of cold unblinking eyes that looked like ancient drops of amber. The mouth was twisted like the gnarly roots of an old tree. Bulbous lips curled over each other anxious to spew out hateful insults. The woman was called "*Am Masana,*" Old Mother." She hobbled about on arthritic legs and wheezed like a leaky balloon. A braided switch of palm fronds was always clutched in her hand, ready to end all conversations with a painful lash.

"*Kunt sawf yuqaddim,*" she repeatedly yelled. "You will submit," spraying a hacking mist of spittle. "Like that Nubian bitch of a mother of yours, you think you are different, better than we. That the will of Allah can be ignored. A stern husband and a few good beatings will teach you correctness. That is if one will have you. Are you a virgin?" she asked, answering the question herself with "you better be. We stone harlots." She smiled a gapped mouth grin of missing and yellow teeth. "Pay attention to your work and you may get through the day without more whelps on your backside."

Na'Taya spent her days rolling a milling wheel, working the spindle that made yarn from the piles of goat's hair, sweeping back the ever-encroaching sand, lugging loads from one place to another, tending to the needs of those doing the cooking and dodging the frequent swipes from the palm fronds. In the afternoons and evenings, she mended torn and worn clothing, worked the loom making cloth, and helped prepare for the next day's chores; all under the disapproving eyes of Old Mother.

One day, Old Mother came to her as she was working the grinding wheel. "I'm your mother now," she said smiling like an over fed cat.

In a moment of defiance, Na'Taya replied. "You are not my mother. I have a mother."

"Not anymore," the old lady laughed. "I am now. That Nubian bitch is dead. Allah be praised. Judgment has been rendered."

"My mother is not dead! You lie!" She shouted.

"Yes, she is." Hissing through missing teeth, raising the palm fronds. "Thank Allah, the stain has been lifted. Our son is free." Na'Taya's eyes began to fill with tears. Her lips quivered.

"Not a drop out of you or I'll beat you with in an inch of your life. It is as it should be." The old lady threatened. "Grab that basket and come with me."

Na'Taya, fought back the tears, remembering her mother's call for strength, and picked up the basket. She dropped the basket and leapt back screaming. A large black Egyptian asp reared up, its hiding place being exposed. The old woman, startled by the action, wobbled and lost her balance, falling to the ground near the snake. She stretched out her hands reaching for Na'Taya. "Help me, child."

Na'Taya looked down at the old woman, but made no move. The coldness and anger in her heart, froze her limbs.

"Help me!" Old Mother demanded trying to scoot away for the viper. Na'Taya watched as the snake wavered like a falling stick before launching itself at the old woman. Pearly white fangs sank beneath the rough cloth and embedded themselves in the old woman's leathery thigh. She screamed as the viper pulled away, coiled and struck her again. Old Mother collapsed and then began jerking and twitching like a dog being held by the tail.

The beast, having addressed the insult of being disturbed, slithered away, disappearing through a hole in the wall. Na'Taya watched Old Mother spasm until she stopped quaking and laid still. A stream of foamy spittle ran out of the corner of her mouth. Her crocked mouth died with a scream still caught on her lips. Her unblinking eyes blinked closed. Na'Taya picked up the basket and went to find her mother.

Na'Taya raised her head and stared into Samel's eyes. Defiance burned behind her stare. She swiped her tongue over her mouth and swallowed the tickle of salty blood. Her voice was full of disgust and anger.

"You are going to kill all those people. You're nothing but a murder. A coward and a murderer."

Samel stopped pacing, faced her and laughed.

"A murderer?" Another laugh, then he frowned. Samel cupped her chin and looked at her with the most penetrating expression Na'Taya had ever seen. His eyes were blank and unfocused like he was looking through her to her very core. The hand was cold and rigid. It felt as if her chin had been placed on a block of ice. A shiver traveled down her spine.

Speaking slowly and quietly like a child reciting a poem remembered long ago, "I am not a murderer. I am justice..." his voice rose when he said the words, "sent to deliver judgment to the undeserving." He swept his arms out in a flourish.

"There are those who know no bounds. Who scoff at common decency. Who would rip the heart from life itself. Those who understand nothing but the fist and the hammer. Well..." he pivoted and restarted his pacing. "I am that fist. I am that hammer. I am a flood to wash the land clean. I am that inevitable retribution that comes with all actions."

"Then strike at those that harmed you. All those innocent people don't deserve to die."

"Child," there was humor in his voice. "...there is no such thing as an innocent person. We are all guilty. We are all deserving of death."

His gaze floated to Spade. "From the smallest to the largest, from the youngest to the oldest. Life itself is a continuing cycle of death upon death. We all owe this debt. We all must pay the price."

"They won't let you do it. They'll stop you."

"They," he said. His eyes brightened. "They who?" She pressed her lips together tighter than a miser's purse and jetted out her chin. Samel rewarded her with another slap. And another. A stream of blood erupted out the of her mouth. She coughed up a mouthful, fighting back the choking flood.

Na'Taya swallowed the growing pool of blood in her mouth, gagging at the effort. With her head tilted down she peered up at him. She spoke in whispers, forcing him to come to her and lean in to hear.

"You are not justice. You are nothing, but another self-righteous madman, doomed to fail. The FBI knows all about you and Calvin Michaels." She swallowed again. "They know about the bridge and..."

Samel laughed. "You are a poor liar. If any of that were true we would not be having this conversation."

Na'Taya melted into the chair, allowing her chin to rest on her chest. She hid behind the sweat-drenched strands of hair covering her face. She spoke through clenched teeth, "The liar is you. Hiding behind a call for justice when all you want is to play God." She spit blood at his feet. "I have known people like you. You're all the same, sad, cruel little tyrants wanting to make others pay because your feelings got hurt."

Samel stopped pacing and looked at her as if she had shot him with an arrow. He opened his mouth to speak, but instead walked to the table and lit a cigar. All the time his eyes moving from Na'Taya to Spade and back again.

Michelle smoked nervously, sensing a storm on the horizon.

30

Roger drove past the warehouse and turned to the left two blocks away. "That was Michelle's car parked in front of the building. The guy standing in front must be one of Samel's men." His foot started tapping the floorboard. "How are we going to get her out of there? They must have guns. We can't just rush in. They'll kill us all."

Salvador was on the phone and held up his hand to silence Roger. "What do you mean, what kind of a game am I playing? False reports...what the..." He yelled into the phone. "Look, buddy. I'm trying to give you a tip that will make your career. You cops are all the same. You think nobody has a brain, but you. Well, if I was as stupid as you I wouldn't brag." He repeatedly jabbed at the end call button shouting, "asshole," over and over again.

"I assume that means your charms didn't work on them?" Roger asked cutting him a sideways glance.

Salvador bit down and shifted his jaws. He waved his arms. "We don't need them. It's probably better if they aren't involved anyway. They've got too many rules they have to follow This is going to take some creative thinking. Some out of the box actions."

Roger turned to him and tilted his head. "You're crazy, we're dealing with terrorists. People that will blow themselves up. Can you imagine what they'll do to us?

MAYBE WE SHOULD JUST CALL the local police and let them handle this."

Salvador crunched his face into a ball. "Do you want to risk Taya's life on what some lousy overweight warriors for hire will do? You just heard me on the phone. If the FBI won't do anything what do you think the local guys are going to say?" Roger looked away without answering. "Listen man, what we need to do is figure out how to separate them." He began waving his hands as if he was doing sign language. "They've got a guy outside, probably another inside. This Michelle chick, the guy that brought Taya in, and this Samel guy. That's five. If we can get two or three of them out of the way, it'll be easier to handle the rest."

"How the hell do you think we're going to be able to do that? Go up to the door and ask a couple of them to go home so we can pull off the great rescue?"

"Come on Roger, man. You're this college boy. Use your head. How about some of those big college ideas. They don't know we're here. So, we have the element of surprise. Let's just put our heads together and figure out something. The Feds aren't going to do anything, and even if they were, do you think they'd be here in time to save Taya? We've got to get her out of there now. Who knows what they'll do to her if we wait."

Roger grabbed the side of his head. "This is crazy. We can't..."

"Think of Taya, Roger. Her life is on the line."

Roger buried his face in his hands. His foot was tapping the floor like a ticker tape.

"Could you stop that?"

Roger slapped his hand to his thigh.

"Think man, think."

Roger leaped out of the car and started pacing back and forth beside it. "I can...no...we can...no...what if ." He repeated to himself.

"Maybe, I can get Michelle and Spade out of there." He yelled, poking his head back into the car.

"How?" Salvador asked.

"Calvin Michaels is out of town, so Michelle is probably in charge. If I set off the alarm at the studio, she'll have to respond. She won't go alone, so she'll more than likely take Spade with her. It won't take long for them to figure out it's a false alarm, but we'll get rid of them for a while."

"That's not half-bad. How are you going to do that from here?"

Roger held up his smart phone. "I'm connected to the system. I installed it, after all."

"And if we," Salvador smiled, "set the building on fire. That'll make the others evacuate the building. Then we can make our move."

"Are you out of your mind? That's arson."

"Only if you get caught." Salvador grinned. "Desperate times call for desperate measures."

"This is insane." Roger said getting back into the car. "I can't believe I'm even considering this. We're either going to get killed or go to jail or worse."

He heaved a couple of deep breaths and started the car. Circling around the block, Roger parked a block from the warehouse. Using his phone, he connected to the system and typed in a command. The screen on the phone flashed red and the alarm blared like a gunshot. Roger silenced the phone and mouthed an embarrassed, "...sorry."

"Okay what do you have in the trunk?"

"In the trunk? What does that have to do with anything?"

"We need something to burn. Do you have any oil and maybe a pressurized can of something?"

"I've got a can of "Fix a Flat" and some motor oil."

They got out and opened the trunk. Salvador looked at the random assortment of things. "What are you doing living in this thing?" Roger cut him a dirty look.

"Perfect," he said grabbing the oil, the can of tire repair and a couple of pairs of socks. "This'll do the job."

"Hey," yelled Roger. "Those are my socks."

"A sacrifice for the cause, my man." Salvador said, heading for the warehouse.

Roger looked at him strutting away and both hated and admired the man. He showed no fear or hesitation. He didn't waver or waste time overthinking a thing, the way he did. He just acted. *No wonder Na'Taya preferred him.* he thought. Roger slammed the trunk shut and trailed after him.

They crept down the street behind the warehouse, peering around the corner of the building to see what was happening. Michelle and Spade burst out of the door, Samel grabbed her arm as she passed him. "Make sure you bring him back here." He growled leering at Spade. "I don't want him out of my sight for long."

Michelle grimaced at the remark. She shook her arm free and ran to the car. "Come along, Spade. You don't expect me to confront burglars alone, do you?" she yelled.

"Yes!" Salvador hissed. "Okay grab a couple of those cardboard boxes over there." He pointed to a pile of debris, scooping up a box himself and dropping his items into them.

"Come on," he whispered, heading up the ladder of the fire escape. With the box secured under one arm, he skillfully ascended the ladder. Roger struggled behind trying to keep his balance.

Samel returned to the center of the room and grabbed Na'Taya's face forcing her to look him in the eyes. He looked down on her with the cold indifference of a butcher picking a calf to slaughter.

"You have the unfortunate luck of knowing too much, little girl?" Na'Taya stared at him with defiant anger. "It is too bad for you. I cannot allow you or your friends to interfere with what must be done."

On the roof, Salvador led Roger to the skylight. Peering through the window, they saw Na'Taya in the center of the room tied to the chair, Samel looming over her.

"There's another guy over by the door." Salvador whispered, pointing him out.

Roger watched Samel grab Na'Taya's face and cried, "You bastard. You better not hurt her."

"Quiet man. Don't forget they've got another guy outside. Just come on." he whispered, leading Roger away from the skylight. "Take the top off that vent."

"Why?" asked Roger. "We can't get in that way."

"Just do it man. Watch and learn." Salvador tore the cardboard boxes into strips and stuffed them in the flue of the vent. He deposited the can in the middle of the pile. After pouring the oil over the pile, he stuffed the socks on top like the wick of a candle.

"Okay," he said. "This won't be too quick, but slowly the cardboard should start to burn and heat up the can. When it gets too hot, it should explode and go through the roof. With any luck the building fire alarm will go off and everyone will have to scramble for the exits."

Roger looked at him like he had just said aliens had landed. "Are you out of your mind? This will never work."

Salvador turned to face him, his fist clenched into balls, the vein in his neck growing with an angry flow of blood. "You got a better idea?" Roger opened his mouth, but nothing came out. "I didn't think so. Either get with the program or get out of the way and I'll do this myself. We don't have time to hold hands and talk things over."

In a voice lost to embarrassment, Roger mumbled a weak, "All right."

Back in the alley behind the building, Salvador continued his instructions. "Go around that way," he pointed to the north end of the building. "I'll go the opposite way. When you get near the guy at the door ask for a light or something. You smoke, don't you Roger? Or are you one of those health freaks?"

Roger held out his pack of cigarettes and fought back the urge to call him a name.

"Good," he nodded. "I'll come up behind him and knock him out." He picked up a random brick.

Roger gave the brick a sideways glance. *That will kill him...* he thought, but held his tongue. Backing away from Salvador, he began walking around the building. Roger paused his steps, but regained his stride when he thought of Na'Taya. Approaching the man at the door, he pulled out his pack of cigarettes. "Hey buddy, you got a light?"

The man, shrouded in shadows, looked at him warily before stepping out of the doorway and reaching into his pocket. He extended an open palm with the lighter in it. As he opened his mouth to speak, Salvador swung the brick sending it crashing into the back of his head. His eyes fluttered, the lighter dropped from his hand and he toppled over like a sack of stones.

The cigarette fell from Roger's hand. He stood over the prone body looking down on him with an expression of shock.

"Come on, grab his feet." Salvador said, tossing the bloody brick aside. "We have to get him out of sight. The explosion should happen anytime now. They should come running out the door after that." Like a robot programmed to obey, Roger blindly did as he was told.

Salvador searched the limp body, taking the guard's gun and money. With a smile of satisfaction on his face, he headed back toward the front of the building. Roger followed in a haze, feeling out-classed and inadequate.

"Boss," the guard on the inside said. "Boss," he yelled again,

"What the hell do you want?" Samel yelled back, whipping around to scowl at the man.

"Do you smell that?" He said sniffing the air.

"What the..." Samel shouted catching a whiff of something in the air. "Go and see what that is." he ordered, waving the man away.

As the dark-haired young man opened the door to the adjoining room, the ceiling exploded, shaking the entire building. A shower of rubble rained down, burying him. A cloud of smoke and dust rushed into the room. The alarm pierced the air like screaming cats. Samel struggled to remain standing, taking several steps backward to regain his balance. Na'Taya screamed as the chair she was tied to toppled over onto its side. Coughing and wheezing, waving his hands, Samel tried to create a clear view of what was going on.

Salvador and Roger rushed into the building. Salvador grabbed Samel by the back of his collar and shoved the gun into his back.

"Make a move and you're a dead man." Samel's shoulders slumped as he raised his hand.

"Get Na'Taya," Salvador shouted. Salvador looked around at the carnage. "I didn't expect it to work that well. It must have been a shitty roof to start with."

Roger stopped to stare at the two men before bending to untie Na'Taya. Samel met his gaze with red eyes full of hate that shown through the dust like hot coals.

"Roger," Na'Taya coughed. "How did you know where I was?"

"Don't worry about that now. We'll talk later. Let's just get out of here."

"Go get the car." Salvador ordered. "I'll be right out."

Roger did not argue or look at him, he was afraid he'd see Samel's death in his eyes. He grabbed Na'Taya's hand and pulled her out the door behind him.

"You are not the police?" Samel asked angrily.

"It doesn't matter who I am." Salvador answered. "The point is I'm the one with the gun."

"I can make you a very wealthy man." Samel offered.

"I'm sure you could and I might take you up on that, but right now I need to get my girl away from here. Surprisingly, she is more important at the moment." Salvador released his hold on Samel's collar and the man turned to face him.

Samel looked down at the gun still pointing at his chest. "I don't care about the girl. You can have her. I just need her silence for a little while longer."

"Yeah, until your fireworks go off." Samel tensed at the reference. "I know all about your plans, Samel." He said the name slowly with a sly smile. "And frankly, I don't care. It has nothing to do with me. If I can benefit from it one way or another, I might be persuaded to ignore what I know."

The sirens of approaching fire trucks could be heard in the distance in between the pulsing noise of the building alarm. Heat from the blaze in the other room began pouring into the room. The cloud of smoke continued to grow more intense and more oppressive.

"Two hundred and fifty thousand, or else Na'Taya and I will have the FBI, the CIA, and Homeland Security all over your ass and you can kiss your plans goodbye." Salvador began backing away. "The foot of the bridge. Yeah, that's a fitting place. At the welcome center." He looked at his watch. "11 o'clock, don't be late." Salvador turned and ran out the door. He jumped into the backseat of Roger's waiting car. Samel stood in the doorway of the crumbling building, coughing and covered in dust. They exchanged hateful glances. Salvador gave him a smiling salute as the car sped away.

"I told you we could do it." Salvador laughed. Roger scowled at him through the rearview mirror. Na'Taya curled into a ball and whimpered, ignoring all comments and refusing to be touched.

Roger opened the door to his room; Na'Taya headed straight for the bathroom and locked herself in. Salvador sauntered in with a self-satisfied grin, plopped down in a chair and put his feet on the table. He glanced over at the bed and frowned.

"That was a neat trick you pulled off back there," Roger said. "Where did you pick up that skill?"

Salvador hunched his shoulders. "It was nothing. Some guys in Montana used the same trick to break out of a county jail. I figured if it worked to break out then it should work just as well to break in. I didn't realize it would work so well." He crossed his arms laughing. "What are you complaining about.? We got what we wanted, didn't we?"

Roger exploded, his voice thick with disgust. "You killed both those guys. And it doesn't both you a bit, does it?

"I didn't kill anybody. The roof was an accident and the guy outside will survive. He'll wake up with a good size lump and a headache that will last a week, but he'll survive. That is if those big ass rats don't eat him." He laughed again.

"I don't want you here," Roger said through clenched teeth. "You're bad news."

"As soon as Taya comes out, we'll be on our way."

"She's not going anywhere with you," Roger spit at him.

Salvador leapt up and stood in Roger's face. So close their breaths assaulted each other like slaps. "The hell she's not. I'm not going anywhere without her."

"We'll see about that. I..."

Na'Taya rushed out of the bathroom and pried herself in between them, forcing them apart. She faced Roger and placed a hand on his chest. Her eyes were red and puffy; her voice was thin and weak. "Roger, let me talk to Salvador...alone please."

"But he..."

"Please, Roger. Trust me." She closed her eyes.

Roger's eyes threw daggers at Salvador. He moved around them stomping out the door and went to his car.

Na'Taya followed him to the door, closed it and leaned her forehead against it. She swallowed a deep breath and turned to face Salvador. "I'm not going with you."

"What? You're choosing him over me?"

"I'm not choosing him. I'm just not choosing you. I'm choosing me. What we had was not real. You don't love me and I don't love you. Our lives together were built on illusions and lies. It was what we wanted the other one to be, not what we are. As soon as the wind blew hard, our house of cards came tumbling down. There was nothing to us, nothing to save."

"You think you can have something better with him? Who do you think is responsible for saving your ass?" Na'Taya winched. "If it was left up to good old Roger you'd probably be dead by now." Salvador held up his hands and stepped back a couple of steps,

"Naw. I'm not going to beg you. If what I've done doesn't prove something to you, then forget it. I don't need this bullshit. I don't need you. I don't know what I was thinking coming all this way. For what? You never..." He swiped his hand as if he was throwing something away. "I've got bigger fish to fry." He yanked at the brim of his hat, gave her a sneer and stormed out of the room slamming the door behind him.

Roger was sitting in his car, his head pressed against the steering wheel, his foot tapping a stampede. The confusion and doubt in his mind and heart was eating holes in his soul. *What if she decides to go with him? What do I do? No, she won't go. She doesn't love him. He doesn't really care about her. She...the bridge...* His head pounded with indecision. *I should go in there and...*

The sound of the slamming door caused him to shoot to attention. When he looked up, Salvador was standing by his window, looking down on him, heaving like an angry bull. His fist balled up and raised like hammers.

"You can have her." He yelled kicking the car door before marching down the block.

Roger slowly opened the door and entered. Na'Taya was standing in the center of the room. To his mind, she looked so small and vulnerable. They slowly walked toward each other, their faces full of questions and doubt. Standing so close, they could see the sadness and uncertainty in the others' eyes.

"Na'Taya, I..."

She placed a finger over his mouth. "Not now. There is time to talk later, just hold me, please."

Roger wrapped his arms around her. They pressed into each other, their hearts matching beat to beat.

31

At midnight, Harrison met Calvin Michaels at the airport. They retired to a table in the back of one of the lounges that allowed smoking. Calvin lit a Panatela to go with his Scotch and Harrison began chain smoking filter less Pall Malls and absorbing bottles of Budweiser.

Harrison was a wisp of a man with large bushy eye brows, probing blue eyes, and the twitchy movements of a rat smelling an unseen cat.

"What do you have for me?" Calvin waved his cigar as if he were sky writing. "Skip the fluff and get to the meat."

Harrison pulled out his notebook like a thief exposing his spoils to a fence. "I had to call in almost all of my markers to get this information." He said, opening the bargaining for his services. "This Michelle Hightower is a contradiction. You know about when she was here, so I'll start after that. She was a stripper in LA putting herself through college one dollar at a time, until she got hooked up with this ex-ambassador, Dumitru Gogean. My guy said she wasn't known to be a hooker, but," he raised his brows signaling his doubts. "Anyway, she shacked up with him. It's reported he had some kinky fetishes. He paid her way through school and left her a pretty penny when he died. I couldn't get a confirmation on it, but it's a good bet they were lovers. She got a job at a big law firm, worked for a couple of years, then all of a sudden resigned. She's next seen jetting all over the world brokering some questionable deals. Then boom, all of a sudden, she drops off the face of the earth. Until boom, she showed up here." He gargled the last swallow of beer, burped, and signaled for another.

"As for Samel Nizam, he used to be a local politician and a UN representative in Afghanistan. That's where he's from. The guy has a PhD from Harvard. After he graduated, he returned home to help his people. You know, one of those liberal pinko do-gooders. During the second Gulf War his village was destroyed. He says that a bunch of Marines in a blood frenzy did it. The whole village including his wife, children, and relatives were killed. The US denied it. He fought it and lost. They say he went crazy and tried to attack the soldiers in the court room. If not for the Prime Minister, he'd had been thrown in jail. Anyway, he disappears vowing revenge. He drops off the radar and reappears as a respectful import/export dealer. Reports started popping up that he had formed some kind of an alliance with some radical groups. No evidence, but he has been placed at the same location when there have been some terrorist attacks."

He flipped his notebook closed. "There are credible rumors that he's involved in drug smuggling." He smiled. "I think you probably already know that." Calvin cut him a sharp look. Harrison, squinted his piercing eyes and added, "Terrorism..."

"Terrorism?"

Harrison nodded. "For hire." He arched his brows. "I thought that my twenty-five years on the force had shown me everything, but how's this for a business model. You hire us and we plan and execute your terrorist attack. You know like contracting to get a deck built."

Harrison downed another beer and leaned back in his chair. "I may have been kicked off the force and denied a pension, but because of my..." He laughed. "...foresight. I managed to lay enough away that I don't need their lousy pension. I do this because the depths of human depravity amaze me. I am constantly entertained. We as a species are some sick puppies." He shrugged his shoulders.

"A guy's got to have a hobby," he smiled and belched. Calvin curled his lip and snarled. Harrison continued.

"It's believed that he and his organization are behind that attack in China three months ago, and the one in the Philippines six months ago. Every agency in the world is trying to get some tangible evidence on this guy. But this he is greasier than a used condom. There is never a shred of evidence. He has covered his track like nobody's business."

"Why are they letting him roam the world, free? I can't believe he hasn't been arrested or taken out?"

Harrison hunched his shoulders. "Probably waiting to get enough to bring the whole organization down. It's most likely one of those things where you give a dog enough leash to think he's free. With things like this you want to smash the foundation, not just cut off one of the head. Most monsters have more than one." Harrison belched and lit another cigarette.

"Besides, my sources tell me he has some very heavy government backing from countries that are not very friendly with us."

"Why terrorism? There are easier ways to make money."

"I think the guy went a little nuts. He wants to avenge the death of his family. By making others suffer; by any means necessary."

"What about him and Michelle together? I believe they're more than business partners."

"She often spends the night. You add it up." He leaned back in his chair and downed the spittle in the bottom of his beer bottle.

"Okay, you've gave me the foundation. Put some meat on this bone." Harrison fluttered his bushy brows. Calvin sighed.

"Yes, you'll get twice your usual fee. Now give me the payoff," he grunted, gnashing his teeth.

Harrison cocked a satisfied half smile. "Nizam has been seen with a guy named Ayham. He's a scientist, a chemical biologist, known for his expertise and knowledge of obscure substances, especially explosives. The FBI would like to know where this guy is. He is known to have assist many terrorist groups." He paused and licked his teeth. "I know he's here in Detroit."

"Are you saying they're planning some kind of terrorist attack, here?"

"One plus one still equals two." Harrison held up his empty bottle to signal for another beer.

"I may be an ex-cop, but I still got the instincts. Something is going down. There are too many coincidences, too many things that add up to something not being right. It must be something big. After all, he holds America responsible for his family's death. Huh, you can bet I'm staying away from public spaces for a while."

"Is Michelle tied up in this terrorism thing too?"

Harrison grimaced. "Come on man. How many secret have you been able to keep during pillow talk? Of course, she's in on it. Right up to her pretty little neck. Like I said every monster has more than one head."

Calvin chewed on the end of his cigar. His mouth fell open. "The concert, on the bridge. My God. They're going to blow the concert." Michelle's words flooded back into his mind. *There are still things that aren't settled between us. You do realize this, don't you?*

Calvin slammed his fist on the table. "That bitch. She's setting me up to be ruined. That sneaky, conniving bitch." The few people present turned and stared at him. The waitress shot him a dirty look. Calvin never noticed and did not care.

"The concert?" Harrison asked. "But, how?"

"I don't know, but I'm sure of it. She's been keeping every detail of this thing under her personal control. And I know her. Something this public is just her style."

"Yeah, that would do the job." He said leaning over the table.

"Never mind, I've got to go." Calvin jumped up from the table and charged out the door.

Harrison rose to leave when the waitress met him with the check. He looked at the substantial amount and sighed. "Damn, stiffed again." He paid it making sure to give the stern-faced waitress a hefty tip.

32

Calvin pulled into the parking lot of the studio. Every light in the building was a blaze. A police car was parked haphazardly near the front door. The patrol car engine was idling, and two officers were seated inside. "What going on?" Calvin asked rushing to the car.

"Who are you?" the officer asked.

"I'm Calvin Michaels. This is my business."

"Sorry, false alarm, Mr. Michaels." The officer answered, exiting the car. The building is secure. No illegal entry. It happens all the time. A power surge, rats in the wiring. Nothing to worry about."

"Why wasn't I informed about this?"

The officer shrugged his shoulders. "Are you tied into the system?"

"Of course, I am." Calvin said grabbing his phone. "Oh, hell. My phone is still in airport mode. I just got back from New York."

"That explains why you didn't receive the notification. Hey, I saw you on "The World Today." That was a pretty good interview."

Calvin grumbled a response and headed for the front door.

"Welcome home, Mr. Michaels." Spade said, seeing him enter the door.

"What the hell happened?" He scanned the room like radar

looking for enemy ships. "And where the hell is Michelle? She's supposed to be in charge while I'm gone. The alarm goes off she should be here." The questions flew out of his mouth like wild birds.

"Where is everybody at? Aren't there supposed to be people working around here? Aren't there things that need to get done? I go away for a few hours and everything goes to hell."

"She was here," Spade quickly, answered following behind Calvin as he marched toward his office. "She headed back to the warehouse after she talked to the police."

"The warehouse? What the hell is she doing at the warehouse? The problem is here."

"She had to get back to Samel and the girl."

"Samel? The girl?"

"Na Taya?" Spade asked.

"What the hell are they doing there?" Calvin cut down Spade in mid-speech. "Never mind, I'll take care of that situation myself." His face twisted into a frown. "What about the rest of them?"

"I think everybody else is down at the bridge setting things up for tomorrow."

"The bridge, that damn bridge." Calvin mumbled. "I've got to stop them from ruining me."

"What did you say, boss?

"Nothing, nothing. Did you check the building and make sure everything was okay?"

"Yes, Mr. Michaels. I..."

"Well, do it again."

"How long do you want me to hang around here, boss? I'd like to get back to the warehouse and..."

"You work for me, not Michelle, and not Samel. Keep your ass here. When I look for you, you'd better be here." he yelled, slamming the door to his office. Calvin turned on his phone. A notification flashed across the screen, *Gala tonight.* He dialed Michelle's number over and over. The call went to voice mail each time. He left no message. Opening his desk drawer, he picked up a silver-handled colt 45. Calvin spoke to it like a father speaking to his child. "We'll take care of them later." He left to dress and make an appearance before the party ended.

Michelle sat in her car, down the street from the burning warehouse. "Samel, what have you done?" The worry was as thick on her face as the billowing smoke that filled the air. Tears reflecting the flashing lights of the fire trucks and police cars leaked from the corner of her eyes. Red tears like blood.

Two body bags on gurneys sat next to an ambulance. Michelle grabbed for the car door handle, but held herself back. Her mind yearned to know. *Who is in those bags? One must be the girl,* she thought. *But the other?* Michelle grabbed her phone and began frantically dialing. *Pick up, please. Pick up, Samel. Pick up.*

The phone stopped ringing, but no one spoke.

"Samel, is that you? Are you there? Are you Okay?"

"It is I," his voice was thin and hushed.

"Where are you? What happened?"

"At the laboratory. Where is Spade? Is he with you?"

"I will be right there." She hung up and sped to join him.

Samel half-heartedly mumbled the details of what happened.

"I know his type. He only cares for what he may profit. Let him have his hush money. It is worth the price."

"How do you know he won't sell us out anyway? You can't be sure of what he will do. We have to abandon this venture and escape while there is still time." A hint of panic was in her voice.

"No!" he shouted. "I will have my revenge. He cannot be allowed to slip away. The time is now. It is providence. He has been brought here to pay with the rest."

Michelle laid her hands on top of his. She closed her eyes and shook her head. "There will be another time. The most important thing now is..."

"There is nothing more important than this!" he shouted, flinging her hands away. Samel jumped to his feet and began pacing, fingering the remote in his pocket. "The time is now."

Michelle faced him, laying her hands on his shoulders. She looked directly into his eyes.

"Samel, get ahold of yourself. You have lost your perspective. You sound like one of those fanatics. Like one of those jihadists. Our life, our freedom is threatened. We have to back off. You must let go. We live to fight another day."

Samel shoved her away so hard she fell to the ground. Standing over her he shouted. "I will not let go until they are all dead. Dead like my wife. Dead like my daughter. Dead like my son. I will kill in them what they killed in me. You can let your retribution fade away unfulfilled. You can let Michaels remain unpunished. Forget about your lost child. But I will not forget about my family."

Michelle stared up at him. His words had struck at her heart. The hate and madness in his eyes made her cold with fear. He seemed transformed, changed into someone she did not recognize. She slowly rose to her feet, staring at him like the gawker at an accident; horrified, but unable to look away. Backing toward the door, she turned to leave.

Samel grabbed her arm, holding her in a desperate grip. "I'm... sorry. I lost myself for a moment." The words forced their way out of his mouth. His expression seemed to soften, but changed when he asked. "Spade, where is he?"

"That's the only thing that matter to you, isn’t it? What this is really about?" Michelle jerked her arm free. "He's at the studio!" She screamed stumbling out the door. "Go get him yourself!"

33

Roger awoke with a mouth full of hair. Na'Taya was layered against him like a coat of paint. The darkness was just beginning to give way to the coming light. *Five forty-seven* glowed on the bedside clock. Roger took in a deep breath, smelling the fruity scent of the shampoo, she used on her hair. It smelled like paradise. The intimacy of last night still lingered in his mind, sending a warmth surging through his body. His arm pulled her tighter to him. He ran his fingers down the length of her body, feeling the smoothness of her skin, the heat. Relishing the touch, Roger felt he had never been closer to anyone in his life. Next to her, with her, he felt strong and at peace.

This is right, he thought. "I think I love you," he whispered, not sure if he had said it or just thought it. She responded by nestling even closer, purring a throaty moan.

"We have to get up." He said in a louder voice. "Today is D-day. We have to find a way to stop them or at least stop the concert."

"I know," she groaned. "Why can't the world go away and leave us alone. Why does life make it so hard to do the right thing?"

"It would be easy if the FBI would just believe us." He exhaled a long breath, kissed the top of her head and jumped from the bed. "I wish we had taped some of what we heard. Without that, it's just our word. We have no proof."

He tossed his hands into the air. "The police are always looking for crime, but you lay one in their laps and they don't believe you."

Na'Taya sat up and ruffled her hair. "If we call the FBI back they might arrest us like they threatened."

Roger shrugged his shoulders. "We don't have a choice. If we don't do something all of those people will die."

"I know...I know...Let's get something to eat and then we'll go directly to the office and take our chances. I don't want to go to prison on an empty stomach," she smiled, threw her hair back, and sighed. "At least if they won't believe us, we'll be with them when it happens and they can't blame us for not trying."

"That's a lousy alternative, but I guess we're out of options." Roger took Na'Taya's hand. "Look, I don't know what's going to happen. But, I want you to know, I meant what I said. I love you."

Dropping his head and looking like a sad puppy he said, "I'm sorry for the way I acted in the car. You're right. I got so caught up in the excitement of the game." He bobbed his head agreeing with himself.

"I was so full of myself. I must've seemed like a real jerk thinking I was going to outsmart the bad guys."

Na'Taya rose up in the bed standing on her knees, coming face to face with him. She playfully punched him.

"Yes, you were a jerk, but you're also my hero. Things were intense. We both over reacted. For my part, I guess I did throw a temper tantrum. I never should have destroyed the phone or left you. I don't want to ever leave you again." She threw her arms around him. "I love you too, and no matter what happens."

Roger stuttered. "You do?" She nodded. "It's not just because of..." he asked, sheepishly.

She smiled. "No, Roger. I know things are moving fast, but it feels right to be here with you. I feel I'm where I'm supposed to be. And I wouldn't want to be here with anyone else."

Roger and Na'Taya sat solemnly over plates of eggs and hash

browns, exchanging worried glances. Each of them in turn was attempting to speak, but having no luck finding words. The eggs had grown cold and the hash browns sat untouched, a thin layer of grease and butter shining on them like a coat of shellac. The hustle and bustle of the restaurant had faded into the distance; only the looming visions of the bridge and the carnage mattered. Roger's foot tapped in double time under the table.

"Roger, I'm worried. What if they still won't believe us? Will they really lock us up for making a false report? And when it happens, will they try to blame us and say we were involved?" Her chest rose and fell like an over-stuffed bag getting ready to pop as her voice grew shriller with worry.

"We don't have any other options. We have to try and stop this. Could you live with yourself if we just walked away? If we just let it happen and didn't do anything to stop it?" Roger answered.

She dropped her head and pushed the eggs with her fork. He reached for her across the table trying to reassure her with his touch.

"Come on," he said, standing up and throwing his napkin into his plate. "We might as well get this over with. The concert will be starting soon. There's not much time left." Roger paid the tab, took her hand and led her out the door.

Standing in front of the restaurant, he shouted grabbing his heart. "Oh, my God, no!"

"What's wrong? What happened?"

"Henry, how could I have forgotten about Henry?" The panic in his eyes frightened her.

"What about Henry?"

"The concert, he's going to the concert. He got a free ticket. We've got to go to Wellington and make sure he doesn't go before we get to the FBI. If they won't believe us, I don't want him anywhere near there."

Ignoring all the traffic laws, Roger sped to the facility. "Where's my brother?" he shouted at the receptionist, bursting through the door.

She smiled and gave him a puzzled look. "Hello, Mr. Beaufort. He's with the others."

"What do you mean? With the others, where?"

"They left early this morning. We decided to make this an all-day outing. Breakfast, a picnic, the concert, all kinds of fun stuff. You know sightseeing, the carnival rides. Letting them get caught up in the excitement. The patients were so excited." She sang out with a smile in her voice.

"Where are they now?"

"Probably down on the waterfront. They've got rides and games and lots of fun things. I can't wait to get off work and join them."

Roger grabbed Na'Taya's hand and raced to the car.

"What about the FBI? Maybe we should go there. We may not be able to find him in time. They could help."

"No, Henry is my responsibility. I'm not going to trust them to do anything to save him." He pounded himself on the head. "Stupid, stupid. I've been so involved with my own self I didn't even think of him."

Na'Taya stopped him by yanking on his arm until he turned to face her. "Don't do this to yourself. We will find him. You're a good brother. Henry knows you love him."

"Thanks," he said, kissing her forehead. Roger took a deep breath and licked his lips.

"Okay, you get on the phone. I don't care what you have to say, who you have to talk to, what you have to do, but make them believe you. Threaten them, scare them, bribe them, make them mad at you, if you have to, but get those assholes down there."

"What are you going to be doing?"

"Driving like a bat out of hell. We have to find my brother." He left skid marks leaving the parking lot.

Calvin stormed into the studio. "Where's Michelle," he shouted at Spade.

"She never came back here, boss. I've been here all night like you said. The only ones who've been here are some of the guys getting stuff to take down and set up for the concert."

Calvin pushed past him, disregarding him like a dropped penny. When he entered his office, Disco was there, playing a handheld video game. He ignored him, grumbled to himself and plopped into his chair.

"How was the party last night, Calvin? Were there lots of famous people there?" Disco eyes were wide with curiosity.

"Where the hell is Michelle?" He snapped.

"I don't know," he shrugged. "Wasn't she at the party last night?"

"If she was would I be asking you about her now?" He added. "The bitch isn't answering my calls either."

"What's wrong Calvin? Why are you so mad?" Disco asked.

"I thought you were going to keep an eye on her for me? Can't you do anything right? Can't you do this one thing I asked you for? I should have sent your ass to Louise like I started too."

"But...but Calvin."

"Shut the hell up and get out of my office," he kicked the desk. "Do I have to do every damn thing around here myself? I'm surrounded by a bunch of idiots."

Disco pouted, hung his head, and slunk out the door.

Calvin called Michelle, then he called Roger. Both calls went to voice mail.

"Where the fuck is everybody? I go out of town for one damn day and the whole fucking world falls apart." He checked his gun and slid it into his belt at the back. "First things first," he told himself, marching out of the office.

"Disco, Spade," he shouted. The two big men appeared, cowering like little boys being summoned by the principal. "Pull the car out front. We're going to take care of some business."

He looked at Spade. "You packing?" Spade wagged his head more like a shiver than a nod. "Good," he said. "Be ready. I plan on there being trouble. Or should I say causing trouble."

"Calvin, I..." Disco started, but was silenced by an angry look from his brother.

Michelle parked outside the lab. It was a four-story brick building in an industrial park near the riverfront a half a mile from the bridge.

The lab occupied the top floor; the other floors were vacant and unused. The building was next to the one Samel used in his import/export business and gave them easy access back and forth between the two. With a clear view to the bridge and with minimal traffic, it was the perfect location to conduct business without interference.

One of her hands rested on the ignition key and the other on the door handle; she wasn't sure which to use. One part of her wanted to go in and reconcile with Samel, to make him snap out of the frenzy he was in. The other part, the survivor, the logical part, told her to save herself and get away from this situation as fast as she could. The feeling of impending doom was itching in the back of her mind and wouldn't go away. Lost in a sea of indecision, Michelle didn't notice Samel exit the building and approach her car. When he opened the door, she jumped.

"I didn't know if you were still here. I thought that maybe you had left," he said, sitting next to her.

She didn't look at him. "I thought about it. I'm still thinking about it."

Samel reached over to take her hand. She pulled it away.

"I'm sorry. I...I know that I lost myself. Something in me gave way and I went mad for a moment. I let Spade's appearance overwhelm me." He sucked in a deep breath and leaned back in his seat. His expression hardened.

"I don't know. All the memories rushed at me, they were so intense, so painful. I was there again looking at their torn twisted bodies. I just don't..." His words faded. "I won't apologize for wanting to see him die. He is the one. He will pay. But, I want to ask your forgiveness for treating you like you don't matter. You know you're the best thing in my life."

A few minutes of awkward silence passed. Michelle clenched her jaws and turned to him.

"When we got together, we were two empty shells. Two people existing on our pain; our loss. I was as empty and lifeless as my womb." Michelle hugged her middle.

"You changed all that. You filled me up, made me believe I could feel something again. I could believe in something besides hate. Made me believe that life didn't have to be just a series of deals, obligations, and compromises. I was tired of using and being used. I know this venture started out as sort of a joke, a back handed way for us to settle our scores, a twisted fantasy, even. When things really started happening, in a funny way I began to feel that we were avenging angels, revolutionaries changing the world. Not with a word, but a hammer. It wasn't just an empty business venture, not just a way to make money. Somehow, I believed what we were doing was actually something worthwhile. We, you and me, would change things, make a difference, wipe out some of the ugly in the world and make way for something. I don't know, something good. Make the world wake up and pay attention to what was really going on, the corruption, the greed, the tyranny, the wanton waste. The fact that we would repay our personal debts and make some money in the process was just a happy coincidence."

She shook her head and stared out the window. "But the way you have been for the last few days. I've started to reevaluate things. You've become obsessed and erratic. I never really understood the depths of your obsession. I don't know what to do. I feel like I don't know you."

Samel gently reached up and swept a loose hair behind her ear. "I'm still me. I'm still the same man who came to you, with what was left of his heart, in his hands. Michelle, this has been emotional and intense for us both. Let's end this, let's kill these ghosts that have been haunting us. Bury our dead once and for all. We are so close, only a few hours and all will be settled. We can start really living. We will disappear and let our souls heal; find our paradise."

Michelle leaned forward and rested her head in her hands. "This isn't like the other times. Then, we went in, did the job and were gone. Here, there are names to these faces. History and connections; a whole city of ghosts. Is this what we want to do? Will this really change things? Change us and put our demons to rest. There is so much more involved. I was handling it all right until you got fixated on..." She hesitated to say the word. "Spade."

Samel flinched grasping his knee. He held out an open hand. "Stay with me." His voice was just above a whisper. "It will all end soon."

Michelle looked at the hand. She looked into his eyes. Carefully, as if his hand were a strange dog, she laid her hand in his. He gently closed his fingers around hers. They both leaned back in their seat, nothing breaking the silence between them.

Salvador woke frowning, smacking his lips against the bitter residue of last night's drinking. Kicking out his leg caused the body next to him to rustle. He looked at her, shrugged his shoulders, smiled, belched, and headed for the bathroom.

"Let's get some breakfast," the woman said when he reentered the room.

He spit into the trashcan. "Can't, sweetheart. I've got an appointment this morning. Wouldn't do for me to be late. Now would it... ugh?" He grabbed his pants and started dressing.

She stood, wrapped in a sheet and crossed her arms. "You don't remember my name, do you?"

"Ugh...Why lie? No, I don't. But, it doesn't matter. We'll never see each other again, anyway. By this time next week, I'll just be a fond memory. You can call me whatever you want." He smiled as his head disappeared into his shirt.

"How about bastard? Last night you talked about us..."

"Last night the whiskey was talking. You know how it goes. This ain't your first rodeo. Besides you had a good time, didn't you? Let it go." He frowned.

She puffed out her lips and marched into the bathroom. Salvador slipped on his shoes, donned his hat, shrugged his shoulder, and mumbled, "Stupid bitch," slamming the door as he left.

"Eight o'clock, I guess I do have time for some breakfast." he laughed, driving away in search of a restaurant.

34

It promised to be a glorious day. The sun was a golden spotlight shining through a clear pale blue sky. A gentle steady breeze waffled in from the south, pleasant and mild. Not a single cloud rode its wind. The temperature was already an exuberant 72 degrees at 8:30 in the morning, threatening to rise to a blistering 90 by noon. The sun, only a quarter of the way up from the horizon, illuminated the riverfront, already alive with activity and gaining strength. Hundreds of people had come down early to claim prime spots. The more committed arrived before the sun had risen, beginning the steady stream of city residents and out-of-towners alike that wanted to be part of the biggest event to hit the area in years. Hard-core fans camped out overnight in sleeping bags and pup tents, setting up makeshift villages like a frontier settlement, up and down the shore.

Modern day mariners spent the night on the water. Vessels of all sizes from tiny rowboats and catamarans to mega-yachts lined the banks. Those with nowhere to anchor, floated up and down the length of the river and back again, searching for a choice spot to claim. Early morning jet skiers were splashing those standing too close to the railings, while waving to excited children who waved back and wished they were the ones skirting the waves.

Jingles, whistles, and singsong melodies were growing ever louder as the crowds began to swell. Vendors opened up kiosks full of hot and cold delights. The scent of spices and tangy sauces was beginning to pepper the air. The smoke of charcoal and roasting meats mingled with the aroma of fresh popcorn and carnival sweets. T-shirts, hats, CDs, DVDs, and posters promoting the "Concert of Love" were on prominent display, intermixed with the usual sideshow fare you see at any other gathering.

Canada's side of the river also bustled with the same party atmosphere. As far as the eye could see, the Canadian party matched the American side smile for smile and mile for mile. Battling choruses of music crossed the half-mile distance across the river between Detroit and Windsor.

The crown jewel of Detroit parks is Belle Isle. The 982-acre island park located east of downtown and straight down the river from the Ambassador bridge. It had so many campers, picnickers, and tail-gaters on it the city was forced to close the MacArthur Bridge that leads to the island park at sunrise to curtail the overcrowding. No matter, the deluge continued. People filled every nook, cranny, and available lot they could find; setting up shop on and off the island.

All along Jefferson Avenue, the thoroughfare used to reach the island, and every side street between it and the Detroit River was carpeted with sellers, buyers, and gawkers. The whole area was like a beehive over run with anxious bees.

"This is not a prank call. Yes, I have called before." Na'Taya yelled into phone. "I don't care if you're tracking the phone. I want you to. I'm trying to warn you. Why won't you believe me? This is real." She shook her head. "I wouldn't risk going to jail for a prank." She sighed and let the phone fall into her lap.

"They put me on hold," she said to Roger. "I can't believe this. We're not going to be able to stop this."

"If they won't believe you then the hell with them. After we find Henry we'll just have to try and warn the security that's there. Maybe we can get somebody to believe us." Roger pushed harder on the gas pedal. "Right now, I don't care about anything but getting to my brother."

"You don't mean that. I know you're worried about Henry and angry with the FBI, but you care about those other people too. You're not some heartless monster that could leave all of those people to die. You're not that kind of guy. It's not who you are."

Roger swallowed and gave her a quick look. "Yeah, I do, but we're doing all we can. I just don't..."

"Want to feel responsible for letting all those other people die?" He nodded. "I feel the same way. We'll do some..."

"Na'Taya," the voice on the phone called out. "Na'Taya, are you still there?"

Na'Taya tilted her head. Her eyes sprang open wide with recognition. "Martin, is that you?"

"Yes, it's me. Where are you?"

"Martin," the smile could be heard in her voice. "Oh Martin, I can't believe I'm saying this, but I am so happy to hear your voice."

"Look, I'm sorry for the way things turned out. I wasn't..."

"Martin, listen," she interrupted. "We couldn't get anybody to believe us. They're going to blow up the bridge, during the concert. You've got to stop them. They'll kill all those people."

"Who is?"

"Samel and..."

"Wait a minute," he said. "stop and tell me everything you know."

Na'Taya took a deep breath and relayed all that had happened to her and Roger since she had last talked to him.

"Where are you now?" Martin asked.

"On our way to the bridge."

"No," Martin ordered. "You stay away from there. We'll handle it from here."

"The hell we will." Roger shouted. "My brother is down there and I'm going to save him."

"Who is that? Is that Roger?"

"Yes, it's me, and I'm going. You can't stop me."

"Look Roger, you're not equipped to handle this. Let us do our job."

"If you had been doing your job," his voice thick with sarcasm and anger, "You would have stopped this a long time ago and we wouldn't be involved at all."

"Okay, there were some errors, but..."

"Some errors?'" he laughed. "I don't care what you say. We've told you all we know. Now it's your problem. You stop the terrorists and I'll save my brother." Roger reached over and clicked off the phone.

Na'Taya placed her hand on his. A smile of pride and approval on her face. "We'll find Henry. Don't worry. Now that we've got somebody to believe us we can concentrate on what we need to do."

Roger nodded his agreement and turned to taking his frustrations out on the growing horde of cars that were clogging the streets. As they got closer to downtown, the traffic became slower and slower until there was no movement and the streets became parking lots, filled bumper to bumper with idling cars.

"We'll have to get out and walk. Downtown is just a little over a mile away. If we sit here, well never get there in time. And we'll never find Henry and..." The words stopped as he pushed the thought of what could happen from his mind.

"Okay, let's do it." Na'Taya agreed.

Roger took the first turn he could make and parked the car in a church parking lot just east of Woodward Avenue, the main street. The two took off at a healthy trot. After a few blocks the unforgiving sun slowed them down to a quick walk. A few blocks later, their pace became just a steady walk, albeit with an urgency in their gait. The entire time they held each other's hand as if the one arm was shared between them. Despite the sweaty palms, neither was letting go. It was as if they were transferring energy to keep each other going.

"How will we find him? We don't know where he is until they head to the concert."

"The concert isn't for a few hours, so they're probably at some of the rides or will be having a picnic or something like that. When we get downtown, let's split up. You head east toward Belle Isle and I'll go west toward the bridge. We're bound to find him. I hope. Whoever finds him first can just call the other. Then we'll get out of here. I figure once the FBI gets started, it's going to be a mad stampede to get everybody away from the bridge." Na'Taya nodded panting against the pace.

"Keep an eye out for Spade and Samel," he added. "We don't want to have to try to pull off another rescue or escape. We've been just lucky so far. I don't want to use up what luck we have left. If we do, we may never find Henry."

His mind flipped to Salvador. Much as he hated to admit it, he thought. *We could use his help.*

35

Calvin nudged back into his seat, feeling the cold steel of the gun pressing against his skin. "Drive to the warehouse before we go to the bridge. I want to see what Michelle and Samel were doing there."

As they drew closer to the warehouse, the harsh scent of last night's fire assaulted their noses. Spade's eyes grew wide as he spied the building from down the block.

"What happened?" he asked, scanning the decimated structure as he opened the door and stood awestruck before the still-smoking ruins.

Calvin leapt out of the car in a rage. The veins in his neck swelled as if they were about to burst. He growled like a wounded beast. Calvin pushed Spade against the open door, grabbed his collar and pointed the colt in his face.

"What the fuck happened here?" he screamed spraying spittle in his face. "You bastard, you never mentioned anything about a fire."

Spade, pleaded more than explained. "It was all right when we left, Mr. Michaels. I swear to you. There was no fire when I was here. I swear. This...this happened after I was gone. I don't know nothing about it." He trembled like a bobble doll.

"Alright asshole, explain to me one more time everything that happened and don't leave out one little detail." Calvin cocked the gun, "or it will be the last fuck-up you ever make." His eyes burned bright red as if they were flames shining through windows in a burning building.

Spade gulped and began telling the story from his first encounter with Samel until he left the warehouse with Michelle, making sure to rethink every sentence for fear he would leave something out. He spoke slowly and clearly, his voice thin and unapologetic.

"I'm going to kill them both," Calvin growled through clenched teeth. Michelle and that mother..."

"You can't kill Michelle!" Disco shouted, jumping into the exchange. "You mad Calvin, but..."

Calvin turned to face Disco, letting go of Spade's collar. The anger in his face caused Disco to take a step back.

"Shut the fuck up. You don't tell me what I can do. You don't understand nothing. You're good for nothing. I'm going to kill that bitch and if you get in my way, I'll kill your ass, too." His free hand, balled in a fist, pumped the air.

Disco curled in on himself and hung his head like a child that had been sent to his room. He backed away from the car, pouting.

Calvin stomped to the building and sloshed through the dirty water and charred remains; muttering curses to himself under his breath.

"I'm going to kill the bitch, then I'm going to kill Samel. And then I'm going to kill Roger. Then I'm going to kill her ass, again." He kicked at a burned chunk of wood.

"I'm going to kill everybody." Returning to the car, he hopped in and kicked the back of Spade's seat, leaving a black footmark on the fabric.

"Take me to the bridge," he ordered. "And don't say another damn word."

Michelle drove into the corporate section of the airport. She and Samel walked across the tarmac. The Bell 407 helicopter, painted red, white, and blue with the words "Concert of Love" painted on both sides, was waiting on the helipad tarmac. Hector Peters, the pilot, a middle aged ex-military man with the propensity and lungpower to talk a blue streak, was waiting like an honor guard. His lazy left eye, the result of enemy shrapnel, clocked them with a whimsical wink. In the midst of his preflight inspection, he greeted them.

"Good morning Ms. Hightower, how's the wind blowing?"

"Fine, Peters. Mr. Nizam and myself want to be on your next flight to the bridge. If you're full, cargo or passengers will have to wait. This is a priority." He nodded.

"Have you been busy this morning?" Michelle asked.

"Yes, ma'am," he said with a Georgia twang. "There's been a steady stream of people since about six this morning. I hardly had time to put my britches on before the phone was jumping off the hook, telling me to get this bird in the air."

"Any problems?" she asked.

"Not a one. It's perfect weather for flying. The passengers have been mostly friendly. People at the heliport down at the bridge have been downright helpful. They've been coordinating between myself and my counterpart from the Canadian side just fine. We're on a rotation. Every 45 minutes one of us flies in, downloads, and flies out, like clockwork. All is A-Okay."

"I'm glad to know something is going as planned."

"Ma'am?" he asked giving her a quizzical look.

"Never mind," she waved off the question. "How long before we depart?"

Peters looked at his watch.

"About 20 minutes. I'm waiting on the shuttle to deliver somebody or another. Hell, I don't know none of these kids. A colorful bunch though," he added. "I suppose you do. Seeing as how you're in the business and all."

He nodded looking for a response. When none came, he continued. "Let me finish my check and you can board. Not many comforts, but..."

She interrupted his rambling. "That'll be fine. We'll just wait in the lounge. Let us know when it's time to leave." She turned and began walking away.

"Sure thing, Ms. Hightower. It won't be long," he waved after them as if he was saying goodbye forever.

"That's the money?" Michelle asked motioning to Samel's brief-case. "I didn't realize that you kept that kind of money on hand."

"There are many things that should be handled strictly on a cash basis. It is quicker with fewer questions."

"So, you're just going to give him the money and that's it?"

"He'll get his money and something extra. Let's call it a bonus." he smiled. Michelle started to ask, but realized she didn't want to know. Samel stopped at the building's entrance.

"You go ahead and have a seat. I'm going to have a smoke." Samel set down his briefcase and reached into his breast pocket for a cigar.

"Samel, what is it? There's something more. I know that look."

He dropped his hands and looked away from her.

"Rala is dead. Last night the police had me come down to identify the body. His fingerprints and dental records had already confirmed who he was, but they needed confirmation from a relative." Samel hurriedly lit his cigar. The tubular rod trembled between his fingers. Michelle raised a worried brow, but did not comment. He puffed up so much smoke it seemed he was trying to create a cloud to hide in.

"What happened? How did he die?"

"Somebody beat him to death. His skull was crushed in," Samel's voice choked up.

Michelle laid her hand on his shoulder. "I'm sorry Samel. I know he was the last of your family. I'm so sorry."

Samel turned and hugged her, burying his face into her neck.

"Spade did it."

"Samel, he doesn't know you two from the war. And if he did, why would he kill Rala?"

Samel pulled away from her and shouted.

"He does," sounding like a petulant child. "He did it. He came to the apartment looking for Rala. When he found him, he killed him."

The hate in his eyes flared like flames.

"He was looking for the girl. Rala was his lead."

"He wanted to finish the job he started in Mosul." His face froze in a malicious sneer. "I guess he'll come for me next. After all I'm the last one."

Michelle stepped back, mouthing the word "no." She turned her head unable to focus on anything except the stranger she was looking at.

"Ms. Hightower, lift off in five minutes. You folks can get on board and buckle in." Peters yelled, passing by with a couple of blue haired young ladies in tow.

Samel threw down his cigar, picked up his briefcase, and headed toward the copter. Michelle hesitated, and then followed slowly behind.

36

Roger and Na'Taya arrived at Hart Plaza, the waterfront park at the foot of Woodward Avenue between Jefferson Ave. and the Detroit River. The fourteen-acre park of stone and grass serves as an introduction point to the Riverwalk, the miles-long park that lines the river. An amphitheater built in the Roman style, anchors the area.

Roger grimaced at the Horace E. Dodge and Son Memorial Fountain; a new age structure that he always thought looked like a urinal in an exclusive upscale New York lounge. Below the upper deck of the plaza are restrooms, dressing rooms, a kitchen, and a host of meeting rooms available for the many cultural activities that the plaza hosts.

Most striking about the plaza is the unobstructed view of the downtown Windsor, Ontario skyline. Most people are amazed at how close the urban areas are to each other. The half mile of water separating them seems inconsequential and makes the fact that they are two different countries seem unbelievable and unimportant.

Na'Taya collapsed breathlessly on one of the stone benches in the plaza. Roger stood, frantically scanning the hordes of people milling about.

"Here's where we split up," he said, surveying the five and a half miles along the Riverwalk, stretching from the

Ambassador Bridge to the Gabriel Richard Park, just east of the Belle Isle Bridge. "We've got a lot of ground to cover."

"Do you think they could be on the Canadian side?" she asked.

"No, I doubt it. You need a passport to cross the bridge these days. The Wellington people wouldn't go to all that trouble."

They walked to the railing overlooking the dark water of the river. There were so many boats in the water you could jump from one to the other and make it across the river. It was a wonder there weren't collisions every few minutes. The crowds on the Riverwalk were so thick it made it impossible to make out anyone specific, except the people on the very edge.

"Okay, which direction do you want?" Na'Taya asked, taking a deep breath, crossing her arms, and pointing in both directions.

Roger made one more assessment. "We'll stick to the plan. You head up toward Belle Isle and I'll go toward the bridge. If you find him, hold on to him and call me. I'll be there as soon as I can. If I find him, I'll call and we'll come and meet you. Then we can get the hell away from here."

She nodded, stepped up to him, and gave him a kiss.

"Good luck. I'll see you soon," she smiled before she tore away and disappeared in the crowd.

Roger watched long after she had disappeared into the crowd knowing that she would be safe away from the bridge. Breathing easier, he dove into the horde and began his search.

Salvador sauntered up to the railing and looked out on to the river. He leaned over and watched the waves splash against the break wall. Being in close proximity to the river relaxed him, reminding him of the placid waters of Lake Washington and Puget Sound back home in Seattle.

A good day to get paid, he thought. Salvador looked at his watch. "Five minutes to eleven, I'll be a little late." He shrugged.

"Huh, it never hurts to make them sweat just a little. He laughed, straightened his hat, and began his trek toward the bridge.

Walking through the gathering spectators, his mind drifted back to the days of picking the pockets of overweight, over-indulged tourists at the carnivals, fairs, and malls in Seattle. He smiled, remembering selecting his marks and devising a game plan.

"You got the touch," Sledge would say. "These ain't good for nothing but busting heads." He'd held up his calloused meaty hands and made his short fat finger dance like animated sausages.

"We all got our talents. I'm tired of nickel and diming my way through. I want to make some real money." Salvador responded.

"I've got something going down and those sticky little fingers of yours could come in handy." Sledge tilted his bald head and lowered his voice.

"You may not have the balls for it. You're still a sapling and I don't know if you're ready for the big time yet, for real money." He gave the thin young man the once over.

Salvador protested. "I'm fourteen. I may not be as old as you, but I'm as good as you. I've been on my own way since I was eleven years old," sticking out his thin chest with pride.

"What about them rent-a-family folk you living with?"

"They don't give a damn about me. As long as I come around when the social worker shows up so they can get their check they don't care if I live or die. Hell, if I died they'd probably prop me up in a chair and swear that I was asleep."

Sledge laughed, bouncing his large head on his thick neck.

"Okay sapling, get ready to prove yourself."

Ten hours later, Salvador started the first of a trio of visits to juvenile detention, eventually graduating to four-

year stretch in the Washington State Penitentiary for armed robbery and grand theft.

"Those days are over and done with," he said to himself with a swipe of his hand.

Salvador eyed a short obese woman in cargo pants and flip-flops. The overstuffed fanny pack at her waist held his attention. *In the day, I would have plucked that fat chicken bald.*

Studying the woman out of the corner of his eye, he decided. *For old time's sake.*

Nudging a young couple holding hands, he caused the girl to lose balance and fall into the guy. He buckled under her weight and bumped hard into the short woman. Salvador moved in like a sudden downpour and with fingers made of crepe paper and glue, relieved her of her purse.

Moving away quickly, he put several yards between himself and the group. Stopping in front of a kiosk selling plastic keepsakes he turned to watch the scene.

Wait for it, he thought. A few moments later, the woman noticed her open fanny pack and shouted. "He stole my purse!" She yelled, pointing at the innocent young man. Salvador laughed and double-timed his steps to the bridge.

Roger moved through the herd of people, gaining the high ground whenever he could, scanning large sections of the crowd. As the number of people continued to increase, it became harder and harder to sort them out. The size of the crowd was a distraction. Picking out one person seemed like an impossible task. The anxiety of worrying he would overlook Henry added to the guilt and apprehension he was already fighting.

The sound of pipe organ music, playing happy jingles, the motors of carnival rides, barkers hawking souvenirs and trinkets, the recorded music of some of the acts that would be at the concert, along with the general noise of thousands of voices and footsteps created a tension and excitement in the air that would have been invigorating if not for the worry in his heart. The noise, the heat, and the worry made it hard to concentrate.

"Roger, Roger over here!" The voice shouted over the din. Roger turned toward the voice. Bouncing up and down on his toe he tried to see over the moving heads.

"Henry," he called out dodging in and around people, pushing his way through without “an excuse me” or a “sorry." Roger stopped near the railing, but all he saw was a young boy waving for his brother to come look at a particularly large yacht motoring down the river.

"Come on Roger, check this one out." he said.

Roger's heart sank as he backed away melting into the crowd.

"This is crazy. I'll just double time down to the bridge. If I see him before I get there, great. If not, then I'll just wait by the entrance and make sure he doesn't get onto the bridge."

Roger nodded his agreement with himself and took off at a jog.

37

"Get on the damn shoulder!" Calvin yelled.

Spade, sweating like a marathon runner, maneuvered the car onto the shoulder of the freeway and skirted around the gridlocked traffic. Horns honked and drivers screamed for him to get back in line and wait his turn. Spade snarled back at them, causing people to lock their doors and shrink down into their seats.

"Ignore those losers," Calvin commanded. "Come up at the next exit and take the streets. The side streets," he directed.

"And hurry up. I need to be down there before..." His thought hung unfinished in the air.

A host of cars began to follow them ignoring the obvious violation. Soon the Lincoln Town car was leading a caravan of a dozen or so other vehicles. Calvin sat in the back puffing violently on a cigar and cursing under his breath. Spade and Disco remained obedient and quiet, not wanting to be noticed.

Spade exited the freeway and began weaving his way through the back streets of the city, heading southwest toward downtown. The usually lightly traveled streets had a noticeable increase in traffic as other drivers with the same idea were making their way into the heart of the city. A dozen blocks from the bridge, the traffic ceased to move. Cars and buses blocked every intersection and alleyway.

HORNS BLARED and voices rose with every moment that passed and every degree that the temperature climbed. Nothing was moving, not even the wind.

Homes along the route had their front and back lawn converted into makeshift parking lots, charging inflated rates for the privilege of easy access parking. Homeowners stood in front of their properties with hand written signs, hawking about the limited space and the need to get your place while they still lasted. Sixty dollars proclaimed one sign, fifty-five dollars offered another, as the homeowners bowed and swept their arm as if he they were maître d's at a fancy restaurant leading you to a prime table.

Calvin flung open the back door. The oppressive heat slapped him in the face. He sucked in a breath, threw his cigar out the door, and stood up looking around at the multitude of idling cars blocking the street. The bridge loomed in the distance, so close he could count the colored balloons circling the girders.

"Park this damn thing and follow me." Calvin started walking down the street in between the cars.

Spade and Disco looked at each other. A shared look of fear and confusion on their faces.

Spade and Disco stood among the idle car. "Get these damn cars out of my way so I can pull in there," Spade yelled, pointing to a clapboard house with a wizened old man standing in the front yard holding a sign.

"How?" Disco asked.

Spade looked around him. His face went from placid to demon warrior.

"Like this," he slammed both fists into the hood of the car next to him. "Move that piece of shit. Get the hell out of our way."

Horrified people began screaming, rolled up their windows, and curling down into their seats. The beaten car had a woman driver and a horde of children ranging from the very small to teenagers. They screamed and pushed to the other side of the car, pressing themselves against the door panel. The woman turned the wheel of the car and inched forward, forcing the next car to attempt the same thing.

Spade growled at the terrified drivers of the other cars. Each vehicle edged out of his way until there was a clear path from the Lincoln to the lot. Disco walked the path daring any car to move in their way.

Spade stomped back to the car like Godzilla rampaging through Tokyo. The people stared in silence. He slid into the driver's seat and rode into the lot, throwing the astounded old man 30 dollars.

"Make sure you take care of my ride." The man held up the thirty dollars and started to protest, but after a leering look from Spade, he pocketed the money and nodded. Disco and Spade double-timed it to catch up with Calvin.

With each step, Calvin grew angrier. The gun at his back rubbed against his skin, adding to his irritation.

"Bitch ain't going to ruin me. I'll send her and Samel to hell before I let that happen."

The two others soon over took Calvin. He scowled at them and returned his focus to the bridge.

Disco cut his eyes at Calvin, giving him angry looks. Lagging behind the other two, he whispered under his breath, "You ain't gonna hurt Michelle. I won't let you."

Na'Taya moved through the crowd scanning every face, listening to every voice, trying to pick up on some sign of Henry; the overwhelming chaos of voices, music, and merrymaking made the task frustrating and difficult. Stopping at every carnival ride, she eyed every rider. At the games, the puppet theatre, the sideshows, the dance parties, the myriad of exhibitions, demonstrations and displays, she mingled among the masses wishing silently.

At a carousel, with unicorns and dragons, a young boy caught her eye. With a yell of recognition, she ran toward him.

"Henry. It's Na'Taya!" She yelled, only to be disappointed when he turned to face her. Disheartened, Na'Taya backed away. Her frustration and desperation growing, she continued her search.

Na'Taya's mind began to wonder. It was as if she had been searching all her life. Searching for love, searching for acceptance, searching for purpose, searching for herself. And she was still searching, always searching for something, somewhere, someone to fill the hole in her heart. Something that could make her feel safe, make her believe that life didn't always have to be pain and disappointment. Something she could count on, be certain of.

"Roger," she said without realizing she was speaking. "No, he is there, but..."

"Na'Taya," the voice said.

"Henry," she shouted turning to face the hand on her shoulder.

"No, It's me..."

"Martin," she shouted jumping into his arms and hugging him like a long lost relative. "I didn't know if you would really come. "

"That's a much better welcome than I expected." He hugged her back.

"What are you doing here? Why aren't you at the bridge? No, never mind I don't care why you're here." The questions came faster than Martin could correlate.

"You've got to get everyone off that bridge. You've got to do it now."

"Slow down Na'Taya. Our people are here coordinating everything. We've got men in route and going to the bridge. We're trying to make this happen. It's a tight deadline. It took me forever to convince the higher ups that you were for real. They still don't believe it one hundred percent, but they at least have us down here to check thing out. Besides, if it turns out you're right and they ignore the warning some powerful heads would roll."

He gave her a stern look. "I thought I told you to stay away from here?"

"We're looking for Henry. He is supposed to go to the concert. We have to find him and get him to safety."

"Okay, okay. He's special needs, isn't he?"

"No, not special needs, he's sick. He has...wait a minute," she scrunched up her face. "How did you know there was something wrong with Henry."

Martin hunched his shoulders. "We had to check out this Roger of yours out. Don't get mad, it's just standard procedure." He gave her a half smile.

"Let me call my people. Facilities like the Wellington always have their own transport. Somebody's bound to have seen the bus. We've got people along the route." He unclipped the radio from his hip.

Na'Taya gave him a wary look. He turned his back and continued to talk.

"The bus is parked in the lot by the amphitheater at Chene Park. Come on, I'll take you down there. They may still be in the area."

"But, I passed that way already."

"It's crowded; you could have over looked them." He took her arm and led her to a white Honda Interceptor DLX.

"A motorcycle? Is that government issue?"

He cracked a devilish grin. "Believe it or not, I do have a life outside this badge." He hopped on, handed her a helmet, and sped down the side street leading back toward Hart Plaza.

Na'Taya and Martin searched the park next to the amphitheater once they located the bus.

"I'm really sorry for the way that things turned out. My hands were tied. I tried to speak on your behalf, but I was over ruled every time by higher ups." He stopped and inhaled a deep breath. "There is going to be hell to pay. They simply wouldn't listen when I tried to talk on your behalf."

Na'Taya looked at him with new eyes. The arrogant, self-assured, no compromise, hard-ass was human after all. His sharp edges had softened a bit. The intimidating figure that had threatened her freedom was replaced by a sympathetic young man only a few years older than her.

The noise of a rowdy game of volleyball drew her attention.

"Henry!" she shouted drawing his attention and causing him to miss the ball. She ran to the game and covered him in a desperate hug.

"Oh Henry, we've been looking everywhere for you. I've got to call Roger and let him know you're safe."

"Of course, I'm safe. We're going to the concert."

"No, Henry. There isn't going to be a concert."

"No concert,' he cried. "Why not?"

"I'll explain later, okay. Let me call Roger and let him know we've found you."

"So, this is Henry," Martin said stepping forward and extending his hand. "Hello Henry. My name is Dwayne Martin." He cleared his throat.

"I'm a friend of your brother's." He twitched at the lie.

Henry drew back and looked at his hand. After an uncomfortable moment, Martin pulled it back and shoved it in his pocket as if he was punishing it for attempting such a thing.

38

The helicopter landed on the helipad moments after the Canadian counterpart took off. The two blue-haired artists looked up from their phones and dashed out the door without so much as a goodbye, thank you, or any acknowledgement that anybody else existed.

"The younger generation, Lord help us," Peters said, deplaning and offering Michelle a hand down.

"I'll be here for another 30 minutes or so before I head back to the airport for another run. I'm sure as the day goes on things are bound to get more hectic, if you need to get on a certain flight let me know soon as you can, so I can have the pleasure of booting a couple of these ungrateful young'uns to the back of the line. I'll enjoy seeing them finally look up from them damn phones." He moved around to the other side of the copter and began unloading the cargo.

"Thank you, Hector," Michelle said. "I don't know how long we will remain, but we'll keep your offer in mind."

She and Samel moved toward the bridge. "Let's get this over with as quickly as possible. I still don't like it, but I suppose we must."

Her voice was sharp and sarcastic. Samel seemed in a haze. He neither reacted to her bitterness nor responded to her attempts to engage him.

THEY TRAVELED past the welcome center that was set up to greet visitors to Detroit and provide them with maps, information and concierge services. Just inside the entrance to the concert venue, a steady stream of roadies and technicians hustled about making preparation for the concert. Samel proceeded, with Michelle in tow, to an elevated level in the open plaza that adjoined the welcome center. He took a seat at a table in the back that still provided an open view of the plaza.

People casually milled about like a great herd during a summer migration. Some celebrities had taken up strategic positions in the plaza, gathering small crowds of admiring fans. They signed autographs and boasted about their latest projects. A few scalpers were peddling over-priced tickets. A bidding war between three couples had started. The sellers were trying to calm them down, lest their enthusiasm start to draw unwanted attention from security.

The smell of fresh popcorn, sticky balls of cotton candy, neon-colored scoops of ice cream, and cold drinks from sodas to ice lattes mixed with the musky scent of sweaty tourists and stagnant river water.

Salvador entered the plaza from the west. He ambled about, casually and cautiously, scoping out the crowd and searching for his payday. Spotting Samel and Michelle sitting conspicuously on the upper level, he wove his way through the thongs of people to join them.

Salvador climbed the stairs to the upper level, scraping under his nails with a knife, a self-satisfied grin on his face. The show of a weapon did not go unnoticed by Samel. Salvador touched the tip of his hat to the lady. Michelle ignored the gesture as if he were just a pigeon begging for breadcrumbs. Samel met him with an icy reception. Salvador shrugged off the reception and took a seat with his back to the crowd.

"Where is the girl?" Samel asked.

"She's back at the hotel recovering from a night of excruciating passion," he chuckled.

"How can we know that you have not reneged on our deal. What assurances can you give me of your fidelity?"

"You'll just have to trust me," Salvador said, flicking away a spot of dry cuticle with the knife.

"I don't give a damn what you people do or don't do. I'm just looking to get paid. Your troubles are your own."

Samel sneered and pushed the briefcase toward Salvador with his foot. "Take your 30 pieces of silver and go."

"Better be a damn sight more than 30 pieces in here," he said, reaching down to retrieve the case and placing it on his lap. Salvador eyes sprang wide as the lid of the briefcase popped open. He stared at the money with the relish of a hungry dog seeing a meaty bone.

Roger entered the plaza from the east. He maneuvered his way around the outside of the bustling crowd. With the incredible crowd of people, he knew his only chance of seeing Henry before he got to the bridge was to park himself near the gate as high up as possible. Moving into position, he spied the trio on the upper level.

Roger watched the scene from the side of a barista selling tacos and lemonade. "Salvador, with Samel and Michelle? What the hell does Salvador have to do with this?" His dislike for the man grew by leaps and bounds. Roger crept closer, winding his way around the crowd. His fear of being recognized caused him to move slower than he liked, but caution over ruled curiosity.

Michelle leaned over and whispered in Samel's ear. She pointed in his direction. Roger ducked behind a couple of tourists. Michelle and Samel smiled and waved to a couple moving along with the crowd.

Salvador laid the knife on the table giving himself two hands to caress the money. Samel leaned forward and took a careful look at the blade.

"May I?" he asked, reaching for it.

Salvador waved him off, too engrossed in the money to care.

Hefting the blade in his hands, he admired the weight and balance. Turning it over he read the etched initials at the base of the blade.

"This is a superior blade Mr...." he tilted his head waiting for a response. Pointing to the engraving on the knife blade, "RN?" he asked.

"Names are not important. We need not pretend to be sociable. Our business is cash, carry, and anonymous."

"Ah, but our business is sociable, even personal. You see I know about blades. This kind in particular."

Samel tossed the open blade up and down a few times catching it by the handle. He lunged forward, planting the steel directly into Salvador's heart. Samel leaned in putting a hand on Salvador's shoulder and pulled him forward twisting the blade into him like a corkscrew. His face wore something between a frown and a smile.

He leaned into Salvador and whispered in his ear. "The owner of this weapon was my nephew, Rala Nizam, RN." Salvador's eyes grew wide at the mention of the name. He groped at Samel's hand, but the knife had him planted firmly into the back of the chair. The briefcase on his lap aided in wedging him in and making moving difficult. Salvador leaned forward and Samel pressed up sinking the knife further into him. The pain and shock of the 6 inches of steel caused him to become limp, speechless, and useless. Samel slapped Salvador's groping hand away and continued to press inward. Falling toward the blade was all that kept Salvador from keeling over.

The action had been so quick and smooth; Salvador had no chance to react. He stared confounded, gurgling his protest. Salvador tried again to raise his fist, only to have it fall limp to his side as his breathing faltered and collapsed to nothing.

Michelle leapt up from her seat knocking over her chair.

"Are you mad?" she looked around nervously.

"He killed Rala. That is the only way he could have acquired his knife. I gave Rala that blade on his 15th birthday. He had it with him, always. I have avenged him." His voice was calm and definite.

"Oh, my God," Michelle said, running her fingers across her

temple. "You said that Spade killed Rala. What are you going to do next, say that I killed him? I'm getting the hell away from here, from you. I don't know you anymore." She headed for the stairs.

Samel took off Salvador's hat and placed it over the knife protruding from his chest. He smiled, wiped his hand on the dead man's shirt, grabbed the brief case and walked nonchalantly down the stairs, chasing Michelle.

Roger looked around him in amazement. His heart was beating like war drums in his ears. He opened his mouth to shout. A slap on the back took the wind and the words from his mouth.

"Hey Roger, glad you could make it. We could use a guy with your skills. We are in need of an extra set of hands. As usual nothing is working the way it's supposed to." Kenny Taylor, the sound engineer said.

"I didn't know you were going to be here, but I'm glad you are," Kenny heaved a canvas bag of wires and components at him. The bag caught Roger in the chest and almost doubled him over.

"Did you just see Michelle and Samel? Did you see what happened?"

Kenny shook his head. "I don't like that Samel guy. He doesn't sweat. My grandmother used to say, 'Never trust anybody who doesn't sweat. They're too close to hell.' He shivered like the thought gave him a chill. "Don't like him. Don't trust him," he sucked a breath through his teeth. "Come on. Let's go."

"But did you see what just happened?" he gazed at Salvador slumped over in the chair.

"Who cares? Come on we've got a concert to put on." Kenny beckoned him to follow.

Roger's phone blared out a siren's call. "Wait, I've got to take this." Turning his back, he curled over the phone.

"Na'Taya," he whispered. "You've found him? Thank God. Okay stay there; I'll come to you as soon as I can.

Should I tell her about Salvador? No, came back the thought. He looked back at Kenny who was tapping his foot and looking irritated.

"I can't explain right now. I have to deal with some of the people from Majestic. Just stay there I'll see you soon." Roger rolled his eyes and sighed.

"I won't go on the bridge. I promise. Look I have to go. I'll be there soon, okay. Just keep Henry safe." He pocketed the phone and followed an impatient Kenny. Roger turned back and looked at Salvador's body sitting as if he had nodded off waiting on a late arrival.

"He wants us to wait for him here. He's coming to us," Na'Taya said.

"Good, then my work here is done. I have to get back to the crew." Martin handed her a card. Here's my private number again. Call me in a day or two. The bureau will want to talk to you and Roger. Hopefully we've got this one under control."

He turned to leave and pivoted back to face her. "You did a good thing, Na'Taya. And I, for one, am grateful." He smiled and gave her a small salute.

"Nice to meet you Henry." The motorcycle revved up and he was gone.

"Where's Roger? And why can't I go to the concert?" Henry pouted, blowing his face up like a puff fish.

Na'Taya took his hand and led him away from the others. Lowering her voice just above a soft whisper she said. "There are things going on, Henry, bad things. Roger is just trying to get us away so we don't get hurt."

"Where is he?"

She looked to the bridge. "He's down by the bridge, but he's coming to get us. We just have to wait here for him."

His face brightened up. "Why can't we walk that way and meet him?"

"No, Henry. He said wait here for him. I know..."

"Roger's in trouble, isn't he?" Na'Taya shook her head and opened her mouth, but Henry spoke first.

"He is in trouble. I can tell. I'm going to help him." He took off running toward the bridge.

"Henry, where are you going? Get back here!" The Wellington handler yelled.

"I'll get him." Na'Taya said waving off the worker. She took off after Henry.

At the entrance gate to the concert, Kenny walked passed security. "He's with us." The guard nodded and moved aside letting them pass. Kenny pointed to a group of confused looking young men.

"Could you go over there and help that group of Einsteins link up the systems? I've got other things that need doing," he looked at the befuddled group and shook his head.

"Thank God for Velcro. I don't believe them boys could tie their shoes without an instruction manual," he added, "one that has pictures."

Roger forced a smile. "Sure, but I can't stay too long. I have to meet my brother and my girl."

"Sure thing, Romeo. But could you at least give us a few moments of your precious time? We're trying to make history here."

"Where the hell is Michelle?" The question boomed out of the middle of a parting crowd. Calvin stormed on to the scene flanked by Disco and Spade. The gathered crew parted like the red sea, giving him a wide berth. Roger saw them and slid into the crowd.

"I said, where the hell is Michelle?" Calvin shouted again.

"Don't know," Kenny said, not paying any attention to Calvin's bravado. "We've been too busy working to keep..."

"I'm not in the mood, Kenny. Watch yourself. You can be replaced, too." He interrupted. Kenny hunched his shoulders and walked away.

"Don't I know that guy?" Spade said pointing at a retreating Roger. "He looks familiar." He pinched his face and squinted his eyes like a he was staring at the sun.

Calvin looked past the crowd. "That's the IT guy, you ape. Of course, you know him. He works for me. That's Roger...whatever."

"No," Spade said moving to get a better view of Roger. "I've seen him someplace else before." Roger turned his back and bent down to hide even more. He started to panic. He moved away from the group and toward the other end of the bridge, ducking and weaving to keep himself hidden.

"Hey Roger, where you going? Kenny shouted.

"Roger," Spade repeated, the wheels turning in his head. "Roger." He shouted his eyes opening wide with recognition. "That's the guy that was with Na'Taya. Isn't it Disco?" Disco hunched his shoulder not sure of what to say.

"Couldn't be," Calvin said. "he didn't start until after she was gone."

"It's him. I'm sure of it." Spade dived into the crowd chasing him.

39

Samel peered down at the bridge as the helicopter lifted into the air. Calvin, Disco, and Spade were on the center stage. The sight of Spade ignited something in him. His fury flared up like a spark on dry bush. Samel flung the door open and cried out.

"Spade!" his voice echoed, booming over the noise of the helicopter blades. He sounded like a wounded animal howling its death knell.

The craft wobbled from the sudden influx of air, jostling everything around.

"What the hell do you think you're doing? Are you mad? Or are you trying to get us killed? Close that damn door!" Peters shouted.

Samel turned and grabbed Peter's shoulder.

"Go back. Go back now." Peters shook him off. Samel whipped out his gun and shoved it in the back of his head. Peters bit his lip, nodded his head, and slowly banked the copter back toward the bridge.

"Samel, what the hell do you think you're doing? We have to get away from here. You killed that man, in public." Michelle screamed over the roar of the motors. The whooshing of the rotor blades and the howling of the battering wind created an echo chamber making conversation almost impossible. But, shrill emotions made her voice ring out loud and clear. She swept back her dis-shelved hair and shook her head.

"Everything has gone to hell. You've let your obsessions destroy everything. I'm not going to jail just because you've become a madman." There was a plea and a condemnation in her words.

"Let him fly us away from here. There will be another time for this insanity."

He was calm and definite. "No, I will not leave," paying no more attention to her words. He dismissed her and continued to stare down at the object of his obsession with cold determination.

"You will pay!" he swore at him.

Calvin stared up at the chopper, seeing Samel. He shook his fist unleashing a magnificent string of curses. The veins in his neck bulged like swollen rivers. Spade, confused by the sound of his name, stopped pursuing Roger and stared up. Samel boiled. His insides erupted. To his eyes, Spade was mocking him, taunting him, laughing at his pain, at his failure.

Michelle grabbed his collar and tried to turn him away from the open door.

"Samel," she shouted! "Listen to me!"

Samel raised his arm and backhanded her, delivering a blow that caused her head to snap back like a spring. She fell hard against the metal handle of the opposite door, a gash opened up in the back of her head. Her lips were smeared with lipstick and blood.

"Get over the center of the bridge." Samel demanded, waving the gun at the pilot. Peters eased the whirling bird over the stage. Michaels, Spade, and Disco stood out against the white backdrop of the stage like paper cutouts on a board. The wind from the copter created its own personal tornado, blowing papers and equipment about the bridge and over the railing. Everyone fought against the noise and the wind, trying to maintain an upright stance. Samel leaned out the door and fired down at Spade. Bullets ricocheted off the stage. Spade moved like a flamingo dancer avoiding the ill-aimed pellets. Leaping in the air and ducking for cover.

"Oh shit. The damn fool is shooting at us!" Spade shouted. "He's trying to kill us!"

Spade and Calvin aimed their guns at the floundering copter and fired. Bullets pinged off and whizzed through the air around the copter. Samel traded fire with them until his gun was out of bullets. He cursed at Spade and threw his empty gun down at him.

Peters yelled, "Oh, hell" and started to pull away. A stray bullet found its mark, crashing through the front shield. Peters doubled over as blood gushed from a wound in his chest. He cried out in pain and fell onto the controls. The copter jerked and spun in circles as it surged forward, heading for one of the bridge's towers.

Samel lost his footing and tumbled out the door. Grabbing a mesh strap hanging over the door, he avoided falling to the dark water below.

"Michelle, help me!" he cried, clutching the strap with two hands as he bounced and slammed into the floundering copter. The slick mesh began slipping through his fingers.

"Michelle," he begged reaching for her as he lost the hold of one hand. Dangling like a leaf on a tree, he swung back and forth against the body of the copter.

Lying against the opposite door, Michelle watched him with disdain and resignation in her eyes. Like dead black lumps of coal, her eyes held no compassion. The kind of look you give a building engulfed in flame when you know it's lost to the flames. She motioned toward him, but rethought it, recoiled and fell back against the door. Samel looked into her eyes and saw nothing in them for him. He turned away. Looking down onto the bridge, he zeroed in on Spade.

"To be so close and be denied," his cried. His rage reignited.

The cluster of people on the bridge looked up from their hiding places and gasped at the seesawing copter with the man dangling out the door. Samel pulled the remote from his pocket.

He looked at Michelle, then at Spade, and then the remote. What retribution he could get would have to do. Samel let go of the strap. With a prayer on his lips, he pushed the button. His body tumbled over itself crashing into one of the high girders and bouncing off. Screams and shouts rose up from the crowd. He bounced off a cluster of the suspension cables and disappeared over the side of the bridge.

Those in boats saw him appear from under the bridge and plummet toward the water. Those on the bridge ran to the sides to follow his descent. Samel flipped over and over until he crashed into the water, narrowly missing the port side of a 40-foot yacht. His body created a large splash and a wave that rocked the vessels around him.

The waters swallowed him like a hungry dog. Everyone stared at the water as if they expected him to spring up like a phoenix from flames. The water settled. A shocked hush fell over the crowd. The world was silent expect for the distressed whooshing of the helicopter.

The antenna atop the lab building swung left then right zeroing in on its coordinates. The machine hummed and emitted an inaudible signal that pierced the air. It could not be heard by human ears, but its vibrations created a tingling sensation to reverberate off the people and the bridge. The itchy feeling of ants crawling on your skin caused everyone to rub or scratch at their limbs and face. An ominous foreboding started to take the crowd.

A look of confusion and dread swept through them; something was happening. The uneasy silence was broken by the popping of the first balloon. One after another the balloons began popping. First one, then many at once and finally a steady string of them like hail hitting a tin roof. People screamed as the powdery hydrofluoric acidic solution floated down and made contact with their moistened skin. When mixed with the sweat it burned like liquid fire.

People ran to the left, "pop, pop." Then turned and ran to the right, "pop, pop." There was no avoiding the splattering compound. Balloons were bursting all over, no matter where you ran, there were balloons erupting and spreading their searing dust. Some rained down from the upper girders, others exploded from the side railings outward. There were hundreds upon hundreds of balloons bursting in rapid succession. Grabbing whatever was close at hand the people on the bridge tried to protect themselves from the ongoing assault.

Covering themselves with tarps and cardboard and loose pieces of metal or wood, anything they could hide behind or under.

The faltering helicopter created a wind that helped disperse the flaky acid everywhere, whipping it through the air. People on the boats below began to feel some of the effects as droplets rained down and burned uncovered skin.

A stampede headed for the exits. Bodies pushed and fell over each other, screaming, shouting and crying. Peters struggled to regain control, but was weak and losing consciousness. One of the landing skids of the helicopter clipped an upper cable. The helicopter spun wildly slamming the tail rotor into the upper girder on the tower. The rotor was sliced off and fell crashing onto the bridge crushing a man who had sheltered his self under a bass drum. The copter spun like it was caught in a whirlpool.

Peters yelled at Michelle. "Help me. We're going down."

Michelle remained seated and did not acknowledge him.

"Help me, damn it," he shouted. She stared straight ahead closing her eyes as if she were going to sleep. Tears rolled down her cheek. The main rotor sputtered and stalled. What was left of the giant whirling blade stopped.

Like a fly being swatted out of the sky, the copter plunged down. It slammed into the side railing of the bridge, teetered for a few moments before toppling over the side.

Michelle was tossed about like soggy clothes in a dryer. Grasping the seat and burying her face in the fabric she whispered. "Mommy is coming, sweetheart." She slowly closed her eyes and let go.

The wounded bird crashed into a cabin cruiser that was not quick enough to get out of the way. Peters could be seen through the front shield groping at the glass like a fish in an aquarium. The copter and the cruiser slowly sank under the water, gurgling and coughing as the water covered them.

The stream of exploding balloons began to subside. People collapsed on the bridge crying and moaning from the acid burns. Most were in shock after watching the crash and surviving the spray of acid. The air was rank and astringent with the stench of burned metal and cooked flesh. The acid clung leaving exposed flesh, blisters and pulsating boils.

The automated antenna pulsed again and let out another signal. The sound wave hit the bridge. The molecules in the paint began to react to the stimulation. A vibration rippled over the structure. The growing heat could be felt in the air. The horde of injured people hobbled toward the exits but stopped when the bridge began to tremble.

The whole structure shook. It felt as if the planet had shivered. A loud snap echoed in the air as if the sky had been cracked like an egg. One of the cables broke loose and swung down sweeping a group of people off their feet and wiping away a bank of amps set up for the concert. The equipment sailed over the side railings of the bridge, taking two of the roadies with them. They plopped into the water like rocks thrown over the side.

The crowd held their collected breath looking around for the next disaster. Another explosion rocked the bridge and tore a hole into the floor. The bridge shifted and creaked like an old man's bones. A blast shattered part of the upper girder. Cables began to rain down as if they were strands of hair falling back into place.

People shocked out of their paralysis, began running and screaming. Spade and Calvin, covered with burn spots, pushed their way through the crowd knocking, pushing and pulling down anyone in their path. One of the main supports gave way. They fell and rolled with the group toward the railing. Several bodies tipped over the edge, crashing into the crowded water below. Disco was clutching a flagpole, crying and muttering Michelle's name.

Spade righted himself and headed for the entrance. A section of bridge exploded under him, sending him flying into the air. He spun above the deck of the bridge like a Frisbee before crashing down inches from the edge. The bridge trembled from the chaos of continuing explosions. Spade slid toward a hole in the deck. With desperate hands, he grabbed the end of a frayed rope stopping his descent. Straining with each motion, he pulled himself back onto a still solid piece of deck. Wheezing like an exhausted racehorse, he lay on his back and tried to calm his racing heart.

Calvin eased his way along the railing, his hands a bloody mess from touching the burning metal. Coming to a section of the bridge blown apart by the blast, he attempted to jump to the other side of the gap. Leaping into the air, an explosion ripped a cable from its moorings. The cable twisted like a snake striking out. It leapt forward, swatted him and batted his body to the ground. The cable tangled itself around him catching him in a twisted knot. In his attempt to untangle himself, Calvin rolled over and fell through one of the growing holes. He clung to the edge, dangling in midair.

Calvin saw Disco close by cling to a pole. He called out to him.

"Help me. Disco, help me."

Disco glared at him, anger in his eyes. "You killed Michelle," he sobbed, his face covered with a mask of tears, mucus, and blood. Disco pounded himself in the head, as if he could knock the vision from his mind.

Calvin struggled trying to pull himself up.

"She...she was planning to take me down. To take us down." Calvin pleaded, puffing with the effort. "I didn't want to hurt her. I just wanted to stop her."

"No!" Disco shouted between sobs. "Michelle would never hurt us. She loved us. She loved me. You're just mean and selfish and now Michelle is..." He dissolved into a soul aching wail.

"Disco, little brother. Listen to me. Help me get back up and .and we can..."

"No!" Disco shouted. "Michelle was the only one who really loved me and you killed her!" His face took on a menacing leer. "Like you tried to do to me when we were young."

Calvin's ire grew. He wagged a clenched fist and growled at Disco. "You, stupid bastard! Get your ass over here and help me up or when I get on my feet, you're gonna regret it! Remember, you're nothing without me!"

"Aunt Louise always said you were no good. She said I should live with her, but daddy said we should stay together." He sniffled and wiped his nose on his shirt.

"Daddy was wrong." Disco released his grip on the pole and began to walk away, weaving a path through the continuing destruction.

"Disco, you dumbass! Get back here and help me!" With every explosion, the bridge trembled a bit more. The edge suspending Calvin loosened with every shake.

"When I get my hands on you I'm going to...to..." He cursed and fought the crumbling bridge, screaming with pain from the sting of the open burns. The section around him began to break away, falling like crumbs of dry bread. Calvin twisted and wiggled, finally getting a firmer grip. He began swaying back and forth like a trapeze artist, trying to swing up on the remaining deck. Generating enough momentum, he swung out and leapt for solid ground. Hitting solid ground, Calvin rolled away from the hole. Lying on his back panting and gasping for air, he muttered. "Disco, your ass is mine, you little shit."

Rising to his knees, Calvin became alarmed when he realized he was on thin strip of ground only as wide as his body. The area around him had broken away. Reacting to the ongoing shifting of the bridge, he wobbled to his feet and moved forward. The ground sank as if he was walking on a sponge. He yanked his leg back.

"Damn it, damn it," he whispered. Taking a step backward he found the same. "Damn it." Calvin took a deep breath and resolved to take a running jump for it. "I'm Calvin Michaels, I don't need anybody. I make things happen. Things don't happen to me." Gathering his resolve and his rage, he leaped into action. The third step gave way and Calvin plunged down toward the water, running in midair as if he were descending an invisible stairway. He disappeared beneath the water with hardly a splash or recognition. One set of teary eyes watched him vanish from view. Disco dropped his head, turned and made his way toward the exit.

40

Roger slipped into the throng of people and started running down the bridge, toward the Canadian side. He ducked and wove his way around and behind people and equipment. Not daring to look back for fear "the tank" would be on him. The sound of Spade growling out his name like a rabid grizzly rose goose bumps on his arms. His heart was a runaway engine.

"Bang, bang," Roger collapsed in on himself, fearing he had been shot. Realizing he hadn't been hit, he dove, along with everyone around him, to the ground seeking cover.

Checking himself, again for bullet holes, Roger rolled down the bridge. He dared to raise his head and look back when he heard Spade's name being screamed. The voice was angry and full of emotion like a booming clash of thunder during a violet storm. The trio of Spade, Calvin, and Disco were staring up into the sky. All their eyes were fixed on the helicopter. Roger saw Samel hanging out of the copter with Michelle trying to pull him back in. He was screaming like a banshee down at the trio. His gun was delivering an erratic spray of bullets. Spade and Calvin had drawn guns of their own and were firing back at the copter. Disco stared up like a child looking at a falling star.

Samel tumbled out of the copter and everyone ran to the railing to watch him fall. People began screaming and running again as the copter crashed into the bridge, sending a bone chilling vibration through its shell. The copter rained debris down like hail, knocking people down, sending jagged metal flying in all directions. Falling over each other, pulling and pushing their way toward the exits, people tried to put as much distance between themselves and the falling bird as possible.

A sense of shock and remorse fell over the crowd. Everyone stopped and stood transfixed, drained by shock and disbelief, not quite sure what to do next. The first bursting balloon basically went unnoticed, except by those shaky souls who jumped or dove back to the ground thinking a gunfight had started again. When the irritating sensation of itchy skin passed through the group, a sense of something happening made the already skittish crowd more anxious. Everyone looked around anxiously wondering what was coming next. As the balloons burst more frequently and in greater numbers, people shouted and screamed. The powdery acid landed on their skin and burned. The flaky substance drifted in the air and floated down like snow. People swatted at their arms and faces as if they were shooing away a swam of pesky bees until the burning began.

"Oh, my God. It burns. I'm on fire!" one man screamed in terror when he looked up and flakes burned his eyes to bloody sockets. A woman's hair sizzled and melted on her head. She cried in agony ripping what strands she had left from her head. People were ripping clothing from their bodies as the acid burned through, exposing their bare flesh to the continuing onslaught. Most ran hollering and wailing toward the exits, suffering the results of their exposure. Their dread grew as the flakes like a winter blizzard, grew thicker and came faster.

Roger grabbed a tarp and tried to cover himself from the falling terror. Men and women grabbed at his cover and fought for a space under the shield. The ones on the outer edge became a wall protecting the ones inside, while crushing them at the same time. All along the bridge, little communities of people were clustered together under tarps, wooden boards, and cardboard boxes, anything they could find to give cover from the falling menace. Even though the acid ate holes in whatever they used, anything was better than being openly exposed.

Jostling to remain on his feet while the mass of people pushed and stumbled against each other, Roger fought to remain in the moment while his mind flashed pictures of the bridge's destruction and his own death.

My God, they did it. They are going to kill us all.

His thoughts drifted to Henry. *Who will take care of Henry? What will happen to my little brother?* His heart pounded harder and harder in his chest. *I'm sorry mama. I know I promised, but...* Na'Taya invaded his thoughts. The feel of her skin, the smell of her hair, her smiling eyes, how good she felt wrapped up in his arms. "Na'Taya" he whispered. "I love you. I'm sorry."

All my life I've worried about dying from a sickness that I'm not even sure I have, never letting it occur to me that I could die from something else. Now here I am about to be killed by this.

His thoughts were replaced by an irritated anger, like a driver who realizes they've taken the wrong turn and are driving away from where they want to be.

A fire erupted inside him. Roger elbowed and pushed his way out of the crowd. "Run," he shouted! "They're going to bring down the bridge! Run!" The community looked at him as if he had just said he was going to fly. No one moved. They just stood shielded under the tarp as it filled with holes.

The last of the balloons popped and the falling flakes began to diminish. An uneasy calm settled over the crowd. Curious and cautious ears and eyes listened and looked around searching out the next surprise. Despite Roger's insistence that they get off the bridge, no one reacted.

"You're crazy. That will never happen." An angry voice cried out.

"It's over," said another. "They failed. This bridge will never fall." The crowd groaned and whimpered like a bunch of disgruntled shoppers. Their crying and wailing drowned out the first signs of the rumbling. The vibrations increased and like a sudden summer storm the first explosion erupted. Pandemonium broke out again. Their sighs of relief were replaced by cries of terror. Everyone ran in different directions. Debris and shrapnel flew in all directions. Some ran directly into erupting parts of the bridge, other into falling metal and holes that had opened up in the deck. Bodies began pouring into the water like a leaky faucet. The stampede knocked down people, who were trampled and disregarded like yesterday's newspaper. Dozens were swept over the side by falling cables, crumbling railings and the increasing birth of holes and slotted paving that marred all paths.

Those on the shore and in the boats gasped in disbelief. Screams filled the air. Tears filled all eyes. The shouts of "No God. No," was muttered from praying lips. Those in boats who did not turn on their engines and jet away, dove into the water and tried to rescue some of the fallen. When they managed to reach someone, they were dead, torn, and broken from the shock of making the one hundred-fifty-two-foot drop.

Roger regained his senses and started running. He darted around some holes and leapt over others. An expanse before him, one hundred yards from the Canadian entrance, the entire floor had collapsed. Moving to the edge along what was left of the railing, he inched his way across the area, pausing when a particularly violent tremor caused the sparse sliver of flooring he was on to waver and give slightly.

Roger's phone rang. Knowing it was probably Na'Taya, he hurried his efforts. He snickered to himself when he thought, *she'll be mad when she finds out I was on the bridge after I promised I wouldn't go. She'll understand,* he thought. *I didn't really have a choice.* Safely on the other side of the opening, he exhaled a deep breath and pulled out his phone to assure her he was okay.

The section of the floor he was on started to crumble. Roger leapt like a flying squirrel reaching for the next tree. Barely reaching solid ground, he watched his phone tumble down and disappear down a hole out of view. Rising to his full height, Roger sprinted for the

Canadian side and safety, Stopping and starting he pressed on. A series of explosions made the bridge teeter. Roger swayed fighting to maintain his balance. Support for one of the main towers buckled and the bridge slanted to the right.

The banner proudly proclaiming, "The Concert of Love" was now a shredded white flag flapping in the wind. Only the word "Love" remained hanging, snagged by a twisted line. The charred and smoldering piece of cloth was an ironic reminder of the all that was happening. Instead of promoting pictures of love and happiness, the white flag seemed to signal surrender and the burned edges to show how heavy the cost was.

The bridge lurched again and wavered like a newborn taking its first steps. Roger, the people, and equipment around him slid toward the broken railing. A half dozen people couldn't recover their footing and jack knifed over the side. Others slid toward holes in the deck and disappeared with a scream. Equipment crashed into the railing ripping it away and raining bodies and debris down on the water below. Roger grabbed a fallen cable and stopped his momentum.

A man ten feet from him was hanging on by his fingertips dangling through one of the many holes in the floor.

"Help me," he begged. "I can't hold on. I'm slipping." Roger saw one hand slip away as the ground around it slowly crumbled.

"Please," the man begged, hanging on with straining fingers. Wrapping the steel cable around his leg as best he could, Roger crept forward on his hands and knees, ever

wary of the unstable ground beneath him. He inched forward until he could see the utter fear in the man's eyes. The man was trying to get a hold with his other hand, as the ground around him kept crumbling away, leaving him hanging on by one hand.

Roger grabbed for the man's hand.

"Give me your hand." He extended his arm into the opening. The man's strength was spent. He tried to raise his arm, but it fell away as if it was too heavy for him to lift.

"I can't," he cried.

"You've got to." Roger stared down at the long fall and his heart became a twisted knot.

"Come on damn it. Give me your hand." He stretched out his arm and wiggled his fingers as if he could draw the hand to him with the gesture.

The man strained and swung his body trying to throw his arm up. The ground around him sagged and began to chip away.

"Come on," Roger demanded, jetting out his arm.

"Hurry up or we'll both go down." Roger grabbed the one arm of the man with both hands as the ground around the hole gave way. The deck crumbed like sand, growing in size. Roger groaned against the jagged edges of the deck digging into his stomach. Hanging into the void from his waist to head, the weight of the man hanging in midair drawing him toward the fall. The cable wrapped around his leg was the only thing keeping them both from plunging into the water. Roger winced as the cable ate into his leg.

Out of the corner of his eye, Roger saw a figure coming their way. "Hey!" he shouted. "Help me. I'm losing him. I can't hold on much longer."

"Then let him go," the voice paused. "Roger." A large boot slammed down on Roger's arm. He screamed as the boot ground his arm into the broken deck. Unable to withstand the onslaught, his hand opened. Roger watched in horror and agony as the man slipped from his grasp and missilled toward the water. His eyes pleading for help, his hand vainly reaching up as if he was trying to climb an invisible rope. Roger, blind with rage, rolled over on his back and stared into a face obscured by sun. He rubbed his aching arm. "Why the hell did you do that? You killed that guy." His teeth gnashed as he chewed out the words. The man laughed.

"Remember me, Roger?" he smiled, his voice dripping with sarcasm.

Roger looked up at a face burned and bleeding, his clothes dirty and torn. "Spade," he whispered, his anger turned to dread. He wiggled to the right. Spade stomped down on the cable encircling Roger's leg causing him to shout out and go stiff from the pain.

"You thought you could out smart me, didn't you? You thought you could get away. Well, you didn't." He spit out the words.

"You didn't save Na'Taya, you couldn't save that guy and now you can't save yourself." Spade shook his head, "tsk-tsk, you're not too good at this superhero stuff are you, Roger?" He bared his teeth and beat his chest.

"Nobody makes a fool out of Spade and gets away with it." he reached down and snatched up the cable. Spade dragged him away from the hole. The strands of the cable dug even deeper into his calf. Roger yelped from the pain.

Spade kicked him in the side. He doubled over in pain.

"That's for making me look bad in front of Michaels." He kicked him again, planting his steel-toed boots into his rib cage. A sharp crack and Roger coughed up blood.

"That's for the window." Spade bent down and punched him in the face. "And that's just because I hate you piss-ass little nerds." He laughed and yanked on the cable. Roger moaned from the pain. Spade's eyes brightened.

"I know, how about we go fishing? You look like a little worm to me." He roared with laughter. Ignoring the explosions happening around them, he dragged Roger toward an opening in the deck. Roger kicked with his free leg and reached for anything that would hold him in place. Spade just pulled harder, scraping him across the bucking and jagged surface.

The section of the deck beneath Spade gave way. His leg, up to the groin, dropped into a hole. He growled as the sharp edges scraped and bit into his thigh, opening a bleeding gash. The cable slipped from his hands as he grabbed at the surface to break his fall. Grasping for air, he tried to pull himself out. Roger took the moment to kick himself free and roll away. He panted and grimaced as he freed himself from the cable. With every attempt to rise from the hole, Spade caused more of the decking to fall away around him.

"Help me," he screamed reaching for Roger.

Lying on his back, Roger stared at the big man. He roughly climbed to his knees, holding his side, he grimaced with the pain.

Straining with the effort, Roger forced his body to stand. His ribs ached. The taste of blood was hot and salty in his mouth. His leg throbbed with pain. Taking two unsteady hops backward he stood his ground.

"Help me, Roger. You know I was just kidding." Spade forced a pained half smile. "I would never have really hurt you. I just wanted to scare you a little. I was mad, just rough-housing. I .I just wanted to scare you a little." The lie came from his lips, but never reached his eyes. Anger and hatred burned in them.

Roger hesitated, and then stepped forward. He paused rethinking his actions. Closing his eyes, he decided, took a deep breath and started again. An explosion a few feet away sent him faltering to his knees. The whole bridge shook and tilted further on its side. Spade sank a couple of inches deeper, yelling at the descent. Roger bent and retrieved the cable; his hands holding on to it like a vise.

"Grab this!" he screamed tossing the end of the cable near the tank. Spade stretched out and connected. Just as he got a good two-handed grip on it, the floor beneath him gave way. He disappeared through the hole like an eight-ball falling into a corner pocket. Spade shouted and screamed like a baby who'd lost his pacifier.

"Ahh, ahh, pull me up! Pull me up!"

Roger held tight to the cable and braced himself. Spade's weight forced him forward, but he leaned back, dug in his feet and managed to stay upright. He began to pull, straining against the cable. The hole grew. Every movement sent agonizing pain through his body. His leg wobbled and threatened to give out. Roger ached all over. As the hole grew Spade inched further and further toward the water.

"I can't pull you up. You're too heavy. You'll have to climb up. When you're close to the top I'll be able to help you onto the deck."

"I can't climb up. The cable is too slippery. It's taking everything I've got to hold on." Spade began to sway like a pendulum on a clock. Every motion he made caused the cable to swing.

"You've got to try. It's the only way I can help you." Roger crept near the edge of the hole and looked down on the swinging man.

"You bastard. You want me to die." Spade growled. "When I get back up there I'll..." The bridge shifted again as multiple explosions went off. Spade yelped as he slid further down the cable. Several suspension cables snapped and the tower they were attached to bowed.

The other end of the cable Spade was hanging on to broke free. The broken end jerked out of Roger's hand leaving a deep gash. It whizzed by him whipping in the air like a streamer. The tail end struck Roger in the arm, he heard the bone crack as he fell into a ball of pain on the deck. The cable vanished into the hole like a snake chasing a rat. Spade cursed, screamed and cried all the way to the water.

The bridge shook and shifted again, leaning closer to the river. Roger struggled to his feet and fell. The deep gash in leg was bleeding badly. The lower half of his leg was swollen and caked with blood. Raw flesh and bone could be seen where his skin had been scraped away. He forced his self to stand on his one good leg and hobbled forward. Weaving his way toward the bridge's exit, he skirted holes and flying debris from the continuous explosions. A trail of blood marked his path. Yards from the exit, Rogers leg gave out and he collapsed on to the deck. On his back, he looked up at the tower. It seemed to be inching toward him. Rolling on to his stomach, he tried to push himself up. His arm wobbled, strained and gave out. Roger crawled, spent and exhausted, dragging his leg like a wheel less wagon. He collapsed onto his face and passed out.

"Henry, slow down," Na'Taya called catching up with him. "Roger wants us to wait for him. He's coming to get us. He doesn't want you or me anywhere near that bridge." She cupped his hands and drew in a deep breath. "There are things going on that you don't know about. Please Henry, let's just do as he asked us to, okay?"

Henry hung his head and looked up at her through half-teary eyes. "Okay," he finally said. "But, will you call him so I can at least talk to him." He paused. "Please, I just want to know that he's alright."

Na'Taya put her arm around his shoulder. "Sure, we can do that. If it will make you feel better. Roger would want that."

The echoing sound of the gunshots snapped the attention of all heads up to the bridge. Na'Taya and Henry watched in paralyzed horror as the man tumbled from the helicopter. When the erratic flying bird struck the bridge and started to fall, Henry yelled, "Roger," and took off again.

Still stunned by the scene, it took Na'Taya a moment to realize Henry was running toward the bridge. Her phone in her hands, she darted off after him.

Henry barreled his way through the crowd of gawkers, pushing a path toward the bridge. The onlookers, themselves were pressing their way toward the bridge, mesmerized by the unfolding events. Everyone wanted to see up close what they couldn't believe was happening.

Na'Taya, just steps behind him, did not try to stop him, but was striving herself to reach the bridge. Henry and the leaders of the mob ran into a barricade of police officers and security guards keeping everyone back from the entrance to the bridge.

"Stay back," they shouted at the curious. "You need to stay back. Get back and make room so the emergency crew can get through."

Henry stomped his feet and yelled, "My brother's up there. I have to go and help him."

"There's nothing you can do, son. Stand back and let the professionals handle this."

"But, Roger..." his words died in his mouth when the balloons started bursting and the people on the bridge began screaming and running. They pressed at the barricade and made the officers step back to regroup. Henry, along with everyone else, kept forcing against the barricade while craning their necks upward to the events transpiring on the bridge.

"What's going on? What's going on?" he shouted in a panic, yanking on the officer's arm.

"I don't know," the officer replied and grabbed his radio. "Cooper, Cooper what the hell is going on up there." All he received in reply were screams, shouts and static.

The onlookers gasped and held their breath. Drawn forward, they inched their way toward the bridge, pressing the beleaguered officers.

The stampede of escaping people crashed into them from the other side, squeezing the officers between the two crowds creating an even bigger scene of chaos.

Henry grabbed Na'Taya's hand. "Na'Taya," he swallowed. "Is Roger up there?"

Not able to take her eyes off the bridge, she shook her head. "No, no, he promised me he wouldn't go on the bridge. He's not up there. I'll...I'll call him. You'll see, he's in the crowd down here with us. He just hasn't found us yet." She wished more than believed. Na'Taya reached to pushed the phone icon that would dial the number when the explosions began. Stopping in mid-motion she covered her mouth with the phone as the bridge erupted in explosion after explosion. A silent scream left her mouth when the first body toppled over the side. With each body that followed she mouthed, "Roger."

Henry pranced in circles, growing more and more agitated. The sights on the bridge were promoting ever-deepening thoughts of dread in his mind. Na'Taya tried to remain calm and quiet him. She dialed the phone and held it out to Henry. "You, talk to him. You'll see that he's safe and nearby." Watching Henry's face grow darker and darker as he held the phone to his ear her heart sank.

Without an ounce of expression in his face, Henry let his hand drop. "He's not there. He's..."

Na'Taya grabbed the phone. "No, no that's not true. I must have dialed the wrong number. I'll call the right one this time."

She held out the ringing phone to Henry. He would not take it, staring at it as if it were something vile and foreign. She put the phone to her ear.

"Ring, ring, ring." Her legs grew weak. Her heart raced and her skin got hot. Closing her eyes, she prayed.

Answer the phone, Roger. Answer the damn phone, please. Slowly her arm lowered to her side. Na'Taya and Henry stared at each other. Na'Taya shook her head. "He's not on the bridge. He's not. He promised." Their eyes like mirrors reflecting, tear for tear, what the other felt. A wealth of words and feelings exchanged in their looks.

Not saying a word, together they stared at the bridge holding on to each other. A silent prayer shared between them.

The explosions grew in intensity. Parts of the bridge rained down like autumn leaves. The structure began to tilt and lend, ready to collapse in on itself. The tower on the American side of the bridge buckled first. It leaned over like a wizened old man unable to stand erect. The snapping cables and breaking metal sounded like old bones giving way as if it was lying down to go to sleep. The tower didn't fall, but laid down into the water. The rest of the structure wavered on shaky legs and then gave in to gravity. The entire bridge dropped into the water causing a giant wave to rush down the river.

Boats rose with the surge like cars climbing a hill. Some teetered and capsized adding more bodies and debris to the crowded waters. Waves raced on to the break fronts washing onto land and whisking away many of the kiosks and stands that were closest to the shore. A few people who did not move back far enough inland were knocked from their feet and washed over the side. Everyone else was doused with a spray of river water.

As the bridge was collapsing, the crowd stared silently, mesmerized by the unfolding events, holding their breath in unbelieving horror. Once the bridge had fallen, a collective wave of silent sorrow swept over the masses. A great chorus of tears and wailing echoed from both sides of the river. People screamed and cried with ear shattering intensity. The crowd trembled with shock and anger. A day that started with the happiest of intentions had turned into one with the darkest of nightmares.

Stray pieces of metal rained down on the barge sitting in the middle of river holding the fireworks that had been prepared for the concert. A thin stream of smoke curled up. The stockpile hissed and sparked. The mound sizzled and exploded into a multitude of blinding flashes of color. Bright streams of light shot into the sky. The boom was ear shattering. The barge twisted in the water sending rippling waves down the length of the river. The ground shook and vibrated. Those on the shore turned and ran. Some were so shocked they stood transfixed and were doused with water and flying debris or trampled by the others. The boom and crackle of the fireworks fought for dominance over the screams and shouts. The brilliant display of pyrotechnics was wasted on eyes too full of tears to enjoy the spectacular kaleidoscope of colors.

A litany of sirens from ambulances, police cars, and news trucks added to the madding chorus. Police tried to herd the remaining people away from the area. It was a scene of total entropy.

Na'Taya's phone rang. A cautious smile sparked in her eyes. "Roger, Roger, where are you?" she shouted into the phone.

"Oh," her excitement vanished as she recognized the voice. "Have you seen Roger?" She looked at Henry. His face lit with anticipation. She spoke carefully.

"He may have been near the bridge. He..." she paused. "We can't. We have to stay here. He will come for us. He'll be worried if he doesn't find us." She held her breath and listened.

"But...but, okay we'll meet you there."

"Who was that? Do they know where Roger is?" Henry asked, almost begging.

Na'Taya took his hand. "That was Martin. He wants us to go with him. He has people searching for Roger. When they find him, they'll bring him to us."

Henry stared at the ground and didn't respond. Na'Taya led him by the hand to the statue of Joe Louis's fist at the foot of Jefferson Avenue near the entrance to Hart Plaza. Minutes later an unmarked car with flashing lights and a siren pulled up. Two black-suited men herded them in the back seat and drove away.

41

The headquarters of the Detroit Police Department was in a state of pandemonium. Everyone had grim faces, red eyes, and raw nerves. The atmosphere was thick with tension and worry. People in and out of uniform were running around from office to office, answering phones, asking and answering questions, while trying to contain and pacify a growing angry crowd outside the building and on the phones. No one seemed to be able to talk without shouting or crying. Women and men alike walked around dabbing teary eyes and turning their heads to avoid personal conversations, whenever possible.

"Yes, the bridge was almost completely destroyed. It is totally unusable," the police chief agreed with the reporter who was interviewing him. "We don't know who did this. There have been no declarations of responsibility. We are not prepared to definitely call this a terrorist attack...yet. But, I will admit that is the most likely scenario. And no, no one has claimed responsibility, yet."

The chief wiped the sweat from his forehead and bit his lips.

"No, The Gordie Howe Bridge was unaffected." He stretched, correcting his stance.

"That's all for now. We have some serious work to do. There will be an official statement at 9 tomorrow morning. Just remind your viewers to stay away from the area. It is still dangerous and unstable." He nodded, turned and walked away. The reporters continued to hurl questions at his back.

In a small office in the back, Na'Taya held Henry's head in her lap and gently rocked him. He softly whimpered, squeezing her hand every now and then for extra comfort. Na'Taya was in a state of disbelief. She kept staring blankly at the door waiting for Roger to burst in and make everything all right. As time dragged on, her wishes deepened into prayers.

Martin quietly slipped into the room. His expression was grim, but he managed a half smile. "Are you guys alright? Can I get you something?"

Na'Taya asked more as a plea than a question, "Is there any sign of Roger?"

Martin shook his head. "We're still searching. Things are a mess out there. He hasn't called and he's not among the bodies..." He stopped when Henry turned an angry face to him.

Na'Taya tried to ease the tension. "Could you do something about getting Henry his medication? We can't leave until Roger is found."

"No problem. We'll arrange something with Wellington." Martin paused and rubbed his hands together.

"I need to talk to you...Uhh, maybe alone," he motioned toward the hall looking at Henry.

Henry's grip on Na'Taya's hand got strong. She patted his shoulder. "Anything you have to say you'll have to say here," she said, bracing herself.

"Are you sure?" His brow rose. She nodded. He cleared his throat. His jitters struck her as strange.

"We found Salvador."

"What do you mean you found Salvador?"

"He is dead. He was stabbed through the heart." Na'Taya stiffened. Henry sat up and wrapped his arms around her. Martin continued. "You said that Roger and he didn't..."

"Roger would never do something like that." Henry interrupted.

His eyes focused on Martin like gun sights. The indignation in his voice was loud and clear.

"He's right. Roger would never do something like that," she added. "Terrorists have just brought down a major American bridge and you're trying to pin a murder on Roger? I don't know why I'm surprised after what you did to me. Roger is a hero and you're trying to paint him as a murderer."

Martin flushed and drew back. "No, I'm not. It's just that I had to ask." He let out a breath.

"Contrary to everything else we still have to try and maintain law and order. There was a murder committed and it may be connected to what happened on the bridge."

"I told you what happened. Neither of us saw Salvador after that," she stuck out her chin and gave him a stern look.

"Are you sure about that?" he asked.

"Yes," she answered defiantly.

The night passed slowly. Na'Taya stepped into the hall to stretch her legs. Henry lay out on the bench, having cried himself to sleep. The chaos of the day had eased some, but a steady stream of activity surrounded them. Blank-faced men and women passed her looking haggard and worn, moving with determined feet, talking in whispers.

Staring out a window at the end of the hall, she could see the ruins of the bridge. A single section of the tower on the Canadian side still stood, slouched and twisted like an old tree that had barely survived a terrible storm. The new bridge, the Gordie Howe International Bridge, stood just west of the ruins, gleaming in the night. Moonbeams danced along the slick curves like fairies sliding down a waterfall. The bridge was magical, shrouded in the midnight mist like a spirit come to pay its respects to the remains of the old bridge.

The frightening possibility of Roger having fallen on the bridge began to gain purchase in her mind. Every time

the thought reared up, Na'Taya slapped it down. With so much time having passed, the reality was becoming more solid, more terrifyingly real and harder to slap down. No longer was it just a wisp of smoke, an annoying gnat of negativity. It was taking shape, becoming a heavy fog that was starting to enclose her, choking her in doubt. A possibility too hard to deny.

"Na'Taya," she turned around to see Martin standing behind her. The grim look on his face caused her heart to skip a beat. She instinctively stepped back.

"Roger?" she managed to say.

He nodded. "We found him." She steeled herself inside.

"He's alive. He's in a Canadian hospital." Na'Taya closed her eyes and let out the breath she was holding, allowing her heart to beat again. "He's in bad shape. The doctors aren't sure he'll make it."

Like a sand castle hit by a wave, the smile washed from her face. She took a moment to secure her legs. "I'll get Henry. We have to go to him."

In the car to the airport, the helicopter to the hospital and even entering his room, Henry held on to Na'Taya's hand with a vise grip. She did not realize it, but she was doing the same to him. Martin let them go in alone, closing the door behind them.

Roger lay unconscious propped up in the bed. He looked like a science experiment. Tubes flowed from every orifice of his body. Bags of clear liquid hung around him like icicles, dripping a steady flow of chemicals down cloudy causeways. Burns and bruises covered his skin from head to toe. He shined with ointment and exposed flesh. His left arm was elevated and encased in a white plaster cast. What was left of his right leg hung in the air, suspended by wires and a sling. Everything below the knee was missing. The leg was no longer than the arm that hung in the air with it. Roger looked like a puppet still under construction.

Henry and Na'Taya gasped at the sight and squeezed each other's hand until their knuckles were numb from a lack of blood. A respirator wheezed and puffed, raising and lowering his chest in an ominous drone. A myriad of machines surrounded his bed; beeping and clicking like a flock of giant mechanical chickens.

Na'Taya and Henry each took one side of his bed, their eyes full of fear and tears.

"I'll be honest with you," the doctor said, drawing their attention to a corner where he was checking charts.

"He's in bad shape. It was touch and go for a while there. He lost a lot of blood and suffered some severe injuries." He paused and motioned to the missing leg.

"There was nothing we could do to save the leg. It was virtually ripped from his body, hanging on by torn and destroyed ligaments. I'm surprised he survived losing it that way. Unfortunately, he's been unconscious since he was brought in so our examination has been limited to the damage we can see. We will have a better idea of his actual prognosis if he regains consciousness."

"If he...?" Na'Taya whispered. Henry grabbed the sheet.

"Yes, 'if'," the doctor said, reluctantly.

"I can't promise he will come out of this coma."

"He'll come out," Henry insisted. "Roger's strong. He wants to live."

Diverting his eyes gave Na'Taya all the answer she needed, but he nodded anyway. The doctor cleared his throat.

"There's nothing more we can do for him right now. So, if you will excuse me there are so many others that need our attention. I'll check back in the morning" His voice sounded with authority and quiet compassion. Serious eyes, heavy from a lack of sleep and a firm up turned chin backed up his words. He tilted his head and left the room.

Na'Taya and Henry laid their hands on the mattress, both afraid to touch him for fear of causing him pain or

making one of the machines sing out in protest. Without talking it over, they set up a vigil. One slept while the other sat by his bed watching, praying and occasionally whispering to him their own secret messages.

On the second day, the respirator was removed. The doctor assured them this was a good sign. On the third day, Roger batted open his eyes. He grunted and coughed, but quickly closed his eyes and fell asleep. On the morning of the fourth day, Henry heard a strained dry voice croak out. "Hey buddy, are you taking care of my girl?"

Henry beamed and nodded yes, too choked up with tears to answer. Roger smiled a pained grin.

"We were so worried about you," Henry finally managed to say.

"I'm here. At least what's left of me. I would never leave you. We're a team, right?" he forced a smile, never taking his screaming eyes off his missing leg. His hand rose and fell back each time he tried to touch it as if he was trying to pet an unfriendly dog.

"Me too. Am I part of that team?" Na'Taya interrupted, offering him some water. Her strained smile full of tears.

"Of course," he said struggling to maintain a calm tone. "Just don't expect me to carry much of the load right now."

The room fell into an awkward silence.

42

When Roger was released from the hospital, he, Na'Taya, and Henry were moved to a safe house. The FBI insisted it was for their protection, but Roger felt it was to keep them from the press and allow the agency to continue interrogating them. The interviews began almost immediately. The FBI, the Detroit Police, Homeland Security, the CIA, the NSA, the RCMP, the CSIS, even MI5 and Interpol took their turn drilling them.

Roger and Na'Taya told their story over and over again; sometimes together, and other times in different rooms. They both became exhausted and then irritated with the process. It turned from an information-gathering exercise to a witch hunt for the right persons to burn.

Blame and responsibility were plentiful and were metered out in large doses. "Why didn't you catch this? How did you let this slip between the cracks? Why didn't you act on this information? Why didn't you share what you knew? Who authorized using the girl? Why didn't anyone believe what they were saying? At least investigate it. Why did it take so long for you to intervene?" The questions and accusations were blunt and threatening, promising that a battle for jurisdiction and blame was inevitable.

Michelle and Samel's complicity was thoroughly invested, but the puppeteer behind the puppets remained a mystery.

After two months at the safe house, Na'Taya found them an apartment. Henry went back and forth to Wellington, spending more and more time at the apartment. Na'Taya played nursemaid, housekeeper, and companion. For the next 6 months Roger convalesced, drifting in and out of depression. His recovery was slow and difficult. Dealing with the loss of his leg made him moody and prone to bouts of self-pity. Roger refused to use his prosthetic leg, remaining unresponsive, irritable, and withdrawn.

"What do you think you're doing?" Roger yelled at Henry.

Henry shrugged his shoulder. "I'm playing golf."

"With my leg?"

"You're not using it. It just sits around getting dust on it."

"That's an expensive piece of equipment. You can't treat it like that."

"At least I'm doing something with it. Not like you, letting it sit around and get dirty."

"Give me my leg."

"No, I'm playing." Henry said and continued to swing at the ball.

"Henry, if you don't stop and give it to me, I'll..."

"You'll do what? Lay around and feel sorry for yourself?" he raised his chin in defiance.

"You've always been my hero, Roger. I thought there was nothing you couldn't do." He hung his head. "But I guess I was wrong. I guess there is something that can beat you." Henry plopped on the floor and hugged the leg to his chest. "You know, Mrs. Cooper at Wellington says that sitting around and feeling sorry for yourself is worse than doing nothing. She says you not only hurt yourself, but you hurt the people who care about you."

He looked up at Roger. His eyes lids hung heavy. "She was right." Henry turned away and began rocking.

Roger opened his mouth, but no words came out. An expression of surprise froze on his face. He stared at the back of Henry's head and a realization came over him. A wave of self-incrimination washed over him. The self-pity and regret that had fed him for all these months left a bitter taste in mouth.

What's wrong with me? I'm not the only one who had lost something. This isn't me, is it? he thought.

Roger grunted, "No," and threw back the covers.

"Give me that thing," he demanded. Henry turned and slowly rose, gingerly handing him the leg. Roger hefted the limb in his hands, looking at it as if it was some strange new creature. Taking a deep breath and nodding to himself, he reached down and strapped it to the stub at the end of his leg. Taking a few moments to let the reality sink in, he looked up at Henry, who was staring back, wide-eyed in anticipation. Roger held out his arm and asked.

"Will you help your big brother stand up?"

Henry's swallowed the doubt on his face and burst into a smile like a sunbeam cutting through fog. His head bobbed up and down as if it had come unattached and was flapping in the wind. He ran to him and wrapped his arm around his brother's waist and gently helped him to his feet. Roger teetered and fell against his younger brother. Henry strained under the weight, but he fought to keep his brother standing. Roger righted himself and stretched to his full height. Henry let him go and slowly stepped back. They smiled at each other and laughed, falling into each other arms, words were not necessary. Na'Taya stood in the doorway watching.

That's a smart little guy, she thought, nodding her head.

The chilly thawing of spring brought days of bright sun and easy winds. Winter had come and placed the events of the past summer into cold storage. The memories, though not gone, had been eased by the passage of time, allowing them to rest unnoticed in a dark corner, silenced, but lingering like a foul stench. Now the promise of spring was all-tempting with a feeling of renewal and the possibility of better days. Roger, Na'Taya, and Henry, still inexplicably tied to that day, ventured down to the Riverwalk. The irresistible need to look at what remained of the bridge was strong. The need to physically see it and confirm it was not just a bad dream lasted all these months.

For Roger, it was like being lost in that moment when you wake up from a dream and don't know if it was real or not. When you're not sure if you're still sleeping or wake, all you know is that whatever it is, it feels real. Your skin tingles with goose bumps, your breath is rapid, and your mind is reeling with unfocused thoughts. Only after you grab a hold of yourself can you begin to make sense of things. Was it a dream or was it real? Always apprehensive and never quite sure if you want it to be real or a stay a dream.

The feeling of having lost something, having left something behind pressed on his thoughts. Losing part of himself, not being whole, not being enough, played over and over in his head like a song you get entangled by. Roger wasn't sure if he knew who Roger was anymore. It wasn't just losing the leg. Though he hadn't totally accepted that truth, he knew in time he would come to terms with it. It wasn't even what had happened to all those people, to the bridge or the city. It was more what had happened to him; inside. Roger always felt he would struggle for life in some sterile hospital room somewhere, alone and unnoticed. But, here he was having survived a battle for his life. A battle he neither expected nor chose. A battle for a life he wasn't sure he wanted.

"Are you alright?" Na'Taya asked. "If this is too much, we can go back."

He smiled at her concern. "No, I'm fine."

Roger took a deep breath and looked at the twisted remains of the bridge. "When I was on that bridge fighting with Spade and all the explosions and screaming and everything was going on, I kept thinking about how much I wanted to live. I knew how much I had to live for." Roger planted his cane in front of his prosthetic leg. Leaning heavily on the cane, he shifted his balance. "It's funny, I'd spent so much of my life worrying about getting sick and dying," he bit his lips. "But when death was staring me in the face I could fought for life. I didn't just accept what I thought was inevitable. I wanted to live. Sick or not, I want to live. I'm no longer afraid of what life sends my way."

He turned to Na'Taya and looked deep into her eyes, the fears of days gone by having burned away. A spark of hope shone from deep within him. "I thought about you, about us, about Henry too." He nodded toward his brother skipping rocks into the water. And how much I wanted to be with you both. I wanted to get off that bridge. I needed to get off that bridge. I wanted..." He swallowed to unclog the knot of emotions that had welled up in his throat. "No matter what's in store for me, for us. I want it. Damn it! I do!" He slammed the tip of his cane into the ground.

Na'Taya took his hand and gently laid her head against his chest. She looked up at him and smiled. "How about we go and plant some orange trees."

The End

ABOUT THE AUTHOR

Franklin R. Wilson is a novelist and short story author. He has three novels debuting during the first half of 2018, with at least two more and a book of short stories to be published the second half of 2018. The first book, titled "Cast A Long Shadow," is a page-turning thriller set in the author's beloved adopted hometown of Detroit Michigan. The second book, part of a multi-book series, is a fantasy story for young adults titled "Hearts of Fire." Franklin plans on publishing at least two more books of the young adult fantasy series in 2018. The third novel, which was actually written first, is a metaphysical thriller titled "Planet of Eden." The anthology of short stories is titled "Small Bites," showcasing the prolific creativity of the author.

When Franklin isn't writing about imaginary people and worlds, he spends his time traveling in the real world, searching for unusual adventures, scrounging through flea markets acquiring collectibles, taste-testing gourmet foods, or racing about in his little two-seat red convertible. You can find out more about Franklin and his books at http://frwilson.com

www.ingramcontent.com/pod-product-compliance
Lightning Source LLC
Chambersburg PA
CBHW070856250626
47159CB00003B/1084

* 9 7 8 0 9 9 9 5 7 3 9 4 5 *